Untaken TWIN

A CALLOWAY BROTHERS NOVEL

samantha christy

Saint Johns, FL 32259

This is a work of fiction. Names, characters, places and incidents are either the product of the author's imagination or are used fictitiously, and any resemblance to actual persons, living or dead, business establishments, events or locales is entirely coincidental.

Cover designed by Coverluv

Cover model photo by WANDER AGUIAR

Cover model – Peter Pisani

A
CALLOWAY BROTHERS
NOVEL

Samantha Christy

Chapter One

Cooper

I haven't felt this alive in years. But as the whitewater churns beneath and around me while I kayak down a narrow river in Missoula, Montana, I almost feel a sense of peace. Maybe it's because I don't have time to think. It's chaotic. I barely miss a cluster of boulders in the center of the water. Then my stomach drops as I go over a fifteen-foot fall. My lungs expel an excited holler.

I shake the water from my face and smile, remembering I'm on camera. I try to provide a bit of narration even as the rushing water beats the hell out of me. After all, this video will be seen by the almost two million followers on my YouTube channel. Gotta make it look good so the money will keep rolling in from that and my sponsors.

I have a camera attached to my helmet. Another is secured to the front of the kayak, facing back at me. Later tonight, while I'm nursing my stiff muscles, I'll edit and release it. Then I'll sit back and watch my bank account get fat. It amuses me that I actually make a damn good living off doing the whole extreme sport thing.

I quickly bank right, narrowly missing a spiky rock jutting out from the river's edge. This sends me into a barrel roll from which I hastily recover. My fans will love that.

There is no calm on this river. Not here, anyway. Once you're in, you're in until about two miles downstream, where there's a small respite area off to the right. Miss that, and it's another mile or so until the next.

No one else is around. It's just me and nature. Exactly how I like it. *Well, fuck… not exactly.*

There were two other guys back at the launch site contemplating whether or not they were going to try it. One said the river was too high today. He wanted to wait for another day and see if the conditions improved. The other called him a pussy and tried to convince him to go. It brought back memories of when Chaz and I would go on our adventures. Adventures when I was the pussy, and Chaz was always wanting to push the envelope. He won, of course. Every time. Whether it was barreling down the diamond trail when we had only learned how to snowboard two days before, or climbing the fence into the no-go zone to watch airplanes take off, he always got his way.

Hell, he even got his way when we shared a womb. He fought me even then, coming out first. Our competitiveness didn't stop there. My parents have videos of us setting up obstacle courses in the house, seeing who could finish faster. Then it was big wheels through the neighborhood. Then dirt bikes. It was no surprise to anyone that we chose to skip college to chase our dream of opening a tour guide business.

But first, we had to learn the ropes ourselves, so we worked odd jobs for months at a time, saving every penny to go on some expedition to see what floated our boat. In the end, we both gravitated toward hiking. Even hiked the Grand Canyon when we were twenty-one. It was then we decided that one day we'd move to Arizona, Utah, or Colorado, rent a small house for the three of us (because he and Serenity were a package deal), and start our business. We just had to hone our skills and save up enough money.

Everything was perfect until that fateful day almost four years ago.

My paddle kicks back, almost slamming me in the face after hitting a passing rock, reminding me to keep my head in the game. It's easy to spiral out of control here, and there's no chance to correct mistakes, not in class five rapids.

The river turns sharply. Another swift drop. More dangerous boulders I need to navigate around. It's exhilarating. Damn, my job is fucking cool. For a fleeting moment, a foreign feeling washes over me. Is it happiness? I can't be sure, because I've forgotten what that felt like. All my happiness was left up on that mountain the day Chaz died.

Guilt consumes me. The moment of whatever that feeling was is over, and I'm back to reality. The reality that has me doing this alone. Without him. Without my brother. My twin. Literally my other half.

I try to push it out of my mind, but it always slips back in whenever I'm doing something like this. Because as amazing as my adventures are, there's always something missing.

A sharp turn has more water drenching my face. I blink the water out, but not fast enough to miss the next drop. I make a wrong move and shift my weight left instead of right, the nose of my kayak getting caught on a boulder, throwing me out of the kayak and into the churning water. I don't panic. I know how to get out of these situations. I've been in far worse conditions before.

When I pop up and get a brief glance of my surroundings, I catch a glimpse of orange twenty feet down river. My kayak is quickly moving away from me. The rapids pull me under again for a moment. A second glance downriver has me seeing exactly diddly squat. *Well, shit, this is just perfect.*

I need to get to the riverbank, then I can hike the rest of the way. It isn't far. But being churned around in rapids doesn't exactly make it easy to find a safe place to climb out. Rocks are my enemy right now. I'm trying my hardest to avoid them as the rapids carry me further and further downriver. I'm at the mercy of the water. Of nature itself.

Then the worst happens. I don't even see it coming. I'm pulled under into a whirlpool. The eddy tosses me around under the water as if I'm in a washing machine, tumbling head over foot so that I can't tell which way is up. Briefly, I get a much-needed breath before getting pulled under again. My training kicks in, and I try to make myself as small as possible. Denser objects will get pulled to the outside of the whirlpool where I'll have a chance to get out of it. I curl up into the tightest ball I can, no easy feat with my bulky life jacket.

I have no idea if it's working. I feel like the metal ball in a pinball machine, bouncing from side to side. My back slams into a rock. It doesn't hurt much because of all the layers: a wet suit, a dry suit, and the life jacket. My helmet makes contact with something hard and unforgiving. White light momentarily fills my vision right before my head starts throbbing. A cursory thought has me hoping the GoPro on my helmet is still functioning. I get tossed into another rock. I uncurl my arm and reach out, hoping to grab onto something, but instead, the water slams me hard, and my arm gets wedged into an underwater crevice.

Now I panic.

I twist and turn my arm, my body still taking a lashing by the water. Every once in a while, if I tilt my neck back far enough, I can catch a breath of air. But it doesn't come without a price; water also enters my lungs, and when I briefly bob above the water, I cough it out, losing more precious air.

The more I try to free myself, the tighter the rock's hold on my arm becomes. I'm exhausted, utterly spent. I don't have anything left in me. I try for one last breath, but the rapids simply don't cooperate.

So this is how it's going to happen?

My body goes limp as I succumb to my fate.

I always thought it would be on a mountain. That somehow, I would go the same way Chaz did.

The darkness surrounding me turns to light, and I see someone coming. The kayakers behind me. No, it's not them. And there are no kayaks. Someone is *walking* toward me.

Holy shit. It's Chaz. He holds out a hand. "It's okay, brother. I've got you."

What the fuck is happening?

I pull away, because he's treating me like a little kid who needs rescuing. *Is he here to rescue me?*

"I'm not afraid to die," I say.

"Bullshit," he says. "Everyone is afraid on some level, even if you know it's coming. Even if you *want* to die." He gives me a sharp look. The look that tells me he knows my every thought. I've seen it a thousand times before.

We're not in the water anymore. We're on a mountain. *The* mountain. Sitting in front of a boulder. He's on one side, I'm on the other.

"You've been on every adventure with me," I tell him. "Every goddamn one."

"I haven't, Coop. I'm gone. Have been for almost four years. You need to find someone else to take adventures with. Someone real."

"I never wanted to do any of this with anyone else."

He reaches over and pats me on the back. "I know. But you know what they say about making plans—God laughs."

"God? You're really going to sit here and talk about God? You think He laughed at us knowing you were going to die the whole time? You want me to believe He even exists if He took you away from me?"

"Shit happens, brother." He offers a shrug and a smile, as if we're talking about a flat tire instead of his grueling death.

"Why are you even talking to me? Don't you hate me?"

"Why would I hate you?"

"Because I'm a terrible brother. Because I couldn't save you." I pause and close my eyes. "Because I broke every promise I made to you." I look in the distance, nothing making sense. The sun is coming up over the horizon, and somehow I can breathe but not breathe at the same time. My chest is tight. I feel like I'm running out of time to say all the things I need to say to him. "We were supposed to live together. Adventure together. Die together. And…" I save the worst broken promise for last. "I was supposed to take care of her."

He just laughs, even as I see parts of him fade away like he's half human, half ghost. "People say a lot of things when they think they're dying. You'd have promised the devil your firstborn if it had gotten us both out alive."

He's not wrong. I remember making all kinds of deals up on that mountain. With God *and* the devil.

"But I failed you in so many ways, both on the mountain and after."

I feel a hand on my shoulder, even though he's not touching me. "You could never fail me, brother. We had quite a life, you and me."

"It hasn't been the same without you. It never will be."

"But look at all you've done," he says, with a look of pride on his fading face.

I gasp for air. "We were supposed to do it together."

"You can still do it all, Coop. Just not the way we planned."

"It wouldn't be the same."

"Maybe it will be even better. I promise there's someone out there. Someone you'll share adventures with. Make memories with." He fades more now. I can just barely make out his shape. "You need to figure out a way, brother."

I shake my head. "I can't."

My head is fuzzy. My chest is about to explode. I need to breathe, but I can't.

"You've never let me down, Cooper. Not one goddamn time." His words float in the air, though he's no longer visible. "And you never will. No matter what happens."

He's gone, but I still feel his hands on my shoulders, my arm. And suddenly, water is churning around me again. It's him. He's trying to break me free. But he can't. My body goes limp, and I feel a peace I've never experienced, knowing I'm about to be with him again. Chaz was wrong. I'm not afraid to die. Not one little bit. Not if it means being with him.

He gives me one last tug. Then everything goes black.

Chapter Two

Serenity

Light awakens me. Darn, I forgot the blackout shades. The clock reads 4:37 a.m. With the days getting longer, the shades are a must at this latitude. It's only mid-May now, but in the dead of summer, daylight will exceed eighteen hours, and the nights will consist of varying degrees of twilight.

Not that waking early matters. I don't sleep well anyway. When I sleep, I dream. And he's always there. I absently twirl the ring around my finger, remembering the day we got engaged. The day we promised we'd be together forever, even in death.

I had no idea what we were pledging.

It's a blessing as much as it is a curse, seeing Chaz every night. Listening to him tell me he loves me. Feeling his breath over my ear, his hands on my body, his lips on mine.

I used to wish I'd never wake up, that I'd stay in the dream forever. The bottle of sleeping pills I keep in the top drawer next to my bed never lets me forget how easy it would be to make that happen.

The passing years have made it somewhat easier to get out of bed each day, although only to go through the motions. I'm not really living. More like passing time. *Until what?* I often wonder.

I turn on my side and stare at his picture in the dim light. My insides still quiver when I look at him. Like they did when I was sixteen and he took the seat next to me in geometry class. It's not that we didn't know each other before then. It was Calloway Creek. Everyone knew everyone. We just hadn't spent any time together. But on that first day, when he was assigned as my partner for our class project, it was as if my soul knew he'd been assigned something more—my heart. Because, BAM! I was in love. It was the insta-love you read about in books and see in movies. The kind that has your pulse pounding and your head swimming because you feel you've been sucked into some kind of vortex from which you'll never escape. And based on the way he looked at me, he felt the same. He may have pretended he didn't, acting like the calm and cool Chaz Calloway everyone knew and loved, but his ice-blue eyes and roguish smile didn't fool me. I didn't need to feel his palms to know they were as sweaty as mine. Didn't need to put a hand to his chest to feel the excited thumping. Didn't need to lower my gaze to see how our heated stare was affecting him below the belt.

The weirdest thing about us falling in love was that he was a twin. An identical one. And if I didn't already know what clothes Chaz was wearing on a certain day, and I happened to see his brother first, those same quivers overtook me. At first, it made me feel guilty that my body had such a reaction to seeing the twin I *wasn't* in love with. But I overcame it when Cooper and I became friends, the three of us spending almost as much time together as just Chaz and I had.

But those quivers were the very reason I left the only place I'd ever called home. How could I stand to look at the man who looked exactly like my fiancé? Calloway Creek is a small town. We were bound to see each other, even if Cooper stopped working at my father's pub. Our houses were barely a football-field apart. At twenty-two, we'd all still lived at home, saving money so we could someday follow their dream. Chaz and I wanted to live together more than anything, especially after getting engaged, but that would have meant having expenses we weren't prepared to pay.

We would save the living together part for when we got married. It had been all planned out. A small ceremony at the pub followed by a reception, again, at the pub. It was the cheapest way to accomplish it. And my dad, owner of Donovan's, the most happening establishment on McQuaid Circle, was so grateful we agreed to wait until we were twenty-three to marry that he offered to pay for everything. We almost gave our parents heart attacks when we got engaged at the tender age of eighteen. They were terrified we'd run off to Vegas and get hitched. They sat us down and had a come-to-Jesus talk, convincing (if not threatening) us to wait five years.

To us, it didn't matter if we waited five years or fifty. We were going to be together forever. So we capitulated—only because of the saving money thing by living in our respective homes. But we happily let our parents think they had won.

I lean back and stare at the ceiling. If only we'd married at twenty-two instead. I would have been his wife. Maybe that would have made things different. Maybe I'd have gone on more of their adventures. If I'd been there, maybe…

Swallowing tears, I get out of bed, tuning out all the what-ifs. I use the bathroom, change, and then hit my usual running trail. Running is how I've coped. I laugh pathetically because I know I'm lying to myself if I think I'm coping. But it makes me feel better.

Sometimes I punish myself and run the entire fourteen miles of roads—the sum total of the roads around Sitka, Alaska.

When I near Harbor Mountain, my pace slows. It's a good location to see the northern lights. And it's a place I feel close to Chaz. The first time I saw the swirling rivers of greenish-blue lights, I swear it was as if I were seeing heaven. And heaven is where Chaz is, I'm sure of it. So in the fall, on days when the weather isn't too cold, I'll stay up all night with a blanket and a thermos of coffee. Thinking. Dreaming. Mourning. Sometimes I even think of Mom being there, in the lights, in heaven with him. And it gives me a fleeting moment of peace.

"Morning, Serenity," someone says, jogging up next to me.

I look away from the mountain. "Hey, Drew."

"Mind if I run with you?"

"Not if you don't mind if we pick up the pace."

I don't really *want* to run faster. I just don't want to have to make conversation. But our increased speed doesn't seem to deter him.

"You're out here early," he says, puffing.

"Mmm."

A sea plane buzzes overhead. It's a common sound given Sitka is a small town on the western shore of Baranof Island along the Inside Passage. The only way here is by boat or plane.

"Sounds like Mr. Cooper is flying in a load of salmon," he says. "Isn't it funny that we can identify some of the planes by how their motors sound?"

I'm not laughing. He said Cooper. And Cooper reminds me of Chaz. And Chaz reminds me of death. And death reminds me of the life I'll never get to live.

Thankfully, we come up to the dirt road my house is on. Well, not *my* house. It's a duplex. I rent my half from Hilda Lohman, owner of the bar where I work. The other half is rented by Yuli Koval, an older Ukrainian immigrant who lives a quiet but happy life being an orderly at the local hospital. He's the perfect neighbor. Sometimes we even sit out on the front porch and have a beer together. Alone. But together.

"Well, this is me," I say, thumbing down the road.

"Maybe I'll see you at the bar later?" Drew asks.

"You know I'll be there." I force a smile.

He waves and happily runs on, glancing back at me in a way I don't like to be looked at. In a way that lets me know he wants me. He's not obvious about it. He's lived here for six months now, working at one of the wilderness lodges. He hasn't asked me out, but he looks like he wants to. Some men are oblivious. Has he seriously never noticed the ring?

~ ~ ~

Today is the beginning of cruising season in Alaska. We get upwards of 200,000 cruise ship visitors each season. Good for business at Hilda's Hideaway, where I've worked since the day after my plane landed. I started as a waitress, quickly moved up to bartender, and now I help manage the place.

Hilda comes in from the back. She usually only works when I'm not here, but today we're expecting a crowd. "Here we go again," she says. "We all stocked up?"

I nod to the coolers, filled to the brim with local brews as well as traditional beers. "Got a big delivery earlier. We're as stocked as we can be. I brought out the extra glasses from storage."

"Looks like you're on top of things." Her hand lands on my shoulder. "I don't know what I'd do without you."

My gaze falls to Brandon, the other bartender, and then Jillian, Ebony, and Brittney—our three servers, all standing at the ready for the afternoon rush. "Any one of them could do my job and you know it. This is a hell of a lot easier than running a bar *and* grill, believe me."

She looks at me sadly. She knows my story. She's one of the only locals who does. Yuli knows, too, having caught me sobbing more than a time or two. Everyone else in town, including my co-workers, knows I wear a ring but that I don't have a man around. They stopped asking me about it long ago. Occasionally, when I go out with friends, someone will drink too much and press me, but they never get far because I refuse to talk about it.

A group of boisterous travelers pushes through the front door. A lady looks around, taking in the rustic tavern. "Oh. My. Gawd," she says with a striking New England accent. "This place is so country chic."

I roll my eyes. What the heck is *country chic?* We've got a few taxidermy animals in the rafters, and the bar is made out of local wood logged from the timber harvest in Tongass National Forest, but really, this place is no different from many other taverns around the country. But tourists tend to think of Alaska more as a foreign country, not part of the U.S.A. I get that it's not exactly mainstream America here, but we're not BFE either.

"Welcome to Hilda's," Ebony says, flashing her pearly smile. "There's a booth over here that would be perfect for the six of you. May I show you a drink menu?"

Someone snaps a picture of Ebony as if she's a foreigner they want to remember. She locks eyes with me. We're all used to it. We laugh about it after hours.

Another few large groups follow a few minutes later, and by two o'clock, the bar is full to the brim. Hilda is happily helping out, bussing tables and refilling coolers as I help Brandon behind the bar. He's happy, too. He knows these are the days we make bank on tips. I couldn't care less about the money. In all honesty, I hate cruising season. It brings out the drunk travelers who think they can hit on anyone with a pulse.

When all three waitresses have turned down the four men taking shots at table six, one of them walks up to the bar and wedges himself between two other patrons. He waves a twenty at me as if that will get me to help him before the two gentlemen I'm already waiting on.

I smile. "One moment, please."

He watches me. I can see him out of the corner of my eye. He's like a predator; a carbon copy of every other douchebag who thinks they can waltz into town, find a pretty 'foreigner,' and have a quickie on the men's room counter.

I hand the other men their drinks and turn to Mr. Twenty-dollar-bill. "How can I help you? Was Brittney not able to take care of you?"

I look over and see Brittney shaking her head and mouthing, *Asshole.*

He smirks. "Not in the way a paying patron might expect."

"I'm sorry to hear that. I'll have a word with her after our shift." *No, I won't.* We'll disinfect our hands of tourist stench and complain about entitled jerks who think just because we live in Alaska, we're easy. Truth be told, Alaska has the highest male-to-female ratio in the country, so women here usually have their pick of the proverbial litter. "We do like all of our customers to be happy. So what can I get you?"

He doesn't take his eyes off me. "How about you surprise me, sweetheart?"

It's not the first time I've been asked that, called that, or gawked at. I turn and grab an expensive bottle of tequila off the back wall, mix a drink, and slide it over to him on a napkin. "That'll be sixty dollars."

He looks at the twenty in his hand and swallows. I stare him down until he digs into his pocket for more cash. He puts two more twenties on the bar (leaving no tip) and turns to walk away, mumbling something about me being a crazy bush bitch.

The men he was crowding chuckle. One of them drops a five into the tip jar. "Nice," he says. "You handled him like a pro."

"Not my first rodeo," I say, wiping the bar in front of them.

"So listen…" the tall guy says.

Oh, Lord. Here it comes.

I put my left hand on the bar and tap my fingers, calling attention to my hand. He eyes my ring and nods to it. "Is it serious?"

"As serious as a dead guy on top of a mountain," I say, my expression terse.

They look at each other confused, wondering if that's some kind of Alaskan proverb or something.

"So that means…?" the guy asks.

Brandon steps over. "That means bug off, dude. She's wearing a goddamn engagement ring."

"I can handle this," I hiss at Brandon.

He holds up his hands and backs off. Brandon was the first guy to hit on me after I moved here. Now, he's more like a protective older brother. Not that I really know what that feels like. Well, I kind of do. Chaz's two older brothers, Tag and Jaxon, were often at my dad's pub and would warn off anyone who gave me a funny look. Not to mention Cooper, who sometimes worked the same shifts as I did. He was the worst of them all. Once, he even shoved a guy against a wall for grabbing my arm. I learned long ago that waitresses and bartenders have to have thick skin. We get hit on, touched, squeezed, pinched, propositioned, and even stalked.

I turn back to the two men, but Hilda is already intervening. "Is there anything else I can get you before I close out your tab?" she asks, staring them down like a mama bear.

"No, ma'am," the smaller one says.

I hand them their check, and they pay me while she continues her visual assault. "Tip my girl well. Her triplets gotta eat."

Suppressing a giggle, I close out the tab. Turns out they *did* leave me a good tip.

When they're gone, I turn to Hilda. "You're terrible."

She squeezes the bony bridge of her nose. "Four months of this is going to make me go prematurely gray."

"You're already gray," Jillian shouts over her shoulder as she passes.

"Shh," Hilda whispers, lifting a finger in front of her lips. Then she fluffs her fifty-eight-year-old tresses. "None of the handsome fellows in here need to know what lies underneath my luscious brown locks."

We all laugh and get back to work serving endless drinks to cruise ship passengers. Hours later, the bar is empty but for the regular locals. All the tourists have left, some wearing ridiculously overpriced Hilda's Hideaway T-shirts that Hilda makes herself in the off-season.

"How was day one?" Brittney asks as we all gather at the bar before she and Ebony end their day shifts.

Brandon tallies up the tips, doling out equal amounts to everyone. "Pretty damn good," he says.

The waitresses smile at their thick stacks. As always, Hilda refuses her share, splitting it five ways between the rest of us. She kisses everyone on the cheek and walks out with Brit and Eb.

Brandon, Jillian, and I stay on for the night shift. It's Tuesday, so it'll be a light one.

Jillian gestures to the front door. "I'll go pick up sandwiches from Penny's if you'll watch my tables."

I hand over some cash. "You got it. I'll have my usual."

Brandon gives her money as well. "Same. But double the fries." He slaps a palm against his gut. "Watching the lot of you get hit on all afternoon has made me hungry as hell."

Jillian chuckles on her way out.

"Like you didn't get your share of advances." I nod to the empty booth in the corner. "The bachelorette party looked like they wanted to eat you alive."

"The maid of honor slipped me her number. Told me to call if I'm ever in the San Diego area."

I shake my head in wonderment. "Who has a bachelorette party on an Alaskan cruise? Aren't there cruises to Cabo for that?"

"Heard someone say the bride has a sensitivity to the sun," he says.

I peek outside. "What, there's no sun up here?"

He shrugs. "Probably not as much as Mexico."

I excuse myself to refill some Cokes at one of Jillian's tables. Then I serve a beer and a seltzer at the other. Back at the bar, I go to wash my hands of the beer that sloshed out of the glass. When I do, my ring falls into the sink. I reach for it, but I'm too late. It goes down the drain. "Oh, shit." I turn off the water. "Shit, shit, shit!"

Brandon rushes over. "What is it?"

"My ring. It slipped off and went down the drain." I try to remove the drain stopper thing but it doesn't budge. Hot tears roll down my face. "No, no, no, no."

"Wait here." Brandon runs into the back room and returns with a toolbox. He gets under the sink, knocks around on the pipes, and two minutes later, sits back on his haunches and hands me my ring with a sad smile.

My breath bellows out of me like a balloon has deflated, and I sink to the floor next to him, holding on to the ring like it's my lifeline. I slide it back onto my finger. It easily goes over the knuckle, the diamond falling to the side. I've probably lost fifteen pounds in the past few years, and it's too loose. I keep telling myself I'll get it sized, but that would mean taking it off for a long period of time.

"Maybe it's a sign," Brandon says, standing. "That it's time to take it off."

"Maybe you should mind your own business," I say more harshly than I should have.

His eyes sweep the premises, then he sinks back down to my level. "Listen, Serenity. I don't know what happened to whoever gave you that ring. We've all speculated. Made up our own stories, even. But all of us pretty much think the man who put it on your finger must have died. And based on what you said to those tourists earlier, it was on a mountain."

I glance over at him, unable to deny it.

"And we think you moved here to hide from the pain."

I get up, not wanting to be psychoanalyzed by a bartender.

"I'm no professional," he says, busying himself putting tools away. "But I'm pretty sure if you saw one, they'd tell you that pain isn't something you can run from. It'll follow you everywhere you go. I've known you for several years now, and you don't seem to be making much progress healing from whatever broke you."

I pull a dollar out of my tip money, wad it up, and throw it at him. "Thanks, *Doctor* Brandon, but I don't need or want your advice." I take the bar rag off my shoulder and throw it onto the floor. "Tell Jillian to put my food in the fridge. The crowd seems light enough for the two of you to handle. I'm leaving."

"Serenity…"

I hold up a hand. "What are you going to do, fire me?" I walk toward the door. "Call me if you're overwhelmed. Otherwise, I'll be at home." I toss him one last look over my shoulder. "You know, so I can sit there and be broken like everyone thinks I am."

"Serenity, come on."

I close the door and run the full mile home in my converse, ignoring Drew, who's probably heading to the bar, along with every other well-intentioned pleasantry that gets shouted my way. I run up the front steps, unlock the door, and collapse onto the floor.

Then I stare at the ring that still tethers me to a dead man, knowing every word that came out of Brandon's mouth was true. I *am* broken.

But better to be broken in a place where people don't know why. Where most folks don't look at me like they feel sorry for me. Like they know what I had and what I'm missing; what I'll *be* missing for the rest of my life. But part of me knows I'm kidding myself. When I booked that plane ticket to Sitka almost four years ago, I might as well have been booking a ticket to hell. Because that's where I've been living.

I crawl into bed, curl up in a ball, and do what I do best—cry myself to sleep.

Chapter Three

Cooper

Water swirls around me. Suffocating me. Drowning me. I begin to shake uncontrollably.

"Brother, wake up!"

I still when I feel arms on me. I clear my throat, surprised to find it free of water. "Chaz?"

"Open your eyes, Coop."

I do what he says, then slowly glance around, my head pounding. "Where is he?"

"Where is who? Jaxon?" Tag says. "He was here yesterday. Said he'd check on you later."

"Wait, I'm not… dead?"

Laughter. Then his stern voice. "You are very much alive, Cooper. Stupid, but alive."

The events of the past few days come rushing back. The kayak. The whirlpool. The hospital. Tag flying out to bring me back to Calloway Creek. *Shit.*

"Dude," he says. "You don't have to look so upset about it."

"About the accident?"

His curt look scolds me. "About not dying."

Tag paces while I continue to get my bearings. Right, I'm in his guest room. I lift my left arm, heavy with a cast covering my thumb, half of my palm, and ending just below my elbow. I ease myself up in the bed and rub my temples. Then I swing my legs over the side and prepare to stand.

"Whoa." Tag rushes over to stop me. "Remember what the doc said. You need to take it easy until you feel better."

"I feel better," I lie.

"Bullshit. Cooper, this is your fourth concussion. Do you know what that means? Get another and you could be dealing with brain damage. Hell, if you ask me, you already have it." More pacing. "Fuck, man. You scared the shit out of us. You're goddamn lucky your arm is broken. Maybe it'll bench you long enough for you to come to your senses. You can't keep this shit up forever."

"This *shit* pays the bills." I stand and pull on a T-shirt. "Besides, I'm almost twenty-six. You can't tell me what to do."

He gets in my face. "I'm still your big brother, so the hell I can't. You're staying here in Cal Creek where I can keep an eye on you."

My head hurts too much to argue with him. I spy ibuprofen on the bedside table and swallow four. "What about my van?"

"You don't need the van. You can stay here. I found your keys and packed a few things for you. Your wallet. Some clothes. Your phone. Moved the van to some parking garage that'll cost you a fortune."

"I'm not staying here. You're getting married soon."

"So stay at Mom and Dad's."

I start to shake my head, then regret it when pain strikes. "No."

"Well, you can't stay at Jaxon's. He's got enough to deal with. But I'm sure he wouldn't mind if you stopped by to help out."

"Me? Help out with three-week-old babies? Yeah, right."

"You have to meet them at least. Aurora and Ashley are adorable. They really do look like twins."

Twins.

I can tell he regrets saying the word as soon as it leaves his mouth. Guilt crosses his face. He grips my shoulder. "We'll figure something out about the van. Maybe we can hire someone to deliver it to you. You can crash here for a few days until then."

"Fine." I sit on the chair in the corner and pull on my shoes. "You don't have to babysit me. Don't you have a business to run?"

"It's Saturday, Coop."

"Right."

He eyes me suspiciously. "Where do you think you're going?"

I grab my phone. "For a walk. Then maybe Donovan's for lunch."

"That is the opposite of taking it easy," he says, standing in the doorway, probably to block my exit.

"Tag, I'm not just going to sit here." I lift up the cast. "I get it. I'm sidelined for a while. But I'm not dead." *Unfortunately.* "So either you get out of the way or I'm going to pile-drive you and end up back in the ER."

He blows out a frustrated breath. But before he moves, he gets in my face. "You do anything idiotic and I will roast your freaking balls on a spit and eat them like s'mores, you got it? Mom can't take one more ounce of worry or heartache. None of us can."

"You're overreacting," I say, sliding past him.

"Am I?"

I ignore him and go to the bathroom, noticing a pack of toiletries sitting on the counter. I brush my teeth and apply deodorant, then I head back out. Tag and his goldendoodle, Sissy, are on the couch. I glance around. "Where are Maddie and Gigi?"

"At the flower shop."

"Tell them I said hey."

"You said hello to them yesterday."

I vaguely remember it, along with seeing Mom, Dad, my other brother, Jaxon, and my sister, Addy. "Yeah, I remember now." I point to my head. "It's just a little fuzzy is all."

"Four concussions will do that to a man. Promise me you'll take it easy."

"Jeez, fine." I'd roll my eyes, but I get the feeling even that would hurt. "Catch you later."

He nods to his dog. "Want us to go on that walk with you?"

"I'd rather go alone. Clear my head."

"Suit yourself. Just stick to sidewalks. Nothing too crazy today."

"Whatever."

He says something else, but I'm out the door before I can hear it. I don't need him babying me. I stand on his front porch and inhale deeply. It's a strange feeling being able to breathe like this after almost drowning.

As I walk toward the park, I can't get something out of my head. The dream I had about Chaz. It was so damn real. I've dreamed about him a lot over the years, but this was different.

Ninety minutes later, walking at a snail's pace (to appease Tag) along one of Calloway Creek's rocky backwoods trails (to give him the finger), I arrive at my destination. I stand at the entrance to the tree tunnel that leads to a small clearing. It was the place Chaz and I used to come to smoke pot. We'd hang out for hours, talking, laughing, planning.

I swallow, slowly walking under the trees, feeling more connected to him with every step. It's a place I've avoided for almost four years even though Jaxon, Tag, and I hike these trails whenever I come to town. Neither of them knows about this place. It was one of our secrets. Not that we didn't get along with our older brothers. We did. The four of us were always close growing up. We kind of had to be if only to stick together and put up a united front against the McQuaid brothers, whose family all but owns the town that bears *our* last name.

Today, however, after remembering my dream, I was drawn to this place. I knew I had to visit it. Visit *him*.

I sit on one of the large rocks with a flat top, the one I'd always sit on, opposite the one Chaz had claimed as his. I stare at the etching I carved into the small grave marker next to his 'stone throne' (as he liked to call it). I can almost hear him laughing at the double entendre. The marker bears one word: **brother**.

My parents had Chaz cremated. While the bulk of his ashes sit in an urn in a special place in their house, they gave a small bit to the four of us kids.

Tag dumped his at Niagara Falls while on a boat tour, something probably highly illegal to do without some sort of permission, but then again, he wasn't one for playing by the rules back then. My parents never had a lot of money when we were young, and the falls were the one place we could go as a family that didn't break the bank. There's still a picture of the seven of us, a rainbow and the falls in the background, displayed proudly in my parents' living room.

Jaxon sprinkled his on the football field at the high school. It's where he bonded with Chaz the most. When Jaxon was the senior quarterback for the varsity team, Chaz and I were sophomores who sometimes got to play. Jaxon will never forget the perfect spiral he threw to Chaz, scoring the game-winning touchdown to beat our rival at the homecoming game.

I still don't know what Addy did with hers. She had her accident the night of Chaz's funeral and was basically laid up for months after. I never asked what happened to them, and she never said.

My share of his ashes is buried right here next to his rock. It was a place I thought I'd visit often but never did until today. *Because you let him down.*

His ghostly voice still echoes in my head. *"You could never fail me, brother."*

I sit until my ass goes numb, the rumbling of my empty stomach reminding me I'm still alive. Then I start back to town, but I take the long way around, passing by Old Man Henson's cabin on the way. There's a for sale sign in the window. A lot of good that'll do; few people come out here. Runners mostly.

Going in for a closer look, I peek through the windows. It's furnished. Everything looks neat and tidy, albeit about fifty years old. *Did he die?* I wonder.

I get my answer when I walk around back and see a small wooden cross bearing his name underneath branches of a tree. I dip my head and let out a sigh. The old hermit didn't want to leave this place even in death. I don't imagine many people would want to buy a place with a grave out back. I peek in a few more windows, then go back to the sign and get out my phone.

When I finally get to the pub, Donny Donovan, owner of the establishment, laughs at my cast. He slowly walks to my table, looking to be in pain. "What hair-brained thing got you into this predicament?"

"Kayaking mishap in Montana. I'll be as good as new in a few months," I reply. He shifts his weight and cringes. I look him up and down. "You okay?"

"Damn hip. Been needin' to be replaced for a while now."

"So replace it."

"It's not that easy, son. It could take months of recovery before I'd be able to work these long hours again." He taps my cast. "Longer than this'll put you out for. And with Lissa planning to take the summer off to travel with that Montana boy…"

"Wait, what have I missed? I knew she and Lucas were fu—, uh, dating. Wasn't aware it was serious."

"As serious as a two-month trip across Europe." He glances back at Lissa, who is happily filling drink orders behind the bar.

She calls over to him, a bit of foam in her hair. "Keg number three just blew."

"We'll get to it in a minute," he tells her, then turns back to me. "I can hardly blame her. On her salary, it's unlikely she'll ever get the chance to do anything like this again. So whether or not she's truly enamored with the fellow, it's an opportunity she couldn't pass up."

"But you'll be down a waitress."

"Lissa's a bartender now. When Kyle quit a few weeks ago to start a summer internship, she got promoted. And now this." He frowns and glances down at his hip.

"You need help behind the bar for a few months?" I ask, an idea popping into my head.

"You know anyone?"

"Yeah, I know someone. Me."

He stares at my cast. "Lotta good you'll do with that thing."

"Donny, it's the perfect solution. I'm laid up for a while, so I'll be in town. You're about to be down a bartender. I've worked here before. I know everything about this place."

"I don't know," he ponders.

I stand and walk to the back. He follows with a limp. I know Tag would skin me alive for doing it, but I enter the walk-in cooler, pick up a full keg with my right hand, and haul it into the kitchen. "Let's get this hooked up."

Donny snorts. "Okay, okay, you've proven your point. When can you start?"

"When does Lissa leave?"

"Monday."

"I guess I'll start then."

He clasps my shoulder. "You're a godsend, Cooper. Even if looking at your face every day will bring back painful memories."

We're both quiet as I carry the keg over to be tapped. He doesn't have to explain how seeing me reminds him of his daughter who ran away and never returned.

He finishes tapping the keg, and I haul the empty to the back door.

"You don't have to do that," he says. "You're not on the clock yet."

"Make me one of your famous French dip sandwiches and we'll call it even."

He points to me. "You got yourself a deal."

As soon as I slip back into my booth, my siblings come through the front door. Addy spies me and runs over as quickly as her prosthesis will allow. She leans down and circles her arms around me. "It's good to see you up and around."

The three join me in the booth.

I raise a brow at them. "You couldn't go half a day without checking up on me?"

Jaxon shrugs. "We have to eat."

I call his bullshit. "Don't you have infants to care for?"

"I'll always make time for *all* my family," he says, pulling out his phone and handing it over. "These are my girls. You should come by and meet them."

Addy bounces in her seat. "Oh my gosh, they are sooooo cute. The way they smell. Their soft tufts of dark hair. Their adorable little fingers and toes."

I stare at the picture. I've seen many photos of them over the past weeks. Mom won't stop posting them on Facebook. Still, I can't believe he has *two* babies. And the way it happened is downright unbelievable. I hand the phone back to him.

"Now that you're in town for a while, you have no excuse to miss the wedding," Tag says. "Maddie will be pleased. She was hoping you'd be there."

"And you'll come to my graduation, won't you?" Addy asks. "It's Friday. We're having my party here after."

"I'll definitely make the party," I say. "Considering I'll be the one serving drinks."

Three sets of eyes are on me. Jaxon breaks the silence. "You're *working* here?"

"As of Monday."

"What the hell?" Tag says. "What do you not get about needing to recover from your injuries?"

I toss him an angry sneer. "What don't you get about me needing to keep busy so I'm not a worthless piece of shit just taking up space?"

He holds up his hands, not wanting to fight.

"Oh, and I'm also buying Joe Henson's cabin."

Tag chokes on his water. "Jesus, Coop. I haven't seen you in four hours, and you've bought a damn house and gotten a job." Then a smile creeps up his face.

I know what he's thinking. "Don't get ahead of yourself," I say preemptively. "The cabin was a steal. It'll be where I crash when I'm in town. A place to stash things I can't fit into the van. And the job is temporary while Lissa goes to Europe with Lucas." I glance at Donny, who's grimacing as he delivers food to table eighteen. "And he really needs the help."

"So the rumors are true?" Addy asks. "I'd heard Lissa and Lucas were getting tight." She takes my hand. "And I'm glad you'll be in town for a while. I've missed you."

I lean over and kiss the side of her head. "I've missed you too, kiddo."

~ ~ ~

"Order up!" Donny shouts from the back.

I hurry through the door before he tries to bring it out himself. I didn't really know just how much pain he was in until my first shift yesterday. Kelly and I share a look. He's the primary cook here, other than Donny himself. He knows as well as anyone how bad things have gotten for Donny.

I take the two plates and deliver them to my customers sitting at the bar.

While my cast certainly makes it more difficult to do the job, I've actually fallen back into the groove quite easily. It feels like just yesterday when I worked here. Nothing much has changed.

I glance at the booth in the corner, the one Chaz and Ren used to share during her breaks. Well—*most* things haven't changed. I shake away the thought, not needing more ghosts ruining my day.

Walking back to the bar, I find myself studying the pictures of Serenity on the wall, wondering what she's been up to all these years. Alaska is a long way from here.

She's been running. Like you.

Her smile is beaming—the kind that seems to radiate happiness. And her dark, exuberant eyes hint at a satisfying and carefree life. Part of me is curious. Does she still smile? Has she lost the glint in her eye?

Suddenly, a crash of plates comes from the back, along with a pained groan. I rush through the swinging doors to see Kelly tending to Donny, who's covered in pasta, meatballs, and sauce, lying prone on the ground.

"Ah, man. What happened?" I ask.

"Damn hip gave out on me," Donny says, moaning. "Stick a fork in me, I think I'm done."

Kelly pulls out his phone. "I'm calling an ambulance."

Donny glances at the mess surrounding him. "You'll clean up before you close up the place?"

I give him a look. "Close? We're not closing."

"Place can't run without me."

"The hell it can't."

He looks between Kelly and me, the only remaining employees he has that are over the age of twenty-one. "You'll need more help."

"Maybe," I say. "But how about you let us deal with that while you go take care of yourself."

Sirens blare in the background. EMS burst through the doors a minute later. They put him on a gurney, Donny's eyes watering as his face is screwed up in a grimace. He tosses me the pub keys. "I'll try and figure something out, but you close the doors if it gets to be too much."

"It won't," I say, escorting him out. "Keep me updated. And don't worry. I've got this."

He winces and thanks me.

After watching the ambulance drive away, I walk back to see Kelly cleaning the kitchen. I glance at the keys in my hand. He does too.

"That's all you," Kelly says. "I ain't never wanted to be in charge, and I don't plan to start now."

"Okay, then. I guess make up a few more plates of pasta. I'll give the customers a drink on us while they wait. And I'll call in an extra waiter to pick up the slack. We'll all pitch in wherever necessary."

"Look at you," he says. "Already pickin' up the reins like they ain't nothin'."

I walk back out front. "Well, there isn't much else to do in this sleepy town," I mumble to myself. "Might as well make myself useful."

Then I remember what Donny said about how long his recovery might take. I glance at my cast, knowing my stay here is only temporary. Yeah… Donny better hope he can work something out, or the place might have to shut down after all.

Chapter Four

Serenity

I sit on the back stoop of Hilda's, staring at my phone.

Brandon comes out the door, throws a bag of trash into the dumpster, and plops down next to me. "That's the face of someone who just got bad news." He glances at my phone. "I hope everything is okay."

"It's my dad."

He scoots closer and puts a comforting hand on my shoulder. "Oh, shit, really?"

"No, he's fine. Well, he's not *fine*. He just told me he's going to have hip replacement surgery tomorrow afternoon, but he should make a full recovery."

"Are the two of you close?"

"As close as any father and daughter can be. He raised me all by himself."

He lifts a brow. "I didn't know that. I'm sure he'll be okay. My grandmother had her hip replaced earlier this year. She's back to playing golf every Tuesday."

"I'm not worried about the surgery. I mean, I am, but that's not what I'm upset about."

"What is it, then?"

I've lived here almost four years, been friends with Brandon for most of that time, yet there are still so many things he doesn't know about me. "My dad owns a place called Donovan's Pub back in New York."

"Ahh, that explains why you were able to hit the ground running around here and rise through the ranks faster than anyone I've ever seen."

"I basically grew up in the bar. There's a room in the back, just off the kitchen. His office. But most of it was made into a playroom for me. I had a little cot in the corner, and a craft table." I laugh. "I'll bet if you looked really hard, you'd still find Play-Doh in the cracks of the plaster. And once I was five or six, I started helping out with small tasks. Folding napkins. Sorting cups. By the time I was fourteen, I knew everything there was to know about the business. And even though I thought I really did know everything, my dad still encouraged me to take restaurant management classes at the local university."

I become quiet again, still staring at my phone.

Brandon chuckles.

"What?" I ask.

"I think that's the most I've learned about you in all the time we've known each other."

I realize what a shitty friend I've been. To him. To everyone.

"I'm sorry." I turn to him. "I feel terrible about how I treated you yesterday after you worked so quickly to retrieve my ring. What I should have said was thank you. So… thank you." I rotate the ring around my finger. "I don't know what I would have done."

"It was my pleasure." He scoots dirt with his shoe. "So let me get this straight. Your dad owns a place in New York. Probably a business he was hoping you'd run one day and even take over after he's gone. And you move three thousand miles away to work in a dumpy tourist drinking hole like this?" He eyes my ring. "This thing you're running from must be pretty bad if you gave all that up."

The trees behind the tavern are swaying in the light breeze. My head still swims with thoughts of what has been asked of me. "He wants me to go back there."

He nods. "Sure he does. My grandma was terrified about getting the surgery. You should be with him."

"That's not why he wants me to go back." I concentrate on the trees. "He wants me to run Donovan's for a few months. Or until he's capable of being on his feet fourteen hours a day."

He sighs. "And that's not something you want to do."

"It's not that I don't want to. I'm just not sure I'm capable of doing it. But I don't want to let him down." Tears flood my eyes. "He's always been supportive of me. Even when I moved here. We talk every week, sometimes twice. We have video calls. He's never made me feel like… like…"

He nudges his shoulder against mine. "Feel like what?"

I swallow and close my eyes. "A coward."

"You think you're a coward?"

Guilt consumes me and I nod, sure that I am. I left my father. My job. My friends. All the people who were also hurting after Chaz's death. It may have been the single most selfish thing I've done in all my life. But I couldn't stay. I couldn't breathe in that town.

"What are you going to do?" he asks.

My shoulders slump. "I know what I should do. I'm just not sure I can."

"Maybe this is the universe's way of making things right."

Huffing out a breath, I give him the side-eye. "The universe is pretty effed-up then, if you ask me."

He laughs. "Yes, yes it is." He stands. "Whatever you decide to do, I'm sure he'll understand."

I eye the ground. "I'll only be a few more minutes."

"Take all the time you need," he says before disappearing back inside.

Fifteen minutes later, Hilda storms through the back door. She forcibly stands me up, rips off my apron, and tosses it over her shoulder. "You're fired."

"What? Why? Because I left early yesterday? It was such a light crowd, I swear. It—" She gives me an empathetic look and suddenly everything makes sense. "Oh, Brandon told you."

She pulls me into her arms. "You know I love you like a daughter, Serenity. I've been very patient, waiting for this day to come. I knew it would eventually. Everyone has to go home and face their fears sometime. This is your time. Now go. I've got you booked on a two o'clock flight to JFK. You'll have a layover in Seattle and then take the red-eye to New York. You'll arrive at 6:00 a.m. New York time. It's all been settled."

"But, Hilda—"

"No buts, honey. Your father needs you. He's been there for you for twenty-five years. This is your time to be there for him."

"I'm not sure I can be."

She holds me at arm's length. "You'll always have a place here if you need it. And I'm going to miss the heck out of you. But truth be told, if you never come back here, that will be a good thing. It will mean you've made peace with the past. And since the day I met you, I've known that's what you've needed." She walks the two steps down to the ground and offers me a hand. "Come now, I'll help you pack. Then we'll swing back here, and you can say your goodbyes."

~ ~ ~

There's a knock on my door. Sleepily, I roll over and look at the clock. It's 12:43 a.m.

I sit up. "Dad? What's wrong?" He should still be at work. It's his night to close.

"It's Jaxon," I hear from the other side.

I'm wide awake now, as much as if cold water had been splashed on my face. If Jaxon Calloway is knocking on my bedroom door in the middle of the night, something is wrong. I spring out of bed, pull on the closest thing within reach—pink shorts that in no way match the old, faded Calloway Creek High football T-shirt I've slept in since Chaz gave it to me five years ago. I swing the door open, heart pounding. "Has something happened to my dad?"

Light from the hallway filters into my room. Jaxon escorts me back to the bed and sits me down. I can tell he's been crying. His face is puffy, his eyes reduced to mere slits.

My throat is clogged with tears. "Jaxon, please tell me. What happened to him? Robbery? Heart attack? Is he…"

Then my dad appears in the doorway, flushed as if he'd run all the way home from the pub.

"Dad?" I look between them. "What happened?"

They stare at each other, both looking terrified. My heart takes a tumble into my stomach. Dad left the bar early. Jaxon is here—Chaz's brother. Chaz and Cooper are off climbing some mountain. Both of the men standing before me look broken. As broken as I know I'll be when they tell me what they came to tell me. I slip off the bed and sink to the floor, my head shaking back and forth, my mind screaming no, no, no, no!

"Don't say it," I choke out.

"Sweetie," Dad says, sitting on the floor next to me.

"D-Dad, I c-can't."

Jaxon flanks my other side. I'm sandwiched between the two as if they think I'll pass out. I might. My head is swimming. I'm having an out-of-body experience, looking down on myself, fearing the words that are about to fall from their lips.

"I'm so sorry, Ren." Jaxon's voice is laced with haunted sorrow. "There was an accident." The words come out strained because he's as destroyed as I'm about to be.

Dad takes over, putting a strong arm around me, his voice cracking when he delivers the news that will alter the rest of my days. "He's gone, Serenity. Chaz is gone."

The plane touching down jolts me awake. I curse my dream as I wipe the tears that rolled all the way to my chin. I pull out my phone and check the time. 2:55 a.m. But that's Seattle time. I turn off airplane mode and it switches to 5:55. I look out the window and sigh when I see the Manhattan skyline just beginning to take shape in the faint dawn. I'm back in New York.

My heart beats wildly.

My palms sweat.

My body shakes.

Breathe.

After deplaning and making my way to luggage claim, I lean against the wall and people-watch. What else is there to do while waiting for my bags? My eyes dart from one man to the next, somehow expecting to see *him*, Chaz's twin, the one person I don't want to see.

Common sense tells me I won't. Although I don't keep up with Cooper, I am aware of his YouTube channel, of his living in a converted van, of his daredevil excursions across the globe. I tried to watch one once, but it just increased the nightmares for a week. How could I look at the face of the man I buried? The face of the love of my life who died far too soon. We should have had at least another half-century together.

I shake off the unwelcome thoughts. Then I think of another fact I'd heard about Cooper—that he tends to avoid Calloway Creek almost as much as I do. It makes sense. People used to joke that they were practically conjoined. And I'm sure everywhere Cooper looks in town, Chaz is there. At the bowling alley we used to go to every Friday night. Behind the ice cream shop where all the teens would convene. At the pub.

The pub. How am I going to go there, *work there*, when I know all I'm going to see is Chaz sitting in the corner booth waiting for me to go on break? Flirting with me from across the room. Flashing me his handsome, roguish smile that made me putty in his hands.

The luggage carousel starts moving. Bags appear, keeping my mind off other, more dangerous things. I watch colorful suitcases, duffle bags, and packages pass by. Part of me hopes mine don't arrive. That somehow it would give me an excuse not to leave the airport. But as my blue-and-white suitcases come into view, I know there's no such luck.

I collect them and check the time. If I hurry, I should make it to the hospital in time to see Dad before his surgery. But only if I take the train. A cab will take too long. I pull my bags behind me and make my way to the AirTrain that will get me to the subway. From there, I can get on the train to Calloway Creek.

My mouth goes dry as I wonder how much going home is going to wreck me.

Chapter Five

Cooper

My arm hurts. My head is pounding. Hell, every part of my body is sore. Seems managing a bar for twelve hours a day is harder than BASE jumping in Dubai or backpacking the Serengeti.

At more than twice my age, I don't know how Donny has done it all these years. He texted me from the hospital last night. Said his surgery was going to happen today. Told me he was working on a solution and thanked me for stepping in.

A pimply-faced teen approaches the bar. He seems nervous. Is he going to try to ask me for a drink? At three o'clock in the afternoon? Fat chance. I couldn't care less if underage kids drink, but Donny isn't going to lose his liquor license on my watch.

"I'm looking for Mr. Donovan," he says.

"Donny's not here."

He fidgets. "Do you know when he'll be back? I can wait."

I look at my invisible watch and then back at him. "July."

The kid's face goes ashen. "Oh, uh… okay."

"Can I help you with anything? Seems I'll be running the show around here for a while."

"I was supposed to have an interview today for a server position."

I massage my temples. "Of course you were."

Just what I need. I contemplate telling the kid to take a hike, but we *are* down a server. Hell, Kelly said they were down one even before Lissa ditched.

"Wait here." I pop into the kitchen. "Kelly, some kid out front wants a job."

"I remember Donny tellin' me last week he had some interviews set up."

"As in more than one? How in the hell am I supposed to hire someone?"

He shrugs. "You used to be a server. You know what the job entails. Just pick someone with a pleasant face, a good demeanor, and a decent work ethic. With finals week at the university, it's about to get a lot busier around here."

Shit.

"I've never interviewed anyone in my life."

"He trusted you with this place. Gave you the keys. I'm sure he'll be happy with whoever you choose."

On my way out, I duck into the office and grab a pad of paper and a pen, just to look like I know what I'm doing. Back out front, I get the kid's attention and nod to a table furthest from the entrance. Then I ask Gino to man the bar along with his tables.

"I'm Cooper." I pull out a chair and sit opposite the kid. "You got a resume?"

"I, uh, not with me. I, um, already gave Mr. Donovan one." He wipes his sweaty palms on his slacks.

"I don't know where they are. Donny had to leave in a hurry. Why don't you just tell me about yourself? Name. Age. Experience. Stuff like that."

He rattles on, stumbling over his words and stuttering his way through as I scribble shit down, wondering if I'm just supposed to hire him on the spot. But Kelly mentioned there were more. And this kid, though old enough to work here being he's eighteen, doesn't have a lick of experience serving alcohol. Not to mention he hasn't made eye contact with me one time. Rule number one as a server: make eye contact. Okay, so maybe it's not rule number one. But it's up there somewhere. He even makes *me* feel nervous. I can't imagine this kid dealing with drunk patrons at 1:00 a.m. on a Saturday.

I stand. "Thanks for coming in, Ken. I'll let you know what we decide."

As soon as he leaves, I see another guy, who doesn't look much older than Ken, waiting with Gino at the bar. I roll my eyes, and Gino sends him over. I go through the same motions, this one much better than the last, but he only wants a job for the summer. He does have experience, however, which gives him a leg up on the adolescent sweaty-hand kid.

I jot more notes down and give him the same spiel.

When he leaves, he holds the door open for my sister. I go over. "Hey, Addy. A bit early for happy hour, isn't it?"

She cocks her head. "That's not why I'm here. Didn't Donny tell you?"

"Tell me what?"

"I'm interviewing for the waitress position."

My jaw falls open. "You want to be a server?" I look at the booth the four of us occupied on Saturday. "But you didn't say anything. And... why? You're about to graduate college with a degree in exercise science."

"I didn't say anything because I knew Jaxon and Tag would get onto me about it. They both have this dream for me that has me earning my Ph.D. and becoming some big-time physical therapist. It's not going to happen. I didn't get into any of the schools I applied to. So I'm going to take a gap year, figure out what I want to do, and then maybe I'll try again."

"And until then, you want to wait tables, serve drunk old men, clean bathrooms, and deal with kids-eat-free nights on Tuesdays?"

"Sure. Why not? I talked to Lissa. She said tips were good. Gave me pointers."

"But you've never done this before."

"I'm a quick learner. Come on, Coop. I'll wear tight shirts and form-fitting jeans to please the men. I'll compliment the ladies. I'll play with the kids."

Even though I don't mean to, my gaze falls to her prosthetic leg.

"Oh, come on," she scolds me. "You aren't going to point out my limitations, are you? If you can do this job with a broken arm, I can do it with this." She kicks her false calf against a stool. "You know I can."

I shake my head. "I also know you're as stubborn as a fucking mule on downers. You won't let this go, will you?"

She walks over to an un-bussed table, pours all the liquid from the glasses into one, stacks them, puts the utensils in the top cup, piles up the plates expertly, and turns. "When do I start?"

I chuckle as I sling the notepad into the trash on our way to the back.

~ ~ ~

Two hours later, after shadowing Gino, Addy declares she's ready to go it on her own.

I toss her a disbelieving smirk. "Addison, there is no way."

"Cooper, I've been coming here since I was a little girl. I know everything on the menu. If I have a question, I'll ask. It's dinnertime. You need me."

"She's right." Gino passes, sensing my hesitation. "She's going to do great."

"Fine. But if you need any help, or anyone messes with you—"

"Yeah, yeah, yeah." She kisses my cheek. "I'll take the next table."

A few minutes later, a family walks in. Man, woman, and two small children. The toddler has a bow on her head, and the older boy looks about Gigi's age—six or seven, maybe. I refill a few drinks at the bar and settle myself by the serving area and listen.

"Welcome to Donovan's Pub," Addy says cheerfully, escorting them to a table. "Aren't your children adorable."

"Thank you," the woman says. "I don't think we've seen you here before."

"I'm new. Sorry, I don't have a name tag yet. My name is Addison, but everyone calls me Addy."

The man raises a brow. "Addison Calloway? Johnathan's daughter?"

"That's me."

"I'm Mitch Wilson. I work for your father. He hired me last month."

She smiles brightly. "Oh, wow. That's fantastic. You're going to love working with him. He's amazing, and I'm not just saying that because he's my dad."

"He's a great boss."

"What can I get you to drink? And while you're looking over the menu, I should let you know that today's special is shrimp scampi. It's to die for."

The boy is staring at Addy's prosthetic. She's wearing a skirt, so it's visible. She never seems self-conscious about it, which I love about her. "What happened to your leg?" he asks curiously.

Without an air of hesitation, she says, "Jumped off a roof, landed on a scooter, rolled right into the street, and got run over by an ice-cream truck."

I laugh quietly. Often, people who don't know her ask about her leg. She always seems to have a witty comeback. None of them are even close to the truth, that she got shitfaced drunk the night of Chaz's funeral and drove herself right into a concrete underpass, severing her left leg halfway down her calf.

The two adults know she's bullshitting, but the boy's eyes are wide.

"Let this be a lesson," Addy says to him. "Don't ever jump off a roof." Then she takes their drink orders and happily goes off to fill them.

The front door swings open, and the asshole brigade walks in. Hawk, Hunter, and Hudson McQuaid make their way to the bar. They are the town trust-fund kids. Only, they aren't kids. They're the same ages as my brothers and me. We all grew up here. Went to school together. And we can't stand each other any more today than we could back then. They're still pissed because one of their ancestors made a stupid bet with one of our ancestors like a hundred years ago, and the town was renamed from McQuaid Plat to Calloway Creek.

They stop talking mid-conversation when they see me behind the bar.

"What the fuck are you doing here?" Hawk asks, being his usual pleasant self.

I can't believe I'm going to have to serve these douchebags. I raise my arm. "Accident. Laid up for a while. Donny needed help. I'm helping." I don't bother asking them what they want to drink.

Hudson chuckles mockingly. "I always knew you Calloways belonged in the service industry."

Addy walks out from the back, clad in her Donovan's apron. Hunter looks her up and down. "I know what service industry *she'd* do well in," he says.

Hawk shoots his brother a fleeting scowl, and I could swear by Hunter's pissed-off expression that Hawk kicked him in the shin. And it occurs to me that Hawk is the only one of them who never speaks ill of Addy.

"Screw you and the stick up your ass, Hunter," I say, always at the ready to defend my baby sister.

"Is that any way to talk to paying customers?"

"You haven't paid shit yet."

Hawk throws a hundred on the bar.

"Guess you got your allowance early this month," I quip.

"Shut your trap and do your damn job. Three shots of Don Julio 1942."

I look at the shelves of liquor on display behind the bar but don't see it.

"In the cabinet," Hudson says, pointing to my left. "Donny keeps it there just for us."

Trying not to roll my eyes, I get out the keys and unlock the cabinet, vaguely remembering this is where Donny kept the stash of top-top-shelf liquor. I pull out the bottle and pour three shots.

Gino walks by and belts out a low whistle. "You celebrating something?" he asks them.

"Yeah," Hawk says. "Tuesday."

It's hard to hold in my disdain for the trio that did nothing for their wealth but be born into the McQuaid family. Rumor has it, they each have a multi-million-dollar trust fund. Ones that are controlled by their grandfather, Tucker McQuaid, until they reach the age of forty. Apparently, Tucker allows them to withdraw a certain amount each month—an amount speculated to be in the tens of thousands of dollars. And the only one of them who even seems to care anything about working a day in their pathetic lives is Hudson, or should I say *Doctor* McQuaid. He delivered Jaxon's daughter, Aurora, last month. But I'm pretty sure he only got into the business for the pussy. Damn, though—you'd think seeing that kind of thing every day, blood and goo and… birth shit, would totally turn a guy off. But based on his dating portfolio, it seems to have had the opposite effect on him. He must be one twisted fucker.

Their sister, Holland, dances through the door, saying hello to everyone as she makes her way to the bar to hug her older brothers.

Hudson turns to me, holding up his empty shot glass. "Better make it four this time."

"Saw your cars out back," Holland says. "Thought I'd come in and see if you wanted to do dinner."

The three jagoffs glance among one another and shrug. Hawk pulls out his phone. "Give me a sec to blow someone off."

Holland pouts. "Are you seriously canceling a date at the last minute? That's so mean."

"Nothing mean about it, Hol. I always tell the ladies not to expect anything until I confirm an hour before." He checks the time. "Well, close enough."

Hunter and Hudson fist bump their brother as if bringing disappointment to others is an accomplishment.

Holland stands tall, hands firmly on her hips. "You are so bad. All of you."

Addy comes over and wraps her arms around Holland from behind.

Holland yelps and turns, then squeals at Addy's apron. "Oh, my god. You work here?"

"Today's my first day. Please say you're going to have dinner. I need the practice."

How our little sisters remain friends when the rest of us hate one another is beyond me. But the twenty-two-year-old beauties carry on like the rest of us don't want to tar and feather each other.

I close out their bar tab, not bothering to point out what a crappy tip they left me, and Addy leads them to a booth.

Four more families, two couples, and what looks to be a soccer team roll in over the next hour, running all of us ragged. I hope Donny comes through with a plan. And soon. I'm not sure how long we can keep up this pace without someone with real expertise running this place.

Chapter Six

"Miss Donovan, you can see your father now."

I stand, my muscles tight, not only from the plane ride but from sitting in this waiting room all day. I could have gone home. His surgery took hours. I stopped by the house briefly to drop off my suitcases, but I didn't stay. Going back to that house will only spark more memories. So sitting here with aching legs, bloodshot eyes, and a headache from reading three dozen hospital magazines was a lesser evil than facing my old bedroom.

"How is he? Did everything go okay?"

"The surgery went smoothly," the nurse says. "He's been awake and under observation for a little while. I'm Scotty, your father's nurse. I'll meet with both of you tomorrow to go over his post-op care when he's not so groggy."

I follow Scotty down the hall and into a private room. Dad's eyes are closed.

"He'll be tired and in and out of it for the rest of the evening," Scotty says. "But we'll have him up and walking in the morning."

"Already? But he just had surgery."

"Don't worry. He'll use a walker at first. And the sooner we get him up, the quicker he'll start his recovery."

"Thank you," I tell him. Then he leaves.

I stand quietly in the doorway, watching my father sleep. Oh, how I've missed him. Earlier today, when I saw him in person for the first time in years, I fell into his arms and cried. I didn't realize until that moment how much I needed him. Tears come, as I'm thankful he's alive and okay.

I go to his bedside and pull up the chair in the corner. It scrapes along the floor, and Dad's eyes open. I cringe. "Sorry. Didn't mean to wake you."

"I'm so glad you're here, Serenity."

"Me too."

Even as I want to deny it, I know I mean it. Because Hilda was right, he's always been there for me. My rock. My mentor. My most favorite person. So, yes, in this moment, I do feel glad to be here.

"You are the absolute light of my life, do you know that? Your mother would have been so proud."

"I hope you know how much I love you, Dad. And I'm so sorry I haven't been back to see you."

"You're here now. That's all that matters."

"How are you feeling?"

"I'm not feeling anything yet. They must have pumped me full of drugs." He cocks his head sideways. "You look like you haven't slept in days, pumpkin. You didn't stay here the entire time, did you?"

I take his hand. "Of course I did. Surgery is a big deal. I wanted to be here."

"You should go home and get some rest."

Home. I wonder if I'll ever be able to call this town, his house, by that word again. "I slept a little on the plane. I'll be fine. I'll stop by the house and freshen up, but then I thought I'd go to the pub and make sure the place hasn't caught fire or anything."

He pats my hand. "That's my girl. I knew you'd hit the ground running." His last words trail off as he drifts back to sleep.

A few minutes later, a doctor comes in, checks a few things on Dad, and assures me everything is fine. "I'm sure you've had a long day. You're good to go home now," she says. "He's doing very well."

My stomach grumbles loudly, reminding me I've put little more in it than bad vending machine coffee and a protein bar that tasted like cardboard. "Guess that's my cue to leave."

"He'll be in good hands," the doctor says.

I keep my head low on the way out of the hospital. I've done a good job at not being noticed so far. I took an Uber earlier today, even though it's only a fifteen-minute walk. But now, I make the short walk home, the setting sun providing camouflage.

I realize it's crazy of me not to want to be recognized. As soon as I walk into Donovan's, the whole town will know I'm back.

You're not back.

Circumventing McQuaid Circle, I duck behind the strip and go through the parking lot behind Goodwin's, the ice cream shop, and the Chinese food place. I stay to the far end, only looking up when the pub comes into view. There are several couples eating out on the patio. A server I don't recognize comes through the back door with a tray of food, boisterous laughter echoing behind him. Seems busy for a Tuesday. It's now that I realize I hadn't bothered to ask Dad who he left in charge. Perhaps Kelly, his long-time friend and fellow cook. Or maybe Lissa, the only other person who was working there back when I was. Dad did mention a few weeks ago that she'd been promoted to bartender after Kyle's departure.

Other positions tend to have more turnover. Not as much as bars and restaurants in larger cities do, but we have our share. Kitchen staff and servers tend to come and go. Worker retention is one of the hardest things for restaurant owners to manage. Luckily, my dad has always been a great boss, so people usually only quit when they leave for college, graduate from Calloway Creek University and get a 'real' job, or move away.

"Serenity?" I hear behind me.

I turn to see Maddie Foster and… oh, my gosh, is that her daughter, Gigi? My mouth is agape. "Maddie, it's so nice to see you. And this little angel! Look at how big she's gotten." I hunch over and hold my hand parallel to the ground about two feet high. "You were only this tall the last time I saw you."

The little girl flashes me a toothless smile. "I'll be in first grade in…" She looks at Maddie. "How many months, Mommy?"

"Three, baby."

"I'll be in first grade in three months," she says, holding up as many fingers.

Maddie hugs me. "I didn't know you were back in town. Makes sense, though. I heard about your dad. I hope he's okay."

"I just came from the hospital. They said he's doing fine after his hip replacement."

"How long are you here?"

I shrug. "I'm really not sure." I notice the ring on her finger, remembering that she got engaged. *To Chaz's oldest brother.* Maddie and I were friends. Not close ones, because her circle was small and tight, but we're close in age and we both worked along McQuaid Circle—she at her flower shop, which we'd ordered from when hosting nice parties at the pub. I try to make my smile seem genuine, because unlike me, *she* gets to marry a Calloway. "Congratulations on your engagement."

"Thank you. We're very excited. I'd love for you to come to the wedding if you're still here next month."

"I…"

I try to think of an excuse, because going to a Calloway event is the *last* thing I want to do.

"Well, I came back to run the pub, so I'll be working a lot, but I'll see."

That appeases her and she smiles. "Great. Well, I'd better get this one home. Tag has dinner waiting."

"Bye, Maddie." I tug on one of Gigi's pigtails. "Later alligator."

"After a while crocodile," she chirps as they walk away.

I let them walk ahead, watching them. I know where they're going and what they'll be doing. I do my best not to think ill of Maddie. She's a good person with a tragic past, but she's living the life I wanted. Raising a daughter with her soul mate. Marrying the man of her dreams. Becoming Mrs. Calloway.

Sniffing back tears, I shuffle my feet slowly all the way back to Dad's house.

I stand in the foyer, eyeing my two suitcases that are right where I left them this morning. A knot forms in my gut when I think about taking them to my bedroom. Has he changed it? Will it still look the same? Oh, God, do pictures of Chaz still adorn the walls?

I pull one of the bags behind me, noticing how the house smells different than when I'd lived here. I'm sure Dad hasn't bothered to put out any air fresheners or fragrance plug-ins since I left. If I'm going to be here for a few months, I'll have to remedy that. I don't want to live in a place that smells like a bachelor pad.

Everything else is the same. The couch he bought when I was five. The recliner off to the side, which faces the television and has worn out armrests and a discolored seat cushion. The small kitchen table with only two chairs—because we never needed more. Even the same old coffee cup he always used is sitting by the sink, the one that reads: **A guy walks into a bar… oh wait, that's me.** It's a stupid mug I gave him for Christmas when I was fifteen. I didn't stop to realize the saying belonged on a pint glass or a T-shirt instead of a coffee mug, but I guess I thought it was funny at the time.

Yes, everything is the same. Which is why my heart is pounding uncontrollably as I enter my old room.

When I cross the threshold, I lose my grip on the suitcase, and it thumps to the floor. Chaz is everywhere. From the collage of our pictures on the wall, to the framed photo by my bed, to the keepsake box on my nightstand, to the binder of every love letter he emailed me (printed out, hole-punched, and sorted by date).

The walls close in. I retrieve my suitcase, retreat into the hall, and shut the door.

Breathe.

I enter the guest room and haul my suitcase onto the bed, my heart still in my throat. I sit and think of anything else, settling on making a mental list of what will need to be done at work, what I'll need to pick up from Truman's Grocery, and how I plan to help my father get around the house more easily.

Feeling somewhat better, I unzip my suitcase, pull out a change of clothes, then use the guest bathroom to freshen up. Looking in the mirror, I see what Dad saw. Which is something just this side of death warmed over. I pop back to the entryway and get my makeup bag, desperately needing to cover the dark bags under my eyes and the paleness of my cheeks. Sitka isn't exactly the place one goes to get a suntan. My skin has become shades lighter over the years. Maybe I'll sit in the backyard and soak up some sun while I'm here.

Instantly, a memory bombards me, and I stare through the small bathroom window. I can almost see Chaz and me painting the privacy fence along our property line. Well, painting the fence and then each other. He flicked his brush at me. I dipped a finger into the paint and ran it down his arm. He tackled me to the grass and painted strokes down my chest. We made love among the mess, my dad none the wiser, as he was manning the pub that day.

My mouth is bone dry. Probably because my eyes are crying all the tears. I sit on the closed toilet seat until I settle down, vowing to make it through the rest of the night without sobbing, but somehow knowing it's a promise I will fail miserably at keeping. Because unless I crawl under a rock, Chaz is everywhere. There's not a restaurant, park, sidewalk, or store in this town that doesn't hold a memory of him.

Why did I agree to this?

I stand and scold the selfish woman in the mirror. "Because he single-handedly raised you. He sacrificed so much so you could have a normal childhood. He's *always* been there for you. The least you can do is put on your big-girl panties and help him out."

After finishing my makeup, my hunger headache has me looking in the refrigerator. I snort. *Typical.* Beer. Coke. Condiments. And a few Donovan's take-out containers. I should know better. My father doesn't cook for himself. He cooks at the pub, eats at the pub, and brings home meals from the pub.

I open one of the Styrofoam lids and turn up my nose. This burger is way past its prime. I don't bother looking in the other. I'll just grab something when I get to work. I don't plan on staying long, anyway. Just long enough to see what's what, get my bearings, and make a plan to go forth.

And get food, my gurgling stomach reminds me.

My mouth waters thinking about Donovan's famous French dip sandwich. I've missed it almost as much as I've missed Dad. Nobody and no place can make one like it. Toasted roll, caramelized onions, marinated beef shaved into paper-thin strips, special seasonings, and provolone cheese. But the secret is in the au jus. Not too thick, not too salty, not too bland—simply perfect.

I leave the house looking forward to my meal.

The sun is down now, and streetlights illuminate the sidewalk. A few people are walking dogs or pushing strollers. I avoid them. My father's house is a mere half-mile from the pub, and the pub is halfway between his house and the hospital. I'm surprised the man even owns a car. He never drives anywhere.

I used to take his car out and drive it around once a week just to recharge the battery. With me gone, I wonder if anyone has even used it. I'll try to remember to start it up later. Surely he'll need to drive places during his recovery. Although I remember reading how he shouldn't for a month after surgery. I'll have to drive him home from the hospital at the very least.

I try not to think about cars, because Chaz is in those too. He loved cars. Especially *his* car. He'd tinker with it all the time, and I'd often watch. I lost my virginity in that car, then I came to love it as he did. Sometimes he'd even let me drive it.

But even though I'm trying not to think about it, it's like the universe is *making* me when a Mustang not much different from his whizzes past me. *The universe.* I recall Brandon's words to me just yesterday about the universe making things right. I puff an incredulous snort of air out of my nose because that will never happen.

I follow the tail lights until I can't see them anymore, then I turn the corner into the parking lot behind the pub. The crowd outside has thinned considerably, only one couple remains at a table along the decorative iron fence. Makes sense—it's Tuesday and it's after nine. Sunday through Thursday, closing time is ten. Some days, when all the customers had gone, Dad would even close up early. I momentarily wonder if he still does that. I guess that's one perk of owning your own business and also being the one to run it. You set the rules.

Hilda would do the same thing. But it wasn't often we would get to lock up before closing time. Seems there was always a group of fishermen or loggers or tourists that would keep us open until the very last minute.

The same server I saw earlier crosses the patio and brings the couple their check. He smiles at me as I pass, then pauses and does a double take as if he knows me. I don't think he does. He looks years younger. Maybe he was one of my friends' little brothers or something.

"Take a seat anywhere you want," he says. "I'll be with you in a minute."

"Oh, I'm not here to—" I shake my head. "Forget it, I'll explain inside."

He narrows his eyes at me, then collects a credit card from the man, staying to chat with him.

I go through the patio door and into the pub, trying but failing not to look at the booth in the corner. I drag my eyes away, needing to look professional when I rally the troops. But when I glance around, there are no troops. There's nobody here. No customers. No workers. It's completely empty.

Then the doors leading from the kitchen swing open.

My world stops.

Chaz walks through.

My brain knows it's not him; it's his twin. But my heart obviously thinks otherwise, because it's imploding, and over the span of ten seconds is reliving every moment I spent with him.

His face is thinner. His beard thicker. His hair longer. His eyes… unhappier.

And those sad blue eyes, they're looking at me like he's as surprised to see me as I am to see him.

I can't breathe. I turn and run straight into the server coming in from outside. I'm shorter than he is, so my forehead collides with his chin, smacking bone against bone. Pain sears through me. But it's not just my forehead that's hurting. It's my heart. My very soul.

I run out the patio door.

"Ren!" Cooper calls behind me.

His voice chills me to the bone. It's the same one that haunts my dreams. The low, familiar cadence that used to wind silken threads around my heart.

I hear steps chasing after me. I run faster. I run all the way home before I look back to see he didn't follow. Then I race into the bathroom and heave up nothing—over and over and over again.

Chapter Seven

Cooper

I walk back into the pub, scrubbing a hand over my beard. *Shit.*

It makes sense, I suppose, having Serenity fill in while Donny is recuperating. But it's not a scenario I'd even remotely considered. She hasn't set foot in this town for years. And now we're supposed to... *work together?*

Her eyes told me everything I needed to know. Donny didn't tell her I'd be here. Just like he failed to mention her to me. What was he thinking?

The restaurant is empty. I pull a bottle of Patrón from behind the bar and pour myself a shot. After pounding it back, I slam the tiny glass down on the counter, almost breaking it.

Gino comes out of the bathroom, rubbing his jaw. "A bruise is forming," he says. "It's going to look like someone decked me." He studies himself in the mirror behind the bar. "Do you suppose people will think I got hit by a girl?"

I'm staring at the door Serenity ran out of.

"Cooper?"

"What? Oh, yeah, no, it's not that bad."

"You didn't even look. Who was that anyway? And why does she look so familiar?" Still examining his chin in the mirror, his eyes must fall on the pictures off to the side. The pictures of Donny with his daughter. "Oh, shit. That was Serenity, wasn't it?"

"Indeed it was."

"Do you think Donny will be pissed at me? We hit heads pretty hard. And then she ran off like a bat out of hell."

"Wasn't your fault." I shake my head. "That's not why she ran. Listen, we're going to call it a night. Can you close up the patio tables?"

"Sure thing."

Now I'm the one looking at the pictures on the wall, thinking how she looks exactly the same yet different. She seemed thinner than she was before. Her honey-brown hair is longer now, falling well below her shoulders. She used to keep it short even though Chaz wanted her to grow it out. She'd complain it would get in the way at work, and she didn't like ponytails. And her skin was pale. Because she lives in Alaska or because she saw me? But the thing that was most different was her eyes. I've never seen them so sad.

Or maybe it was rage I saw in those chocolate irises. I know she hates me. How could she not? I couldn't save him. I hate me, too. So it will be impossible for us to be around each other.

I get out my phone.

Me: What the hell were you thinking, Donny? Call me in the morning.

I send the text and take another shot.

My phone rings ten seconds later. I answer. "Didn't you just have major surgery? It's almost ten o'clock. You should be sleeping."

"I slept for two damn hours during the procedure, and about six since. What's on your mind, son?"

"You know exactly what's on my mind. How could you hire me and then bring her back here without telling either of us?"

"Figured I'd just throw caution to the wind. See what happened."

"What happened was she saw me, turned white as a fucking ghost, and hightailed it out of here."

He sighs. "I'm sure it was a shock seeing you. Maybe I didn't go about this the right way, but she'll settle in and get used to it."

"I should quit, Donny. With her back, you don't even need me."

"The hell I don't. With Lissa gone, I need both of you. Hell, I need *more* than both of you."

"Oh, yeah. I should probably tell you I hired a new server today."

"Good for you. See, you're already acting like a manager."

"Don't you want to know who?"

"Well, if it wasn't your sister, I'd say you're a pretty shitty brother."

I laugh. "So nepotism isn't a problem for you."

He chuckles.

"Still," I say. "I just don't see it panning out—Serenity and me working together."

"It won't be all the time. Just during the busy nights. You can split the other shifts between you."

"I'm not sure that's going to suit her. You didn't see the look on her face. She wants me here like she wants a bullet in her head."

"Just give it a try. It's my best hope for keeping the place running while I'm gone."

"Only if she agrees."

"Fair enough. How was business today?"

"Good. A soccer team came in. Addy's already covering her own tables. Nobody sent their food back."

"Sounds like you're doing a great job, Cooper. Thank you."

"Sure thing. Now get some sleep. I'll talk to you later."

I glance back at the pictures on the wall, believing this may be my last shift. No way will she agree.

A half hour later, the place closed up, I'm walking back to Tag's house, my temporary living quarters until I move into the cabin this weekend. The sale doesn't officially go through until next month, but they said I could take occupancy. I pick up the keys tomorrow and plan to spend Thursday and Friday morning cleaning up the place. My van, with the rest of my stuff, should be here by Sunday.

Tag's best friend, Amber, and her husband, Quinn, are sitting around the table with Tag and Maddie, having drinks and discussing wedding plans.

"There he is!" Amber sings, jumping up to hug me. "I can't believe you've been in town for five whole days and I haven't seen you."

Amber and Tag have been best friends since they were kids. A few years ago, she went to a wedding down in Texas, got laid up there with a broken leg or something, and met the man she would ultimately marry.

Quinn shakes my hand, eyeing my cast. "How's the arm? I heard what happened. Sounds like you got lucky."

"Yeah, lucky. That's me."

"So guess what?" Maddie says. "Chris Montana is offering their vineyard for our wedding and reception. We don't have to have it at the Eighth Avenue Reception Hall. And Quinn is going to fly Gigi and me over in the helicopter and then fly Tag and me to the airport after."

"Helicopter?" I narrow my brow. "Isn't Chris's vineyard only thirty minutes away?"

"Yeah, but it'll be like arriving in a horse-drawn carriage, only better. Gigi is so excited."

"That reminds me," Tag says. "Gigi is staying with Josie's nanny, Sophie, when we're in Barbados for our honeymoon, but her cat and our dog don't exactly get along. I'd ask Jaxon to take her, but he has his hands full. Do you think Sissy could crash with you that week?"

"You want me to dog sit?"

"She's very well behaved," Maddie says. "We've had her trained. And she'll love the cabin, I know it."

"What about when I'm working? I'm at the pub for twelve-hour shifts sometimes." I pull out a chair and sit. "That is, if I still have a job after tonight."

Tag snorts. "What did you do, burn down the kitchen?"

I suck in my lower lip, making a hissing noise. "Serenity Donovan is back."

Nobody seems surprised. Word must have gotten out. Yet all eyes are on me.

Amber is the first to speak. "It's about time. Is it for good, or just to help out Donny?"

I shrug. "Don't know. At this point, I don't know anything. Except she came into work a little while ago, saw me, didn't say a damn word, and marched right back out the door."

Amber covers her gasp. "Her dad didn't tell her you'd be there?"

"Nope. Didn't tell me she was coming either."

"Sneaky bastard," Tag says. "What's his endgame?"

I cock my head. I hadn't thought about Donny having some kind of ulterior motive.

"My guess is he's trying to get her to confront her demons," Amber says. "It's been a long time coming."

I thumb to the hallway. "I'm beat. I'm going to hit the hay."

"Listen, about Sissy," Tag says. "Jaxon has a dog walker I can hire for the week, so there should be no worries about you being at work."

"Yeah, sure. Whatever."

On my way to bed, Amber's words echo in my head. *Demons.* Does Serenity have them? And if she does, are they as bad as mine?

Chapter Eight

Serenity

My alarm goes off at 8:00 a.m. I snooze it three times. My body is still on Sitka time.

"Alright!" I yell at my phone the fourth time the incessant noise startles me.

Light filters through the drapes in the guest room. I crane my neck and look at the words painted in an arch above the headboard.

May our home be warm and our friends be many.

In high school, Dad commissioned my best friend, Allie, to paint it. She was always super talented. He insisted on paying her even though she didn't need the money. After all, she is a Montana and one of the heirs to her father's profitable winery.

I should call her. She would be so mad to hear from someone else that I'm back in town. I'll make it a point to call her and Mia Cruz, my other best friend, before the day is over. But first, I've got things to do.

1—start Dad's car

2—visit Dad

3—go to work

It's the last thing on the list that has me staying in bed longer than I should. Cooper looked surprised to see me last night. Dad obviously kept it from both of us. Probably because he knew I wouldn't have come back had I known Cooper was in town, and definitely not if I'd thought Dad expected me to work with him.

He won't be there today, I tell myself. He was only there to pick up the slack until I came home. Based on what I've heard about him in the last several years, Cooper Calloway would never be happy bartending for a living. It was a favor to Dad. A temporary solution.

Feeling a modicum of relief, I swing my legs out of bed and make my way to the bathroom. I rip the Band-Aid off my head, noting last night's collision wasn't as bad as I'd thought, and finally take a much-needed shower, after which, I scoop coffee grounds into the coffee maker, making it extra strong to get me through the morning. While it's brewing, I walk through the laundry room and get a set of keys from the decorative **K.E.Y.S.** holder by the door to the garage, thinking there are more sets dangling from the letters than I recall being here before.

I open the door to the garage and reach inside. Muscle memory has my fingers landing exactly where the automatic opener is. The garage door lifts, bringing more light from outside into the garage with every inch.

Dad's blue Hyundai Santa Fe looks virtually untouched since I left. I walk around to the driver's side, stopping in my tracks when I round the back bumper. My stomach tightens. My breath hitches. My legs almost fail me.

Chaz's Mustang is parked right next to Dad's car. I close my eyes tightly, certain I'm hallucinating. But when I open them, the apparition doesn't disappear. His car is actually here. My heart hurts as if it's being squeezed by a vise. A dozen memories bombard me all at once. Chaz picking me up for our first date. Us dressed to the nines on our way to prom. Him picking me up from the airport after I went with Allie's family to Mexico for spring break.

Us making love in the back seat in the parking lot behind the train station.

Frantic to maintain control of my emotions and keep myself from spiraling into a pit of despair, I focus on my other senses—the smell of the fragrant jasmine lining the driveway, the sound of dogs barking in the distance, the feel of sharp edges of a key on the keychain.

But looking at his car... It's too much. I race back to the laundry room. I push the button to lower the garage door before I slam the door shut and press my back to it as if a serial killer is on the other side. I slide down the door until my butt hits the floor, knowing I won't go back out there. Because what's on the other side *might* actually kill me.

~ ~ ~

I walk into Dad's hospital room, happy to see him sitting up in bed but having a hard time expressing my happiness, because, well... the Mustang. I can't think of anything else.

"Why is his car in your garage?"

His face softens with empathy. "I wasn't sure how to tell you. I suppose I figured by the time you came back, you'd be ready to move on."

"Seems you didn't tell me *a lot* of things."

Empathy turns to guilt, and he rubs his hands together. "Guess we have a few things to discuss."

"We do." I sit and give him a hard stare. "The car?"

"Johnathan and Libby knew how much you liked it. And since Chaz always drove you everywhere, and you didn't have a car of your own, they thought he'd want you to have it. It was very generous of them, don't you think?"

"Generous of them to give me something that reminds me of my dead fiancé every time I see it? I'll never be able to drive it, Dad. We should give it back."

"Or maybe it's too early to make that decision."

"Whatever. It's your garage. I don't know why you'd want a second car in there, being as you never even drive your own."

His eyes follow the motion of my hands as my fingers twist the engagement ring around. "You didn't get the gift I left you?"

"You got me a present?"

"I left it on your dresser."

I shift my gaze and look out the window. "I slept in the guest room."

He seems disappointed. "Oh, well, when you're ready, you can go in and get it. It's just something small I picked up in the city last year. Thought you might be able to use it."

"Well, thank you. I'm sure whatever it is will be amazing. Your gifts always have been."

He winces as he pushes himself up a little further in bed. "Okay, come on, let me have it. You know you want to have words. Just remember, I'm an old man in a hospital bed." He points to his chest. "The old ticker ain't what it used to be."

"Please." I roll my eyes. "You're one of the healthiest fifty-somethings I know. But, yeah, I want to have words. I mean, Cooper Calloway? What were you thinking?"

"Pumpkin, I hired him before this happened."

"Why would he even want to work there with all his daredeviling and gallivanting?"

"Guess you didn't notice the cast."

"Cast?"

"Broke his arm on one of those crazy expeditions of his. He needed something to do in the meantime."

"Well, he can find something else to do," I say. "I'm here now."

"You want me to fire him?"

"Yes."

He shakes his head. "I can't do that."

"Why not?"

"Because I'm not the manager right now, you are. Or he is. Not really sure. We could call you co-managers."

"You made him a manager? Why not Kelly or Lissa?"

"Lissa's taking some time off to travel. And I've tried promoting Kelly a dozen times over the years, a fact you're well aware of. He doesn't want anything to do with managing. You want Cooper gone, you'll have to do it yourself. But it would be a mistake. It's a lot of work, that pub. I'm used to the shifts than can last up to fourteen hours. Got nothing else to do but run the place. I know you're young, but hours like that, day after day, they take some getting used to."

"I managed Hilda's."

"Not by yourself. And managing a bar is a lot different than a restaurant."

"So I'll hire someone else."

"Because running the pub *and* training a new manager seems like the much better option. Pumpkin, Cooper worked there before. He knows the place. He jumped right in. And the timing is right, as he only needs a temporary job anyway." He cuts me a sharp look, challenging me to argue.

"How can I work with him?"

"Serenity, I understand what Cooper represents to you. But have you forgotten what good friends you were? How he tutored you in Calculus senior year. How you two were always trading shifts so the other could go on a date. How he stepped up and helped you when you sprained your ankle when Chaz was off running that half-marathon in Central Park. How you never made him feel like a third wheel. And I could name a hundred more things. You and Cooper were as close as you and Allie or Mia. When he lost Chaz, he lost more than his brother. He also lost you as a friend. You'd do well to remember that."

I scrub my hands across my eyebrows and down the sides of my face. I know what he says is true. But that won't make it any easier to work side by side with the man who reminds me of Chaz even more than the Mustang does.

He takes my hand. "Give it a chance. Take turns closing. The only times you'll have to work together will be the weekend nights."

My phone vibrates with a text.

Mia: Girl, are you seriously back in CC? My friend Janine heard from Regan who heard from Ava who said Amber told her you arrived yesterday. You better call me.

I'd almost forgotten how quickly word travels around this town. Everyone knows everybody's business.

"Dad, I'd better go if I want to be at work to open."

"So you'll give it a try?" he asks, his expression hopeful.

"Honestly, I haven't decided yet."

"You've got a good head on your shoulders, Serenity. And a good heart, too. That, you got from your mom. I know you'll make the right decision."

"Way to guilt trip me, Dad."

"I'll stand by whatever decision you make, even if I don't agree with it."

I know he speaks the truth. After all, he's supported my decision to live in Sitka all these years, and I'm *positive* he didn't agree with that.

I make my way to the door. "Good luck walking today. I'll check in on you later."

He winks and smiles.

Just down the street from the hospital, I run into Nicky Forbes. Or is it Calloway? I don't know what she goes by these days. She's pushing a baby stroller. When she sees me, a smile brightens her face. We were close once, both of us dating Calloway brothers.

"Serenity! I heard you were back in town."

I'm not back. "Hi, Nicky." I lean down and admire her baby. "Congratulations. She's beautiful."

"Thank you."

"I saw you on XTN earlier this year. You've really made a name for yourself. I imagine it's everything you've ever dreamed of."

She gazes at me sadly. Probably because she knows I'll never get to live *my* dreams. I look away, not wanting any more pity.

"We're on our way to a well-baby checkup, but we should do lunch soon," she says. "That is, if you don't mind this little one tagging along."

"Sure. Come by the restaurant anytime you want. I'll have Kelly make us something special."

"It'll be nice to catch up." She draws me into a hug. "I've missed you."

I continue on my way and remember I need to call Mia.

She squeals upon answering. "So it's true?"

"Yes, I'm in Calloway Creek. Sorry I haven't had a chance to call. Everything happened so quickly."

"When can we get together? Oh, my gosh, does Allie know? She must not know. She hasn't texted me. We *have* to see you, Ren. It's been, like, four years."

Three years, ten months, one week, and four days to be exact.

Part of me wants to tell her to stop calling me Ren. It's a nickname I picked up early on in this town. And it's the only place anyone ever uses it. Just another reminder of my past life.

"I'll call her. Maybe the two of you can pop by the pub after work. It's Wednesday so it won't be so busy that I can't have a drink with you and catch up."

I hear her clap. "Perfect. Can't wait to see you."

"Me too."

By the time I'm off my second phone call with Allie, I'm staring at the back door of Donovan's, dreading going inside. Will he be here?

I inhale a cleansing breath and open the door. Kelly immediately reacts to my presence. "Well, look at what the cat dragged in," he jokes. "Damn glad to see ya, squirt."

Chuckling, I don't bother reminding him I'm almost twenty-six years old, not the little girl I was when he started cooking here two decades ago.

I wrap him in a hug, because I have missed him. "You, too, Kelly. And just so you know, I've been craving a French dip sandwich since yesterday. My mouth is watering just thinking of it."

"I'll make it now."

"Aren't you still prepping?"

"Almost done. I was just gettin' ready to put my desserts in the oven." He nods to a man chopping vegetables. "Allen's doin' the rest." He waves his arm. "Boy, get on over here and meet your new boss."

"New boss?" Allen says, confused. "I thought—"

"You thought nothin'," Kelly says. "This here is the very talented, incredibly tenacious Serenity Donovan."

"Donovan?" Allen gives me a cock of his head. "Right, you're on the wall." He wipes a hand down his apron and holds it out. "Nice to meet you."

I shake. "You, too."

A woman walks in from the front, carrying a tray of ketchup bottles. Kelly introduces us as well. "And this is Katie. Katie, this here's Serenity. Donny's daughter."

Katie smiles. "I've heard so much about you. Your dad sure does love telling stories about when you were growing up."

"Allen and Katie," I say, committing their names to memory. "We'll find time later to get to know each other a little better."

Katie goes to refill the ketchup bottles, and Allen resumes his prepping.

Kelly picks up a bag of rolls. "I'll get started on the sandwich. You want it in the office?"

"Uh, sure," I say, not knowing what, or more specifically *who*, I'll find when I go in there. "I'm just going to look around for a bit first."

"Nothing's changed," he says. "Except for you not being here to brighten everyone's day."

I offer a smile. Little does he know I'm not good for brightening *anything* these days.

Holding my breath, I push through the swinging doors to the front. I do a visual sweep of the restaurant. Empty. I breathe a little easier. I walk behind the bar and go on autopilot, filling the napkin trays and straw bins from the stock underneath, realizing Kelly was right, nothing has changed. Everything is right where it's always been.

I take quick inventory of the liquor bottles lining the shelves, then the glasses hanging from the rack over the bar. I glance around at the tables and booths (taking care to ignore *the* booth) seeing that the salt and pepper shakers have been filled. The utensil bin is full, the napkins having been securely wrapped around pairs of forks and knives. Once the ketchup bottles are in place, the front of house will be all set.

Going through to the back, I take a clipboard off the wall, looking at the food inventory. I walk into the cooler, eye the spare kegs and cold ingredients, then take a glance at the pantry food. There's only one thing left to do—go to the office. I approach it slowly and test the knob as if fire may be behind the door. I push through and enter, relieved to be the only person in the room.

My heart back to a normal pace, I scoot behind the desk and sit, the familiar feel of the cushy cherry leather office chair surrounding my hips. I press the spacebar on the keyboard, and the black computer screen morphs into a picture of me. I remember the day Dad took the photo. It was the last vacation he and I went on together. We didn't get many of them, considering we ran the pub together, but it was a rare weekend. He surprised me with a trip to the Jersey Shore. He said he knew it would be our final father-daughter trip, what with Chaz and I set to be married the next summer, so he wanted to make it special. In the photo, I'm sitting on the beach sipping a fancy drink I can't remember the name of. Ironic since I'm a bartender. But the most surprising thing about the photo is how happy I look.

Happy isn't even an emotion I'm capable of anymore.

The door opens and I glance up, my stomach turning at the person walking in. He sees me and thrusts his hands into the pockets of his jeans. His forehead creases into a frown, and his entire face morphs into a pained grimace. I look back at the computer and busy myself with the mouse, trying to ignore the powerful rush of emotions making my throat sting. "I, uh… thought you weren't here," I mutter.

"Bathroom," Cooper says. He shuts the door and sits on the small couch in the corner.

I'm silent, because if I talk, he'll talk. And if he talks, it will be like Chaz is talking. And I don't want to hear Chaz's voice.

But no such luck.

"Are we going to talk about this?" he asks, his voice laced with remorse. "Or are you just going to sit there and ignore me all day?"

I can't tell if he wants to be here or not. I was hoping he wouldn't want to be. That he'd quit before I could fire him.

I clear my throat nervously. "There's not much to talk about. I'm here now, so you don't have to be."

"I talked to your dad last night after you ran out. He said he needs us both."

"I can do it on my own," I say to the computer screen.

"Donny could barely do it on his own, and he had thirty years' experience."

"You have no idea how to manage this place."

He huffs a sigh of annoyance. "I've done pretty good the past two days."

There's a war going on in my head over whether or not to look at him. Because I know if I look at him, it's not Cooper I'll see. I'll never see Cooper. I'll only see Chaz. And I'll see the life I never got to live. The experiences I never got to have. The love I'll never get to feel again.

"Two days?" I say melodramatically, still pretending to work on the computer. "Oh, well, then by all means, you're an expert restaurant manager now."

"That's not what I meant." I hear him shift his weight on the couch. "Are you ever going to look at me?"

"Hadn't planned on it."

"So that's how it's going to be?"

I shrug and spare a fleeting glance at him.

Powerful arms cross his chest. "Serenity, we can't work together and not look at each other. I get what I represent to you. Sometimes I can't even look in the mirror. But this is the situation we're in, like it or not."

"Not," I say flatly, setting my mouth in a grim line.

"Well, Donny wants us to do this together."

I snort. "The extent of your knowledge about running this place is how to inventory bottles of liquor and drink mix. You forget I used to work with you, Cooper. But there's much more to it than that. Hiring staff—"

"I've already done that. Addy started yesterday. She's up to speed."

"You hired Addison?"

"I *am* one of the managers."

"Not for long. My dad gave me the okay to fire you."

Silence.

"He… did?" he asks quietly. In my periphery, I see his shoulders slump. "So are you?"

"I haven't decided yet."

"Just tell me what to do and I'll do it. I told Donny I'm here to help."

"I don't have the time to train you. Do you understand how much there is to know? Inventory management, menu pricing, CoGS numbers, stock wastage calculations, demand forecasting, supplier management, dish profitability, payroll, bank reconciliation, customer retention, profit margin determination—"

He holds up a hand. "Okay, I get it. Yeah, I don't know shit about most of that. So decide what's the easiest for me to handle, and I'll take that load off you."

"I…" I try to look directly at him but can't. "I don't think it's a good idea. I think you should consider this your last—"

He stands so quickly it startles me, and my eyes finally meet his. I immediately realize the mistake.

Those eyes. Those amazing, bold blue eyes. The same ones I thought I'd be looking into for the rest of my life. They destroy me. I bite back the sob rattling around in my chest.

"I'm not going down so easily," he says. "I'll take off now. You run the day shift. I'll be back around seven to finish up and close. I'm sure you're still jet lagged."

"Cooper…"

"Just don't make a decision yet. Not until we give it a try."

My eyes close momentarily. "Don't you get it? I can't look at you. I can't listen to you. I can't even smell you."

Guilt crosses his face. "I know."

"Then why are you fighting this? Why do you even want to work here? If there are any two people in the world who shouldn't be working together, it's the two of us."

He holds up his cast. "I'm benched for a few months. Not much more to do in this Podunk little town. And I owe it to

Donny. He was always a great boss. Time off whenever I needed it. Advances when I was short on cash." He pauses poignantly. "Besides, we were friends, Ren. We lost more than just him that day. We lost each other."

We lost each other. The words echo through my head like he'd shouted them into a deep cavern. Everything my dad reminded me of earlier comes rushing back. The antics. The good times. Our unwavering support of each other. But the regret I feel over the loss of our friendship isn't enough to overcome the crippling pain that tears through me when I look at him.

Unable to bring myself to fire him after what he said, I get up, stride to the door, and open it. "Fine. You can leave now."

"Fine?"

"That's what I said. But maybe don't get too comfortable here." I gesture to the desk. "The office is mine. You can find someplace else to do… whatever it is you're going to do."

"I don't need an office, Ren. I'm going to fill in wherever I'm needed. Making drinks. Serving food. Cleaning tables. Hell, I'll cook if Kelly needs help." His fingers brush over his thick facial hair. "I'll even wear a beard net if I have to."

"Like I said, don't get too—"

"Comfortable. Yeah, I heard you the first time." He walks through the door and looks back. "See you at seven."

"No, you won't. I'll be gone by 6:55."

He exhales in frustration. "Fine."

"Fine," I scoff back and shut the door.

I plop down onto the couch, head in my hands, the scent of him still lingering. How do they even *smell* identical? And even though my whole body is warning me against it, I'm drawn to the warm suede cushion he vacated. I lie down, breathing him in.

They say scents can evoke the strongest memories.

Whoever *'they'* are, they're right.

Because the floodgates have opened once again.

Chapter Nine

Cooper

I sneeze at the dust that gets stirred up when I remove the sheet covering the couch. I assess the decades-old piece of furniture. It will have to go, like most of the other furniture here. I've slept in my share of questionable places in my life, but I'm not too keen on sleeping in Old Joe Henson's bed. Especially when it's entirely possible he could have died in it.

Glancing around, I realize how much I like this rustic cabin. It's my kind of place. Small. Secluded. Off the beaten path. And most importantly, although it's in Calloway Creek, it doesn't hold any memories.

I get my cleaning supplies out of Jaxon's Honda. I'm not sure why he still drives the thing. His wife is making bank working for one of the top cable news networks in the country, but he insists he doesn't drive much, so what would be the point of a fancy new car. I'll have to run it through a car wash before I return it. There are no paved roads leading to my new abode, only dirt ones that aren't much wider than the arm span of an NBA player.

Walking back to the front steps, movement on the hiking trail catches my eye, and I find myself amused that I'm now the proud owner of a one-room cabin on one of Calloway Creek's most popular outdoor pastimes. I hesitate before entering the cabin, figuring I'll be neighborly and wave to the passerby. But when said passerby gets closer, I realize my faux pa.

Serenity sees me. Her steps falter and she tumbles to the ground, grimacing in pain.

I drop my bags and trot over. "You okay?"

She looks up, her dark eyes fringed by full lashes. "Why must you show up *everywhere* I go?"

"You're the one running past my house."

Her gaze falls upon the cabin. "*Your* house? You bought Joe Henson's cabin?"

"I did. Well, as soon as the sale goes through."

She pulls her knee up. Blood trickles down her leg, dirt and pebbles stuck inside a gash on top of her kneecap.

"Damn, Ren. That looks bad." I thumb to the cabin. "Let's go see if there's anything inside to clean you up with."

She shakes her head vehemently. "I'm okay."

I laugh smugly. "Your sock is turning red from the blood, and who knows what's in the dirt inside the wound—animal feces maybe. You have to clean it."

Her nose turns up. She assesses her knee. "Fine."

She really seems to like that word.

I hold out my hand to help her up, but she refuses it. "I'm not an invalid. I can walk."

My hands go up in surrender. "Just trying to help."

She doesn't want your help. And can you blame her?

She follows me inside. I pull out an old, rickety kitchen chair and sit on it first to make sure it can handle the weight, then I stand and motion for her to take a seat.

"There has to be something in here we can use to fix you up." I go back onto the porch, retrieve the bags, and rip off a few strips of paper towels. I wet them and hand them to her. "Hold this on it while I look around."

There aren't many places to look in this tiny cabin. There are exactly two upper cabinets in the kitchen, filled with an eclectic mishmash of flea market housewares. The four lower cabinets hold more of the same. I stomp on a spider as it scurries out of a saucepan. There's a fire extinguisher under the sink that expired ten years ago, and a container of Clorox wipes that has long since dried up.

"I'll just check the bathroom," I say.

I stare at her on my way. She isn't looking at me. She's looking everywhere *but* at me.

I chuckle when I enter the bathroom. If there's one thing the old man spent any money on, it's this. Makes me wonder just how much time the old geezer spent in here. There's a shower/tub combo that looks like it came right out of one of those bath-fitter commercials. A vanity sink that was probably last year's Home Depot model. And a toilet with a… *bidet* fitting?

Bingo! In the cabinet under the sink is a first aid kit that appears might have been bought in this millennium. I carry it out and set it on the table, taking a seat next to Serenity.

"We got lucky," I say, perusing the contents. "Antiseptic wipes. Bandages. Tweezers. But first, we need to get it cleaned out. Let me help you to the bathroom."

She shrugs my hand away when I put it on the soft skin below her elbow. "I can do it."

I pull back and watch her hobble to the tub. She sits on the edge, turns on the water, and makes a hissing noise when she dips her knee under the stream.

"Here." I hand her a fresh wad of paper towels.

She pats her knee dry and goes back to the chair. I stand to the side as she sifts through the medical supplies and opens an antibacterial wipe. I wait for the yelp when it touches her knee, but it never comes. Her face gives nothing away. It's as if she's numb to the pain.

It's hard not to notice her snug jogging shorts, and her light-green top discolored with dampness between her breasts. Her hair is pulled back into a ponytail, the beads of sweat dotting her brow having evaporated over the last minutes. And her pale skin… It's as flawless as virgin snow.

I turn away when something stirs inside me. Because something should definitely not be stirring. Of all the women in all the goddamn world, *she* shouldn't be the one to stir me up.

While she patches herself up, I catch her glancing up at me. Is she testing the waters? Seeing if looking at me is easier today than it was yesterday?

Then I think of last night. True to her word, she was gone when I showed up at seven o'clock, the only communication being a note tacked to the outside of the office door outlining a schedule of when I would be working. She alternated days with me opening and her closing on Sunday, Tuesday, and Thursday, our shifts just barely overlapping during the busiest dinner hours; and her opening and me closing on Monday and Wednesday. Friday and Saturday nights are the only time we're scheduled to work more than an hour or two together.

"The pub gets pretty busy on both Sunday and Tuesday nights. I'm happy to swap the closing shift with you for one of them."

Without looking up, she says, "Thanks, but I think the more experienced manager should work the busier nights."

This is going to be a long few months. Maybe I should just stay holed up in my new pad like Henson did. Become a hermit. I think I could get used to that way of life.

But I promised Donny.

"Fine," I say, apparently favoring the word myself. "But you'll let me know if you need the extra help."

"I won't." She wads up the bloody paper towels and other trash and then leaves them in a pile on the table. "I'm good now." She goes for the door, still not looking at me. "Thank you," she says quietly, as if it pained her to utter the words.

"No problem. I can give you a ride back to town."

"I said I'm good. Don't be late for work."

"I'll be there by five."

She heads toward the hiking path, each step more determined than the last as she gets farther away from me, only pausing long enough to give me a brief glance over her shoulder like maybe she wants to say something else. Instead, she flicks her arm in the air as if to acknowledge my prior statement.

The over-the-shoulder look—I've seen it before. A memory hovers in my periphery. Then it slams into me with the force of a Mack truck.

"Are your Apple Jacks stale?" I ask Chaz, watching him push them around his bowl for the tenth time without taking a bite.

"He has his big speech today," Mom says, pouring me a serving. She kisses him on the head. "You'll do fine, sweetie. When you practiced it for me last night, I thought it was very informative."

"It sucks," Chaz says, dropping his spoon into the bowl before taking his uneaten cereal to the sink. He leans against the counter. "How come I can play football in front of five hundred people, but the thought of standing in front of

twenty, talking about the ancient Mayan civilization for three fuckin' minutes, makes me want to vomit up last night's pizza?"

"No cursing," Mom says. She picks up her keys. "I'm off to take Addy to school. Just stick to your notes and remember to make a little eye contact with the audience."

Chaz grumbles. Mom leaves. We're alone.

"Fuck, I hate school," he says.

"You don't hate school. You hate speeches."

He follows me to the bathroom and stands in the doorway, waiting his turn while I brush my teeth. He catches my eyes in the mirror. "Do it for me."

"Funny." I shut the door on him so I can take a leak.

"I'm serious, Coop," he says loudly through the closed door. "One: you don't want me to throw up in the car on the way to school, because the smell of vomit makes you vomit. Two: you don't want me to fail this class, which would make me have to take summer school, which would ruin our plans, and this speech is thirty percent of my grade. And three—"

I flush and open the door. "There is no three. Dude, we haven't switched places since we were in fourth grade."

"And three"—he pulls out his wallet—"I'll give you fifty bucks. I was saving it to buy Ren something nice, but I'll just mow extra lawns for the next month."

I could use the money but shake my head anyway. "I'd bomb it. There's no time to prepare."

"There is. It's not until sixth period. I know you had a bunch of tests last week, so you're probably not doing shit that matters right now. And I have second period study hall, which will give you a lot of time to prepare. Then there's lunch. Come on, you know you can learn it. I have flash cards that say everything." He pulls another twenty out. "This is everything I have. I'm at your mercy here. Please?"

"Stop begging, you idiot. It makes you look like a pussy." I stare at the seventy dollars in his hand, then pluck it from his grip. "Fine, I'll do it."

He snatches the twenty back. "You'll get this after I get a B or better."

I roll my eyes. He starts taking off his clothes.

"Dude, what are you doing?" I ask.

"You have to switch clothes with me or it will never work. I never wear button-ups. And you should stutter a few times during the speech or Mrs. Hornsworth might catch on. Everyone knows I stutter when I'm nervous. I'll help you prep during lunch. It'll give us an excuse to skip the cafeteria and avoid our friends."

"You'll have to tell Ren."

"Screw that. She would string me up by the balls if she knew I paid you to do it."

"But you have two classes with her," I say. "Including *sixth* period."

"You mean *you* have two classes with her." He hands me his shirt. "We sit alphabetically in English. Harper Davis is between us. She's an uptight nerd and won't let Ren and me get in a word around her. Walk Ren to Mr. Wilkins' Spanish class after."

I toss him a look. "Walk your girlfriend to class?"

"I'm not saying you have to shove your tongue down her throat, Coop. Jesus, help a brother out here."

"If she suspects, I'm not going to deny it."

"Fine. Whatever. She won't. We barely have four minutes between classes. It's not like she'll have time to suspect anything. Meet me in the bathroom by the cafeteria right after seventh. We'll switch clothes and by the time Ren meets us at my car, nobody will be the wiser."

I remove my clothes and put on his, not quite believing I'm agreeing to this. "If there's a pop quiz in Pre-Calc and you fuck up my grade, I will kill you."

"If there's a pop quiz, I'll fake being sick and go to the nurse."

"You've got an answer for everything, don't you?"

He checks the time. "Come on, we'll be late, Chaz."

I shake my head on our way out, feeling like I'm seven and not seventeen.

Six hours later, after a performance that should earn me another forty bucks instead of just twenty (I added extra stutters just in case), I'm walking out of the classroom, Ren trailing behind.

She pulls me aside. "You did great. See, I told you not to stress over it." She raises a sultry brow. "I thought you looked really sexy up there."

I glance around, more nervous than I've been all day. "I, uh…"

Without notice, she takes a fistful of my shirt, pulls me toward her, and leans up to kiss me. Okay, granted, I have to lean down, *because she's shorter than me, but in the point three seconds I have to make a decision, I figure Chaz would rather have me peck her on the lips than him be in the doghouse for the next week.*

But the peck on the lips turns out to be more. She deepens the kiss, putting her tongue in my mouth. I haven't kissed a girl since I took Joellen Gellerman to the homecoming dance two months ago. Before that, I'd kissed my share of girls, messed around with a good handful, and slept with a few I probably shouldn't have slept with. None of them, however, had my blood pumping and my knees going weak like I'm feeling right now. None had my skin tingling at the mere touch of fingers brushing against it. Or my head going all fuzzy like I'd taken a few shots of Dad's rotgut whiskey.

Luckily, a teacher clears her throat and reminds us we have two minutes to get to our next class.

"See ya," Ren sings happily, smiling at me as she dances down the hall toward her AP History class. She stops walking for a beat, hesitating, then starts again. Before she disappears around the corner, she turns, tossing me a look over her shoulder like she wants to say something. She doesn't. And then she's gone.

Me—I stand here like a goddamn fool.

Or maybe a traitorous twin.

Because, fuck… *I think I might have a boner for my brother's girl.*

Chapter Ten

Serenity

"Something wrong with my car?" Dad asks when the Uber pulls up to the hospital entrance.

"Wouldn't start," I say.

He eyes me sideways but doesn't press the issue. If he did, I'd have to tell him I haven't been back in the garage.

Or my room.

Or the backyard.

Work and home. Home and work. That's all I can manage at this point.

And running. But even that has its unfortunate complications.

"Careful." I help him into the back seat and hand him his cane as the orderly loads his bag into the trunk.

"Pretty soon, I'll be able to walk between here and home," Dad says. He taps his leg gently. "With my bionic hip and all."

"Easy now. I know they want you up and walking, but don't overdo it."

"Don't plan to. I haven't had a vacation in years. This might be nice."

"Vacation? You call convalescing at home a vacation?"

"Sure. It'll give me a chance to catch up on all my shows."

"What shows?"

"*Seinfeld. The Sopranos. The X-Files.*"

I chuckle. "I'm not sure any of those are still being aired. Besides, you need to update your repertoire. Maybe try *Game of Thrones* or *Stranger Things.* Don't you ever watch television at work on your downtime?"

"There's always something to do at work, pumpkin."

"You work too hard."

"Said the pot to the kettle."

"That's not true, Dad. Nobody works harder than you do."

"Well, when you have a goal in mind, it makes it easier."

"Goal?"

He pats my hand. "To have something to leave my daughter when I'm gone."

I swallow hard. "That's not going to happen for a long time."

"From your lips to God's ears."

At the house, we get out of the car, and I cringe at the front porch steps. I take Dad's elbow. "I'll help you."

"They already had me do some work on this step thing they had at the hospital. I'm almost a pro."

He's right. He goes slowly but without trouble. Inside, I get him situated in the living room. "I don't think I should go to work today."

"Nonsense. There's a party tonight. It'll be all hands on deck."

A *Calloway* party. Precisely why I shouldn't go. I haven't seen Chaz's parents or older brothers since I've been back. Maybe they're avoiding me as much as I am them.

"I'm sure they can handle it without me."

"I brought you here to run the pub, not be my nurse. Besides, there is a home health aide coming by later to get me started on some physical therapy. There's no need for you to babysit me, Serenity."

"Well then, I should really be there by one. I've stocked the kitchen with snacks and some microwave meals."

He turns up his nose. "Instant meals? No, thank you."

"You can't eat all your meals at work now. I'll bring food home for you when I can, but you have to stay nourished."

"Tell you what. When you get there, send Allen over with a cup of chowder and a Reuben. That'll suit me just fine."

I raise a brow. "So Donovan's delivers now?"

"Donovan's does whatever the hell we say it does, pumpkin."

"Fine."

"Everything ready for Addison's graduation party? Did you get the flowers ordered? The extra liquor?"

I shrug. "Don't know. Someone else was taking care of that."

"You mean Cooper?"

"I suppose."

"But he's going to her graduation, no?"

"That's why I have to go in by one." *But he'll return after, along with every other Calloway in town.*

"You'll make sure everything is set up when you get there? I have a big cont—"

"Container in the back full of streamers, signs, and banners. I know, Dad. I did work there almost my whole life."

"Yes, you did," he says. "Almost."

"Are you okay out here? Can I get you anything?"

"I'm good. There's one thing you can do for me, though." He nods to the hallway. "Go into your room and get the box on your dresser."

"I really should get ready for work."

He stares me down without saying anything. He's good at getting a point across without having to use words. It's why he never had to raise his voice at me growing up.

"Dad, no."

"You have to go in there sometime. Now's as good a time as any."

When I don't move, he just stares at me some more.

I roll my eyes. "Fine."

I stomp down the hallway and open my bedroom door. Squinting so as to blur my vision, quick and purposeful steps take me to the dresser, where I feel around on top, grab a small rectangular box, and hastily retreat back into the hall.

Proud of myself for completing the task without having a mental breakdown, I'm now excited to see what Dad got me. I take a seat near him and hold up the box. "What's the occasion?"

"Consider it a thank-you gift for dropping everything to come help."

I narrow my eyes. "But you said you got this a while ago."

"Just open the damn thing."

I slide the ribbon off and remove the lid from the box. Lifting the tissue paper reveals a silver necklace with a pendant on the end resembling a horseshoe. I drape it across the palm of my hand. "This is pretty. Does it have a particular meaning?"

"No particular meaning. But it has a specific use."

"Use?"

"Look at the little card that came with it."

I take the small instruction packet out of the box and examine it. The necklace is a ring holder. The picture shows a diamond ring nestled around the top edge of the horseshoe charm. I sigh, place the necklace back inside the box, and put the lid on. "Thank you."

"You're not going to use it?"

"I—"

"Pumpkin, it's time." He nods to my left hand. "That ring on your finger symbolizes something that no longer exists. Believe me, I know. I wore mine for a good bit after I lost your mother."

My throat stings at the thought of removing it. "How long?"

"Almost ten years."

"Ten?" My gaze snaps up. "It hasn't even been four for me."

"It's different. I had a daughter to raise. A business to run. I wasn't in a position to have anything else in my life."

"I'm not either."

He reaches over and takes my hand. "Serenity, you're young. You have your whole life ahead of you. But men need to know you're available."

"I'm *not* available. And you're one to talk. When is the last time *you* went on a date?"

"Well, you got me there. Been a while. But I'm a lot older than you."

"What does that matter? Plenty of people in their fifties date. They even have apps. Services. If you wanted to take out a woman, you would. So don't sit there and lecture me about moving on."

"You're right. How can I expect something of you that I'm not willing to do myself? I should have set a better example." He holds out his hand for the box. "I'll return it."

I feel guilty. After all, he must have put a lot of thought into it. I open the box again and get out the necklace. "No, don't do that. It's beautiful. I can still wear it just as it is."

He watches me put it on. "You're what's beautiful. You make the necklace look good, pumpkin, not the other way around."

"Thanks, Dad." I look down at my ring, still safe on my finger.

Suddenly, I feel a rush of emotion toward the man who worked so hard to raise me as a single father. I slump down next to him, mindful of his hip, and tuck my face into the crook of his shoulder.

He runs a hand down my back. "What is it, Serenity?"

"I just missed you so much, Daddy. I'm sorry it took you having surgery to get me to visit. I've been a terrible daughter after everything you've done for me."

"Hush now. If anyone understands the process of grief, it's me. I'm just happy you're here, for as long as I can have you."

I hug him hard before pulling away. "Well, I'd better get ready. I promise to have that food sent over."

~ ~ ~

"A little help?" I bite at Cooper as I haul a heavy box of liquor from the back.

He gets up from the table, where he's been sitting with his parents and siblings. He trots over, helping me the best he can despite his casted arm. "Sure, because there aren't three dozen other able-bodied people here to do this."

"It's *your* job."

He silently unboxes the liquor, slides the bottles into place, breaks down the box, and takes it into the back. Then he resumes his spot with his family.

Everywhere I look, there are Calloways. And if they aren't Calloways, they're related to them. Aunts, uncles, cousins, second cousins, cousins once removed, cousins-in-law, half cousins, and the list goes on.

And they've all been staring at me for the past two hours. Few have approached me for more than a simple greeting. It's like they'd all been told to steer clear of me.

I eye Cooper. *Were they?*

Allie and Mia sit at the bar, both of them here for me but related to Addy nonetheless. Allie, being a Montana, is a second cousin, or maybe a first but once removed (it's hard to keep it all straight). And Mia, as a Cruz, is a third or fourth cousin (again, who the hell can remember), or as she likes to say, not any more related to the Calloways than to some rando walking down the street. It's true. We looked it up once when we were younger and Mia was in love with her third cousin, Wyatt. Apparently, third cousins may or may not share more DNA than random strangers. And as she so vehemently insisted, even first cousins are allowed to marry in a handful of states (eeeew).

"Ren," Mia says, her voice so quiet I have to lean closer. "I say this with affection, because you know how much I love you, but girl, you are being a total bitch to Cooper. Have been all night."

Allie nods, both of them apparently in agreement. "It's not his fault that he looks like Chaz. You should quit punishing him for it."

"That's ridiculous. I'm not punishing him."

They both cackle and shake their heads.

"And I know it's not his fault. But that doesn't make it any easier to be around him."

"Still," Allie says. "Cut the guy a break. You may have been the fiancée, but they were twins. They shared an umbilical cord, for Pete's sake."

"Placenta," Mia says. "They shared a placenta. They each had their own umbilical cord."

Allie snorts. "Whatever, Miss Smarty Pants."

"I'm not a smarty pants, I'm a twin."

"You and Dax aren't identical," Allie says.

"No, but I still know things. Like monochorionic twins are genetically identical twins that share a placenta. Whereas Dax and I are dizygotic twins. Fraternal twins like us almost always have two placentas."

"Can we stop with all the twin talk?" I say.

Allie nods to the main Calloway table. "All I'm saying is he's hurting too. And word around town is that he'd be okay joining his brother."

"What?" My jaw drops. "You think he's suicidal?"

I'm frozen at the thought and swallowed by fear. Because as much as I hate looking at him, I've also somehow found comfort in being near him. In the recollections of the good times we shared. The talks we had. The memories we made.

Out of the blue, something happens. When I look over at Cooper, it's *Cooper* I see. Not my dead fiancé. Not my past. I see the man who was once my ally. My confidant. My friend.

"Have you even seen his YouTube videos?" Mia asks. "The man has a death wish."

"He's always been adventurous."

"There's a line between adventurer and monumental risk-taker. And he's definitely crossed it."

I step away to fill some drink orders. When I glance at the end of the bar, Chaz's mom, Libby, is waving me over. Can I pretend I don't see her?

"Serenity!" she calls.

I walk slowly, slinking around the bar and her as if she'll burn me. She motions to a quiet corner.

"It's so nice to see you. I can't tell you how often I think of you." She offers a sad smile. "Is it okay if I give you a hug?"

I nod and she wraps me in her arms. *I will not cry. I will not cry.*

"Oh, honey. I've missed you."

"You, too, Libby."

Over her shoulder, I see Cooper staring. I stare back, thinking of what Mia said about his risk taking. His body is sleek and lean. An athlete's body. His snug faded jeans fit all too well. He looks rugged, handsome, and deadly—a poster boy for adventure.

He goes over to man the bar in my absence.

"Now, I know I wasn't supposed to corner you. Cooper warned us all that you're still… dealing. But I just couldn't come here and not talk to you. We were so close once."

She's right. Libby became like a mother to me. She took me shopping for a prom dress. Included me in all their family gatherings. Even took me to her gynecologist when it became evident that Chaz and I were getting serious.

She pulls back and looks at me from head to toe. "You're too skinny. Beautiful as always, but skinny. I need to have you over for dinner. Say you'll come."

"I…"

My hesitation causes a pained sigh to escape her. "It's okay. Cooper doesn't like to visit the house either. We'll go out. Lunch maybe, on an afternoon off?"

"I think I can manage that."

"Perfect."

"And thank you for allowing Cooper to work here. He'd go stir-crazy without anything to keep him busy."

With all the guilt-tripping placed on me by Dad, my friends, and now Libby, any attempt to fire him would surely make me the enemy of the state. I muster a smile. "No problem."

She returns to her family. I go back to the bar, where Allie and Mia have been joined by a woman and a toddler. The woman extends a hand. "I'm Sophie, and this beauty is Josie."

"Sophie is Josie's nanny," Allie says.

"And Josie is?" I try to place the name. "Sorry, I've been away a long time."

"Josie is Amber and Quinn's daughter."

Quinn. Right. The stranger over at the table with all the Calloways. I stare at the group, thinking so much has changed. Yet everything has stayed the same.

Cooper passes me without a word, avoiding me like the plague. He's been doing it all evening. Since yesterday, in fact. But as the night grows long, I start to wonder about his recent and conspicuous aversion toward me. It could be that Allie and Mia are right and he's just plain tired of the way I've been treating him. Could they also be right about his recklessness?

After closing, I stay late, forcing myself to watch Cooper's videos. The man has done everything: dangled from a skyscraper in Chicago, swam with jellyfish in Palau, cave diving, bungee jumping, cliff camping, hang gliding, free climbing, hell, even tight-rope walking.

My hands are shaking, and my heart is in my throat after watching clips of each.

We're two sides of the same coin, he and I. I sit passively, waiting out my time until death eventually claims me. But Cooper—he's actively seeking it.

Chapter Eleven

Cooper

Pulling up to the cabin in Tag's SUV, I glance at the sky, hoping the rain will hold off until this afternoon. My brothers will join me later and help move the rest of the furniture from Tag's garage, where it was delivered, but I wanted to get a jump on things and try to beat the weather.

The cabin has been cleared of all things old-mannish. The furniture, the housewares, the bearskin rug—all of it. Only one single relic remains, an old rustic sign that hangs on the wall next to the kitchen cabinet. It appears Old Joe and I had one thing in common. The sign reads: ***Home isn't a place, it's a feeling.***

I glance around at the fruits of my labor. With the floors scrubbed and the windows cleaned, it's ready for a new owner. I step to the back window and let my eyes fall on his grave, somehow feeling a connection with the geezer. Maybe because we're both outcasts in our own way. The hermit of Calloway Creek, he rarely was seen in town, and only then to pick up deliveries that trucks refused to make out here.

I'm going to like it here. It'll be the perfect place to hang my hat while I'm in town.

The sky turns an even more ominous shade of gray, reminding me of the job I came to do. I go back outside and pop open the liftgate. I study the contents of the SUV Tag and I loaded last night, then look at my cast wondering if this wasn't a hairbrained idea. Maybe I should wait for them after all. Thunder rumbles in the distance. No, I need to get this stuff into the cabin before the ground turns to mud.

I manage to carry in the bags and boxes without too much effort. It's the chair that's giving me trouble. Luckily, the back of the recliner is removable. As I take it inside, sprinkles dot the brown leather. I don't have much time. I hurry back out to get the heavier bottom piece and struggle to get it out of the back of the SUV. I lose my grip and it ends up face down in the dirt.

Shit.

Sprinkles turn into big, fat raindrops. The dirt is quickly darkening into mud. And trying to get a grip on it from the ground is exponentially harder than doing it from the back of the SUV.

It's pouring now, and I almost give up and leave the brand-new recliner outside. I can afford a new one. My bank account is still fat from all my sponsorships. But I decide to give it one more try. I lean down, slide my cast underneath the front, hold it tightly with my right hand, and hoist it up. My foot slips in the mud and my ass hits the ground, bringing the weighty piece down right on top of me.

"Are you okay?" I hear behind me.

I push out from under the chair and see Serenity walking up. Her running clothes are soaked. I stand, feeling mud in places mud should definitely not be. "I was trying to beat the rain."

Shocked to see anything but a scowl on her face, I can't help but stare when her lips turn into something resembling a smile. "I could say the same." She motions to the massive oak tree across the trail. "I was taking cover over there." She bends down next to the recliner. "I'll help."

"Screw it. I think it's ruined."

"It's leather. It can be cleaned. Are you going to help me get this up on your porch or not?"

And there's the scowl.

I lean down and grip the other side the best I can. "Careful, the mud is slippery."

"I could see that based on the comedy show I just witnessed."

We get the chair up to the porch and set it down under cover. "You were watching me? Gee, thanks for the help. I'll remember that the next time you're struggling with a hundred-forty-pound keg."

"I helped."

My gaze falls on the muddy chair. "A lot of good it did me."

"Just let the mud dry. It'll wipe off easier." She looks at my dirty cast. "You really shouldn't get that wet, you know."

"I'm well aware." Thunder crackles and the sky flashes. "Gotta love these spring storms. I'm pretty sure I can scrounge up some coffee if you want to come inside and wait it out."

She hesitates, almost like she had forgotten who I was for a minute, but then it came rushing back. She peers out at the muddy trail and then back at the cabin door.

I force myself to look away from her pouty pink lips, telling myself they are not, in fact, sexy.

Finally, after an ungodly amount of uncomfortable silence, she follows me in, and I feel an unwilling smile tug the edges of my mouth.

She glances around. "You did all this since Thursday?"

"Moved all of Joe's stuff out yesterday morning."

"Yourself?" she asks, looking at my cast.

"Not myself." I gesture to the chair outside. "Obviously. My family helped."

I busy myself wetting some paper towels to get the mud off my cast, but all it does is smear it and shred the paper towels.

"You're making it worse." Ren comes over. "Do you have soap and some sort of cloth towel?"

"Somewhere." I dig through the bags I brought in earlier until I find a bottle of Dawn and a dishrag.

She makes a sudsy mixture in the sink. "Use this. It's okay to use soap since your cast is fiberglass, but ring out the rag. It should only be damp, or you'll ruin the cast."

I hold it up. "Think it's already ruined." I dip the rag into the mixture, squeeze out the excess, and wipe it over my cast. But doing it one handed is not as easy as it seems.

In my periphery, I see Ren's head shake. "For Pete's sake, you'll destroy it. Let me do it." She blows out a breath like the last thing she wants to do is touch me, then she takes my cast in her hands and starts cleaning it.

She's doing a pretty good job of it when she puts a hand behind my elbow, her fingers accidentally grazing my skin. Heat scorches through me. I pull away and clear my throat. "That's good enough."

For a moment, our eyes meet and I wonder what she's thinking. Is she thinking how disgusted she is that she touched me? There's no way she's thinking what I am. Because what I'm thinking should earn me a one-way ticket to hell in a fucking handbasket.

She steps back. "Now that that's done, you might want to think about cleaning the rest of you." She dumps out the contents of two plastic bags and hands the empties to me. "Wrap your arm in these while you clean up. I'll get the coffee going."

"Yeah, thanks." I take the bags and my duffle and disappear into the bathroom.

I turn on the shower but don't get in. I stare at the guy in the mirror, knowing what a bastard he is to have even a fleeting thought of her.

She was looking at you. Talking to you. Helping you.

I shake my head. It doesn't mean anything. Other than maybe she's getting used to being around me. Or just that she saw a guy in need and decided to dial back her bitchiness.

Since the day I kissed her, junior year, I never once acted on my feelings. I pushed them deep down inside, ignoring every pang of want, each instance of longing. What else could I do? She was his. And if she ever wasn't, she still couldn't be mine. There was a code. *Is* a code. And I would be a goddamn snake if I broke it.

But now I'm feeling emotions I'd conditioned myself not to feel. And I curse myself when I realize my dick is hard. Then I damn myself when I step into the shower and do something about it. I fantasize about those dark-chocolate eyes, that petite little ass, her heart-shaped face. The glossy strands of hair that escaped her ponytail. Her hint of a smile that let me know a part of her is still alive.

I sink down and sit on the edge of the tub, fully aware that I'm a pitiful excuse for a person. I rip the bags off my arm, willing the damn thing to heal. The faster it does, the quicker I can get out of here. Away from everything. Away from her.

When I return to the other room, it's empty. She's gone. And I find myself disappointed as much as I am relieved.

I walk to the front door, open it, and catch a glimpse of her legs as she rounds the corner onto the trail.

It's still raining. Still thundering even.

A thought occurs—she'd rather risk her life than stay here with me.

I slam the door.

Chapter Twelve

Serenity

Not able to sleep, I wander the dark house. I try to find something to watch on TV. I thumb through pages of a magazine. But nothing can keep my mind off what today is.

I find myself standing in front of my bedroom door. It's probably the worst thing I could do, but I do it anyway. I turn the handle. Flick on the light. Walk to my bed. Sitting down, I focus on the soft squares of the quilt. It's sewn in diagonal stripes and geometric patterns, with every third square a solid pale blue. *Blue—like his eyes.*

I reach into my nightstand and pull out the small picture book Chaz gave me one Valentine's Day. I trace his handwriting on the first page that reads: **All of my favorite moments with you.**

I page through, tears wetting my pillow as I wonder if anyone has ever cried more tears than I have.

Homecoming. Prom. Graduation. The beach. It's the last one that has me sealing the book back in the drawer and covering my head with my pillow. Finally, I cry myself to sleep.

"Pull over," Cooper says. "I have to take a leak."

"Can't you wait?" Chaz asks. "We're almost there."

We've been driving all night, the two of them taking turns, and as dawn breaks, we're approaching our destination—Cocoa Beach. It's the trip we've been talking about for months. Our graduation trip. Just four eighteen-year-olds, a few thousand dollars, and the open road.

Except now it's just three of us. Cooper and Missy broke up. They started dating right after spring break, when Chaz and I set them up. Missy dumped him when he forgot their three-month anniversary, they fought, she claimed he was never that into her, and he agreed.

Cooper leans in from the back. "Unless you want me to piss in your car, pull the fuck over."

"Alright already."

I point. "There's a parking lot over there."

Chaz turns in, Cooper hops out, and I stare in the distance, just now realizing where we are.

"Chaz, look! It's the beach. And the sun is rising." I open the car door. "I have to go see it."

We pass Cooper, who's standing to one side of a walkway. Chaz flicks his shoulder. "Can't you go in the dunes or something, you derelict?"

Cooper points to a sign. "It says you can't walk on the dunes, jagoff."

Chaz stops walking and stares ahead. "Holy shit."

"I know," I say, taking in the awesome view of the sky and the water connecting as the sun casts its rosy hue across them. "It's beautiful."

He turns back toward the car. "You go ahead. I'm going to grab my phone."

As he runs off, I notice his phone is in his back pocket. "Chaz!" I shout. But he doesn't stop. I don't run after him. I'm not about to miss my first beach sunrise.

I walk down the path, the sand getting thicker under my flip-flops with every step. I slip my shoes off and squish the soft, cool sand between my toes. I don't even stop when I step on the sharp edge of a seashell. I have to feel the surf against my legs as I experience this amazing sight.

"Pretty sick," Chaz, or maybe Cooper, says (I don't bother to look) as he comes up to my side.

"It's the most beautiful thing I've ever seen," I add.

"It's not the most beautiful thing I've ever seen," I hear behind me.

I turn and Chaz is on the sand, looking up at me, surf licking his knees. And he's holding out a ring.

My heart thunders.

He swallows hard. "I was planning on doing this sometime during the trip." He nods to the ocean. "This just seems like the appropriate moment."

I fall to my knees, all thoughts of the sunrise gone, and look into his hopeful eyes.

"Serenity, I know we're still young, but I've known since the day I first kissed you that I wanted to marry you. We don't have to get married tomorrow, or even next year. I just need to know that you're going to be mine forever."

Happy tears cascade down my cheeks. I drag my knees across the thick, wet sand until mine are touching his. "I'd marry you tomorrow, Chaz Calloway, or any other day."

"So that's a yes?"

I laugh. "That's a yes." I squeal. "Put the ring on me, dummy."

He does, and then we kiss.

When I open my eyes, Cooper is watching. But in a way that makes him look sad. I guess it makes sense. He probably feels like he's losing a brother.

"What are you waiting for?" Chaz says to him. "Get over here and congratulate me and my fiancée."

"I..." Cooper hesitates, then closes the gap between us. "I'm really happy for you guys. You belong together and everyone knows it." He hugs me, pats Chaz on the back, then quietly gazes out over the ocean.

I awaken, my happiness turning into sorrow like it has so many times before when my eyes open and reality hits. I turn off the light and close up the room, scolding myself for entering. It's still dark out, but dawn is coming soon, so I dress in my running clothes and head outside, needing to run the memory right out of my head.

As I jog down McQuaid Circle and past the pub, I think about the last few weeks and how uneventful they've been. Cooper still comes to work. I still let him. It's become easier to be around him. I no longer see Chaz every time I look at him. And with the passing of each day, I notice more and more differences between the two of them.

He may still be working with me, though we seem to be avoiding each other more now than ever. Or should I say *he* avoids *me* more than ever. At least he acknowledged me before. Now, he treats me like the unwanted stepchild.

Part of me gets it, though. I hadn't treated him well when I first came back. Not to mention that the past week has been difficult for us both. We knew what was coming. *Today.* Today was coming. Their birthday.

Chaz would have been twenty-six. We'd have spent the day climbing some mountain or exploring a new trail. Maybe even with a child in tow.

It's hard to cry and run at the same time, so I push myself harder, running so fast that thinking about anything other than my feet and my breathing isn't an option. I run through the park, down the trail, through the woods. Dawn begins breaking when I stop in front of the tree tunnel. I haven't been here since long before he died. It's where we had our first kiss. Where we'd come to plan our future. Where, at sixteen, I knew I wanted to be his wife long before he asked me. Why am I here now? I should keep going.

My mind and my heart are at war, one telling me to run fast and far, the other to stay and hold onto any shred of him that I can.

As usual, my heart presides, and without putting another thought into it, I step forward and walk through the tunnel. I get to the clearing, and my eyes play a cruel trick. Chaz appears.

His watery eyes look upon me as my brain makes a realization. *Cooper, not Chaz.*

Breathe.

"What are you doing here?" he asks, his voice an aching rasp that sends shivers through my soul.

"I, uh… This was our place."

"This was *our* place," he quips possessively.

"You and Chaz came here?" I ask.

He looks at the ground next to the large rock Chaz used to sit on when we'd have our long talks about everything. About nothing. "I guess there were some things he didn't tell the both of us." He runs a hand across a smaller rock. "You haven't noticed this?"

I go over and squint, the sun not up far enough, and my eyes not clear enough for me to see. I lean down and read the word 'brother' carved into it.

"That was never there before," I say.

"It's been here for almost four years."

I glance around sadly. "I haven't been here since—"

"It's him," he says.

"What do you mean it's him?"

"Some of his ashes are buried here."

My throat thickens and I sink to my knees, staring at the grave marker.

Cooper sits and leans against Chaz's rock. "Everyone says I'm reckless."

I look at him through my tears. "Aren't you?"

"I'm not trying to die." He picks up a twig and swirls it through the dirt. "But it would be okay if I did."

I lean forward and brace myself on the ground with my hands, short of breath because his words have punched me to the core.

"Ren?"

I shake my head, swallowing the lump. "Nobody has ever been able to put it into words until now. That's exactly how I feel."

"You want to die?" he asks softly.

"No. Sometimes. I don't know."

We stare at each other, possibly being the only two people in the world having the same emotions over the same person at precisely the same moment. Tears stream down our faces. I watch as his get absorbed into his beard. He follows mine as they drip off my chin.

When we surge toward each other, it's simultaneous, as if we're drawn together by a force out of our control. Our lips collide, a salty culmination of years of despair that only the two of us could understand. The kiss is filled with desperation. But also something else. Need.

Need for what, I'm not sure. The need to live. The need to die. The need to feel something other than the utter agony we've both been drowning in.

I ache to have him closer. But it's more than an ache; it's a feral necessity.

His strong fingers weave into my ponytail, then free my hair from the band. A pained moan escapes him when he clasps the nape of my neck and deepens our kiss.

Hands roam everywhere, the hard edges of his cast prickling me with sensation. He caresses the small of my back, the curves of my hips, the flesh of my outer thighs. Mine grasp his arms, his waist, his broad shoulders, searching for purpose.

Neither of us pull back to breathe. We pant into each other's mouths, never breaking the seal our lips have formed, while our tongues explore as fervently as our hands.

His erection strains against me. I shimmy my hips into it, wanting more, needing more. Needing more like it's the air I need to keep breathing.

I break away from him and peel off my running top and sports bra. He stares at my breasts as if he's never seen any before. Carefully, gingerly, he puts his right palm on one, his eyes closing as he draws in a ragged breath. Before I can even enjoy the sensation of his hand, he lowers his head, putting his lips on my skin and taking a nipple into his mouth. My head falls back at the intense feeling.

He follows the motion and steadies me as I sink to the ground, never losing the contact his tongue has with my flesh. I arch into him. He grinds his hardness against my leg. I press back. His hand travels between my thighs and rubs me over my shorts. It's electrifying. Tingles zing through my entire body as if it's being awakened after a long sleep. A deep sexual hunger stirs to life inside me, an explosion of both pleasure and necessity.

Wanting nothing between his hand and me, I work my shorts down as he feasts on my chest. He pulls back, seeing me naked, and I can almost feel the heat of his gaze as his eyes wander over me. But there's a moment when his gaze meets mine and the heat disappears. Something behind his eyes is so distant it's like he's not even here. I trace the outline of his erection through his shorts. "Touch me," I say.

He does what I ask, and I shiver. When he slips a finger inside me, he curses, then moans. His hand retreats, and his clothes are off before either of us has time to decide if what we're about to do is a monumental mistake.

Naked and hovering over me, he perches on his elbows like he's waiting for a sign. For the sky to fall? For God's hand to strike him down? For lightning to hit?

But before any of those things happen, I reach between us and caress his velvety-soft, hard-as-steel penis. His eyes close. His head drops to my chest. His fingers find their way back inside me.

The feel of his tongue on my nipple, of his thumb on my clit, of his fingers exploring; it all has me building, winding me up like a coiled spring needing release.

"Please," I beg.

Without hesitation, his penis slides in, stretching me, filling me with sensation, emotion, awareness. I grip his shoulders. He's not close enough. I grip his hips. I need more. My palms press against the globes of his ass, keeping him tightly against me as he rocks into me, grinding me into the earth below.

His breathing changes. He hums against my shoulder. He works a hand between us and does amazing things to my clit. "Oh God," I breathe out in a heavy sigh, my belly and hips tensing as an all-consuming, euphoric rush explodes through me.

My walls clamp down and a low, guttural growl escapes him as he comes.

He collapses down on me and stills, both of us panting like we just ran a marathon.

I look up at the trees, rays of sunlight punching their way between the branches, and I realize I'm feeling something I haven't let myself feel in a long time.

Alive.

Chapter Thirteen

Cooper

I glance to the side, Chaz's grave marker staring me square in the face. My stomach churns. I roll off her, stand hastily, and dress without giving her another look. Because I know if I look at her, she won't be looking at me. She'll be looking at *him*.

What have I done?

"I have to go," I say and jog off toward my cabin.

I half expect her to call out after me. Chase me. Or chase *him*. She came here for the same reason I did, and I went and fucked up everything even more.

I have to stop and heave into the bushes before I get home, knowing I'm the worst brother to ever walk the face of the earth. Then, despite the early hour, I go into my cabin, grab a bottle of Jack, and drink myself into oblivion.

~ ~ ~

The climb has taken us half a day, but finally, we reach the summit. Chaz and I glance at each other, grinning. We both know this is what we were made for. This is what's going to be our future livelihood. Somehow, some way, we're going to turn our love for the outdoors into a business.

"Holy shit," I say. "Will you check out that view?"

He nods to a grouping of boulders. "It'll look even better from up there."

I point to the sign that clearly states **No climbing on the rocks.**

Chaz laughs. "You pussy." He tosses me his phone. "At least get a picture of me while you're cowering down here."

"You're going to get yourself killed one of these days."

"Yeah, but what a way to go." He climbs up on the large pile of rocks, some of them as big as cars, and works his way to the highest point. Then he does a double-biceps pose, and I snap his picture.

"Dude, you have to come up here. I swear I can see all the way to North Carolina."

"I'm sure you can. It's only twenty miles away."

"I need my phone," he says. "I can get some great pictures from up here."

I hold it out. "Come and get it."

He stares me down. "How in the hell are we going to be adventure guides if you won't pull the pansy stick out of your ass and become a little fucking adventurous?"

I roll my eyes. Chaz has always been the crazy one, pushing us to the limits, making us do things I never would have done. "Jesus Christ. Fine." I stash his phone in my backpack and approach the rocks, finding careful footing as I climb. It doesn't scare me. It's just that I'm a rule follower—unlike my twin. It's the one area where we diverge.

He's the one who got us grounded when we were fifteen by taking a six-pack of beer from our garage refrigerator and convincing me to drink some. One summer he almost blew us up with fireworks, somehow getting ahold of the illegal kind and then daring me to help him set them off. Not to mention he's the only one who ever wanted to trade places. The first time he pretended to be me, we were five and he tricked our mother into buying me, a.k.a him, another ice-cream cone. I never said anything. Because, well, I disliked ice cream. And we're brothers. I wasn't going to rat him out. We always had each other's backs.

I reach the top of the pile of boulders. As usual, Chaz was right. The view is spectacular. There's a break in the tree line, and I can see the winding road below, figuring it's about a mile away. On the way up, the trail followed the road for a bit and then veered off into a steeper climb.

"Hand me my phone?" he asks.

"Get it yourself." I lift my chin, still admiring the view. "It's in the outer pocket."

In my periphery, I see him leap from the rock he's standing on. When he lands on mine, the earth shifts beneath us, the rocks come out from under our feet, and we go tumbling down, along with the fucking boulders. A smaller rock scrapes my arm, another bounces off my foot, and when I finally hit the ground, twenty feet down the mountain, my leg is pinned.

My heart is beating out of my chest as I take stock of my body. Other than my leg being trapped and the shit being scraped out of my arm, I'm okay. "Holy shit!" Then I stop breathing. "Chaz?"

"Yeah, I'm here."

Relief floods through me. "What the hell just happened?" I tug on my leg, but it doesn't budge. I start laughing. "I can't believe you got us into this situation, you dumb motherfucker. If my leg weren't trapped, I'd tear you a new asshole right now. Will you get the hell over here and help lift this rock off me?"

"Can't, bro."

"Well, why the hell not?"

The pause is long. Too long.

"Chaz?"

"Because I'm pinned beneath this goddamn boulder."

I wake up, head pounding from the amount of alcohol I drank this morning. Not that I need to be anywhere or do anything. I'd pretty much planned on being drunk all day anyway. Mom tried to convince me to go to dinner. Not a chance in hell.

When I sit on the edge of the bed, this morning comes rushing back to me. I put on my shoes, grab the bottle, and head out the door.

I try not to make a sound when I go to the clearing. Surely she won't still be here. One of us had to be at work today. She didn't schedule me, for which I was grateful. Still, after what happened, I didn't know if she'd changed her plans. But she's nowhere to be found. I stare at the spot next to his grave, the leaves and dirt displaced from what we did earlier.

From what *I* did.

I unscrew the cap and take a long drink, fully aware that I betrayed him in a way no brother should be betrayed. I sit next to his rock. "I'm a shitty fucking brother." Another drink. "It was you she was fucking, not me." Another.

My mind races with thoughts of Ren. Her soft, supple skin. Her lips plump from kissing me. Her magnificent orgasm that took me to the edge of insanity and back.

I can't stop thinking about how she was looking at me. An unexplainable heat exuded from her gorgeous, sad eyes. There was a fire behind that sadness I'd never seen before.

Him. She was looking at *him.*

I gulp two large swallows. Because even though guilt is eating away at me, inch by torturous inch, one realization remains: I don't want to take it back.

Fuck.

Chapter Fourteen

Serenity

Dad keeps glancing over at me from the booth. He walked here with Patricia, his physical therapist, and they've just finished an early dinner. I'm pretty sure that's above and beyond the duties of any home health aide, but who am I to question it.

He comes over with their dirty dishes and puts them on the bar when he sees me struggling with the heavy dish tray. "Hey, pumpkin, can I help you with that?"

I take glasses out of the tray and slide them into place in the rack over the bar. "I've got it, Dad. You aren't supposed to be working, remember? Besides, you can't just leave your date alone at the table."

"Date?" His eyebrows touch his hairline.

"Oh, come on. I've seen the way you two look at each other when she's at the house. She's single, right? Didn't her husband pass a while back?"

"Eight years ago, from one of those heart attacks they call a widow-maker. She's got two sons about your age—Jeremy and Jason."

"I remember them from school." I give him a look. "Considering how much you seem to know about her, I'd say this is *exactly* a date."

He studies me. "You look pretty today, Serenity. Seems you got some color back in your cheeks."

"Thank you," I say, glancing over as a family walks in.

"You keep looking at the front door. Are you expecting someone?"

"Just trying to make sure people are greeted right away." I turn and give him a gentle nudge. "Best not to leave Patricia waiting."

"You're doing a great job here," he says over his shoulder. "Knew you would." He returns to the table and winks at me before starting a conversation with Patricia.

As I watch the two of them, one word comes to mind: smitten.

Gino passes, stopping to whisper, "Go, Donny."

I chuckle.

A couple walks in, and I realize Dad was right. I look up every time someone walks through the door. It's not like I expected Cooper to seek me out after what happened yesterday, but I thought we'd at least talk about it. He ran off. I get it. I didn't exactly know what to do either. Sleeping with my dead fiancé's brother? There's not exactly a playbook for what happens after. We crossed a serious line. My insides are still all tangled up thinking about it. Is what we did good? Bad? Is it going to happen again?

I touch my lips, still fresh with the memory. We were both hurting. We turned to each other for comfort. But was it more?

For the past thirty-six hours, I've been trying to separate the two men in my mind. The small subtleties that differentiate them. How over the past few weeks I've noticed that the inflection in

Cooper's voice is different. The way he walks through a room. How he runs a hand through his hair. Then there was the scar. The small imperfection over Chaz's right eyebrow that he got when they were rappelling down rocks in Sedona when they were nineteen. I laugh when I remember how he said that would put an end to them ever switching places again.

My breath hitches. Did I just… *smile* at a memory?

"Ren?"

I look up. Addy is staring at me, holding an empty tray.

"Right. Drinks." I get to mixing more margaritas for table twelve.

When I place them on the end of the bar for her, she cocks her head sideways. "You're different."

"What do you mean?"

"I can't put my finger on it. You seem almost happy. Don't get me wrong, it's great. Amazing even. We never thought… I mean, I never thought… Well, *nobody* ever thought, really." She shakes her head. "Anyway, I'd better get these drinks over."

I gaze after her, absorbing her words. How could I possibly be happy?

Holding up my hand, I study the ring on my finger, wondering if one day—one reckless incident—has somehow freed me from the prison of my past.

What if it wasn't just Chaz I've been mourning this whole time? What if somewhere along the lines of my grief I stopped missing *him* and started missing what we had. Closeness. Human contact. Sex.

I inhale deeply at the epiphany.

The front door opens, my eyes shift, and I see him walk in. He stops. Our eyes meet. Neither of us moves.

"What happened to your leg?" I hear a drunk customer at Addy's table ask.

"Tussle with an alligator," she rattles off.

Spittle from the man's mouth must reach Cooper. He breaks eye contact and wipes off his arm. Then he marches past me into the back. When I don't follow, he looks out at me through the window of the kitchen door. Well, looks is not the right word. Glares is more like it. He's glaring at me from the other side of the window. *So we're doing this right here, right now.*

"Gino, can you watch the bar?"

"I'm on it," he says.

I don't miss how Addy watches me curiously as I go to the back. When I get there, Cooper is nowhere to be found. Kelly lifts his chin toward the office. "Man went in there with a mission, I'd say."

Cooper hasn't been in the office since the day I kicked him out of it. I know it. Kelly knows it.

I eye the door, then turn back to Kelly. "I'll just… be a minute."

He smirks. "Take all the time you need."

When I enter, Cooper is on the couch, slumped over, forearms resting on his knees. I shut the door behind me and give him a wide berth as I go around the desk and take a seat in the office chair.

He scrubs a hand down the side of his face and across his hairy jaw. He looks up at me, guilt consuming his handsome features as lines of angst collect at the edges of his mouth. I stand and move to the couch, leaving a respectable amount of space between us. "I know what you're thinking. Believe me, every thought that has gone through your head has gone through mine. You can't beat yourself up about it. What happened happened."

He doesn't speak. He just looks at me—my hair, my eyes, my lips. His eyes stop there. Something happens inside me, and I don't think. I just lean over and kiss him. Oh, how I've missed being kissed. Being touched. Being held in a man's strong arms. Instantly, his hands wrap around me and his tongue darts into my mouth desperately, like he's drowning and I'm his air. Nothing could have prepared me for the intensity of this kiss. It's like a drug, one that's leaving me mindless, shaking, and yearning for more.

Suddenly everything becomes clear to me. I want this. I want him. However wrong it is.

The office phone rings. He pulls back.

"Let it go," I say, arching forward again.

But he moves away, ejecting himself off the couch and crossing the room as if I'd burned him. He rakes a hand through his hair. "I can't do this."

"I know it seems… weird. But it's okay, Cooper."

"It's *not* okay. It's so far from okay that okay isn't even on the same goddamn planet." He nods to the spot on the couch he vacated. "You weren't kissing me. You were kissing Chaz. And yesterday, it's him you were fucking."

My mouth slackens. "What?"

"How can you even deny it?"

"Because it's not true, that's how."

"Bullshit, Serenity. You leave town for four years, come back and almost fire me, are a complete bitch to me for weeks, and then sleep with me next to his fucking ashes."

I swallow. "I'm not saying it hasn't been confusing. But Cooper—"

He strides over and takes my hand. Maybe he's coming to his senses. Instead, though, he lifts my hand between us. "You're still wearing his ring, Ren. I'd say that's a pretty damn good indication that it's not me you wanted to be with." He drops my hand. "Now if we're done here, I have work to do."

He walks out the door, leaving me in a muddy pit of uncertainty. Everything he said is spot-on. Could he be right? Is it Chaz I want?

I twist the ring around my finger for a full five minutes before I muster up the courage to go back out front.

The night is filled with awkward glances between us. We look. We look away. We look again. Thank goodness it's busy, because otherwise my mind would be spinning, demanding answers I don't have.

As the night winds down, he brushes against me as we pass behind the bar, and I could swear I hear his breath hitch. Just like I'm pretty sure he heard mine. It's hard for me to concentrate with him so close. With his longish chestnut hair that curls over his ears and at his collar—the kind of thick waves a woman aches to draw her fingers through. The way he pushes those curls off his forehead absentmindedly as he talks with patrons. How his dark brows dip together over the bridge of his nose when Gino asks him a question. The way his lips fold thoughtfully when he catches me staring.

At closing time, everyone is gone but the two of us and Addy. She finishes mopping and perches her hands on the upright handle as Cooper comes out from the back.

"What is it with you two tonight?" Addy asks, her eyes bouncing between us. When neither of us speaks, her face slackens in surprise. "Did something happen between you?"

Cooper strides over and takes the mop. "You can go now, Addison. Good job tonight."

"But—"

"Come on," he says, pushing her out the door. "I'll walk you to your car." He glances back but doesn't make eye contact. "I'm out until Sunday. Wedding tomorrow."

Before I can even acknowledge him, the door slams shut, and he locks it from the outside.

I sit on a stool, lean over, and let my head fall to the bar. How did my life become even more messed up than it was?

Chapter Fifteen

Cooper

Maddie walks down the aisle on her grandmother's arm, eyes glued on Tag as he waits for her under the trellis of flowers at our cousin's winery. On Maddie's other side is her daughter, Gigi.

After Grandma Rose takes her seat, nobody else is standing but the three of them and the officiant. Tag didn't want to have to choose between his brothers and his best friend, Amber. And Maddie didn't know how to pick either, her list of close-knit friends having grown long over the past year. To simplify things, they decided to go it alone at the altar.

They couldn't have picked a better day for the wedding. Few clouds dot the sky. The June temperature is moderate. And there's just enough breeze to make Gigi giggle when her veil, a replica of Maddie's, tickles her face.

This whole day hasn't just been about Tag and Maddie; it's been about them becoming a family. Although they've been living together as one for the better part of a year, this makes it official. Tag is going to be much more than a stepfather to Gigi. He's going to be the man who raises her.

His life has purpose. What a change from just a year ago when he was the playboy bachelor of Calloway Creek. It's a title that's been bestowed on both of us at one time or another. My womanizing days were after high school graduation and went all the way up to when we lost Chaz. I'd sleep with just about anyone, but rarely more than a few times. After we lost him, there just didn't seem to be a point. I took pleasure in my adventures, not women. I've had female companionship when I've needed it, but it's few and far between.

Female companionship.

And now I'm thinking of Serenity again. I grit my teeth tightly together, keeping my emotions under control as I force myself not to long for what I can't have. What's forbidden.

I toss her out of my mind and focus on my brother, the happy motherfucker. He's getting everything he never knew he wanted.

I spare a glance at Jaxon, sitting next to his wife, Nicky. He's finally living his dream life, too.

And my parents, sitting to the left of Addison, though they've navigated some bumps in their marriage, are happier than ever.

Everyone around me is happy.

How can they be? My parents' son is still dead. My siblings' brother is six pounds of ash.

Addy and Mom are blubbering as Tag and Maddie say their vows. Tag added extra vows just for Gigi. I can practically hear ovaries exploding around me.

Knowing Dad would rake my balls across hot coals if I got my phone out, I busy myself looking at the landscape, the buildings, the vineyards in the distance, and the kid picking his nose in the row behind Maddie's grandmother.

After the whole ordeal, I have to suffer through a thousand family pictures before finally being offered alcohol. I drain my entire glass of whiskey in one swallow.

"Looks like I might have to drive you home," Addy says.

"I'm responsible for getting Tag's car back to his house."

"The hell you are after drinking. You don't think I can drive a Range Rover?"

"Great. Looks like I can have another one of these, then." I point to my empty, and the bartender gives me a refill.

"Are you ever going to tell me what happened between you and Serenity?"

I sip the next drink slowly, thinking how my brother would not take lightly to me being fall-down drunk at his wedding. "No."

"But something did happen."

It wasn't a question.

"Don't you have some wedding duties to perform?" I ask, irritated at her incessant meddling.

"Actually, I don't. I helped set things up, but now I just get to enjoy the reception. Come on, Cooper. Spill. The way you acted around each other last night was…" Her eyes roll. "Let's just say you couldn't have cut the sexual tension with a bulldozer."

"You're crazy. You were seeing things."

"No, I wasn't. Everyone was talking about it. Gino. Katie. Even Kelly, and he *never* gossips."

Jaxon sidles up to the bar. "What's up?"

"Cooper and Serenity are what's up," Addy says.

I choke. "Give it a rest, Addison."

"What's this?" Jaxon asks. "As in *you and Ren?*"

"Addy is overreacting," I say and take another sip.

"I'm not. Jaxon, you should have seen them, stolen glances at the other when they didn't think they were looking. Looks of longing that would put a starving man at a buffet to shame. And don't even get me started on when they disappeared into the office together, and then this one came out looking like his dog died."

I hold my glass out for a refill, some liquor sloshing out of the glass as I make my hasty retreat. "I don't have to stand here and listen to this shit."

Jaxon follows me past the dance floor and outside, where random smokers are lighting up.

I turn and face him. "Drop it."

"So Addy's wrong? There's nothing between you two?"

"Fuck." I stomp away and find a bench to sit on, feeling fifty fucking shades of confused.

Jaxon sits too. "I'm not here to judge you, Coop. But I can be a pretty good listener. And it looks like maybe you need to get something off your chest."

I'm quiet for what seems like minutes. When he makes no move to leave, I talk, because I feel like my head is about to combust. "We didn't mean for anything to happen. It was a few days ago, on my birthday. *Our* birthday," I correct. "We were in the woods off the trail at a place… It doesn't matter where, but we were both wrecked, and it just happened."

"As in *it?*"

I don't have to look at him to know his brows are hitting the sky.

"I'm going to hell."

Laughter fills the air between us. "Brother, if you were going to hell, it would have been for the dozens of women you slept with before Chaz died, not the one you slept with after."

"There's been more than one."

"Okay, three. Seriously, this is what has you hiding like a damn tortoise in a shell?"

"It's *Ren*," I say.

"Yeah? So? It's not like you stole her from him. He's been gone for almost four years, Cooper. It even makes sense somehow, the two of you comforting each other."

"It wasn't me she was sleeping with. It was him."

"You've talked since?"

"Last night."

"And she told you as much?"

"Not exactly."

"What did she say?"

"Some shit about it being okay that it happened. And then she kissed me."

"Wow. So not a one-time thing?"

"No, it was. It *was* a one-time thing. It should have been a *no-time* thing. Why the hell did she have to kiss me?"

"Oh, the kiss is what you're concerned with. Did you enjoy it?"

"Which part?"

"The kissing? The *it?*"

I close my eyes and nod, admitting to him what I can barely admit to myself. "That's what's so goddamn wrong. I'm kissing her and she's kissing my dead brother."

"That's not how it sounds to me."

"You weren't there."

"No, but I think you should give her the benefit of the doubt, Coop. Talk to her. What you hear may surprise you."

"I doubt that very much. She's still wearing his ring, Jaxon."

"What's this I hear about you and Serenity?" Tag says, walking up behind us.

"Jesus." I stand. "Addy needs to keep her big mouth shut. If anyone says another fucking word about it, I'm leaving."

Tag backs off, laughing. He and Jaxon share a look. I expect it to be judgmental as hell, but it's not. It's more of an amused look. I take my empty glass and head back inside, pissed that I seem to be the sole provider of my family's entertainment.

Chapter Sixteen

Serenity

Following my afternoon run, I'm walking by my closed bedroom door when I suddenly have an urge to open it. I do. I walk in, expecting feelings to overwhelm me. But it doesn't happen. Yes, the mementos around the room are still painful reminders of a past that went horribly wrong and a future that won't ever happen, but as I run my hand across the edge of the binder containing Chaz's love letters, I realize I'm no longer broken.

It's the ultimate irony, though, that the day that broke me the most—his birthday—also ended up putting me back together.

A second realization hits me like a ton of bricks. I haven't dreamed about Chaz. I haven't dreamed about him in days.

I get his old CCHS T-shirt from the drawer, remove photos from the wall, gather up every keepsake in the room, and carefully place them inside a box. One of the photos in the photo collage falls to the floor. It's the one where Chaz didn't shave for months because of a dare between him and his brothers. And for the first time when looking at a photo of him, it's not him I see. It's Cooper.

And something shifts inside me. I should feel betrayal over the way my body reacts. I should feel guilt. But I don't. Instead, I slip my ring off. Then I unclasp my necklace, thread it through the ring, and let the ring fall to rest on top of the horseshoe. Putting it back around my neck, I take a deep breath. Breathing is easier than I thought it would be after removing the ring.

I tuck the box into the back of my closet and go to the guest room to retrieve my things. After putting them away in my room, I sit on the bed, wondering what I'll fill my walls with now.

"Well, look at you," Dad says from the doorway.

I shrug. "Thought it was time I moved back in here."

His eyes home in on the necklace, and I can almost see the relief cross his face. "I'm glad to hear it." He starts to walk away, then turns. "Grief can be a funny thing. You may feel like you're drowning in it, then—Bam—suddenly you realize you're no longer surrounded by water."

My father. If anyone knows anything about grief, it's him.

"So listen," he says. "I was thinking of inviting Patricia for dinner. Maybe on Wednesday. Perhaps you could join us?"

"Cooper closes on Wednesdays, so yeah."

"Good. Well, I'm off to watch a show. Have a good day at work, pumpkin."

"Thanks, Dad."

I lie back on my bed and stare at the ceiling, enjoying the feel of my cheeks as they form a smile.

~ ~ ~

I find myself checking the clock constantly throughout my shift. And the closer it gets to dinnertime, the more anticipation I feel over seeing him. And the more confident I am in knowing it's Cooper I want to see.

He was wrong the other day; I wasn't kissing Chaz. I've had time to think about it. I've concluded that the same things that drew me to Chaz also draw me to Cooper. After all, they are alike in more ways than they're different. And once you get past the forbiddenness factor of me wanting a relationship with my dead fiancé's brother, it almost makes sense. To me anyway.

I glance around the pub and wonder what everyone in Calloway Creek would think if I moved on from Chaz with his twin.

My lungs deflate with realization. They would all believe I was trying to replace him.

Just like Cooper does.

The object of my newfound affection walks in. But even as my heart leaps, I make a split-second decision. We need to be friends. Anything else can wait. My eyes train in on his cast. Well, maybe not for too long. He'll be gone as soon as they cut it off him. But for now, I resign myself to making the best of our tenuous situation. We were friends once; we can be again.

Our eyes meet and I see it. The hesitation. The indecision.

Friends, I remind myself. *You can do this.*

"Hey," I say, adorning my best friendly smile.

He glances around. "Looks like it might be busier than a usual Sunday. Where do you need me?"

As my eyes fall to his lips, many answers to that question pop into my head. I voice none of them. "Behind the bar would be good."

"No problem," he says with the hint of a smile.

As he walks past me, I try to decide what was behind the expression. Was it a sad smile? A polite one? Or maybe it was a

Pan Am smile—the one Dad always told me to have on my face when I served customers—derived from flight attendants who were required to keep smiling even when they wanted to throw peanuts at unruly passengers.

"Serenity?"

I turn and wait for more. Then I realize he didn't call me Ren. I lift my brows, anticipating his words.

He shakes his head. "Nothing." He blows out a breath. "I'd better get to work."

Frustration festers inside me. It definitely was not *nothing*. What was he going to say? I go about my duties, but it's hard not to wonder. For two hours, it's hard. Not even the influx of patrons gets my mind off it.

I spend a lot of time chatting with customers. It's what Dad does a lot. He believes a friendly manager is one of the reasons people come back. I say it's because Donovan's Pub is the only happening place on McQuaid Circle.

You've got Lloyd's Restaurant, an upscale establishment over on the roundabout; Goodwin's Diner, which doesn't serve alcohol; and a few fast-food eateries. The only other place to really hang out within walking distance is the bowling alley.

I'm floating between tables when I come upon Hawk McQuaid and some girl I don't recognize, who I question is even old enough to be on a date with him. "Good evening," I say, stopping at their booth.

"Hey, Ren," Hawk says. "I heard you moved back."

I go to tell him I haven't, that I'm only here to help until Dad is fully on his feet, but before the words come out of my mouth, I stop them. Because suddenly, I have a thought. *Am* I moving back?

"Nice to see you."

I paste on my Pan Am smile, because, well… he's a McQuaid. At one time or another, he and his brothers all tried to sleep with me while Chaz and I were dating. It was like a game to them to see who would get me, or Jaxon's girlfriend, Nicky, to cheat on our Calloway boyfriends. All part of the stupid feud they refuse to let go of.

"How's your dinner?" I ask.

He looks thoughtfully at his Philly cheesesteak. "As expected. Not as nice as Lloyd's. Better than what I'd get at Goodwin's."

Unsure if I should consider that a compliment or not, I say, "Well, we appreciate you coming in." I turn to the girl (because I'm not exactly sure I can call her a woman) and extend my hand. "We haven't met. I'm Serenity Donovan."

She wipes her hands on her napkin and shakes. "I'm Sydney Montana. We've actually met before, but it's been a long time." She picks up a lock of her hair. "And back then, I was going through a pink-hair phase."

My biting gaze settles on Hawk. "Is she even old—"

"Pipe down, Donovan. She's nineteen."

I lift a brow. "And you are?"

"Thirty," Sydney says, looking at him with dreamy eyes. "He's thirty."

My protective instincts scream to take over when someone appears at my side. I turn to see an old classmate of mine. We were on the cheer squad together. "Shannon?" Then I notice her protruding belly. "Oh, my gosh, you're pregnant? When are you due?"

"Why don't you ask the baby's father?" she says, glaring at Hawk.

My hand comes to my mouth to cover my surprise. Not that I should necessarily be surprised that a jerk like him would knock someone up and then take a woman-child to dinner.

Hawk scoffs. "That has yet to be determined since you refuse to take a test, which means you most likely know I'm not the father, and you just want me to support the little bastard."

"I've told you a million times I hadn't been with anyone else in six months."

"Says you."

"Shannon?" her stepsister says, waiting by another table. "Do you want to go someplace else?"

Shannon shakes her head, looking sad, and walks over to where Melissa is waiting. I take her elbow. "Hawk McQuaid, really?"

She shrugs. "It was a moment of weakness. You know how he can be."

I laugh. "Yeah, I do. Which is why most women won't touch him with a ten-foot pole."

"We were drunk."

"Ahh. Dangerous."

"You're telling me."

At the table, I greet Melissa as Shannon sits with her back to Hawk. She rubs her belly. "This little nugget will make an appearance in two months."

I gesture back to Hawk's table. "And him?"

"I doubt he'll be involved. And I *will* get a paternity test once the baby comes, because if nothing else, this kid will at least have a carefree life being a McQuaid and all. But I figured I'd let Hawk sweat it out."

"She's hoping he'll see the baby and change his mind about being with her," Melissa says.

"I am not."

"Shan, you've wanted a McQuaid since we were kids. I should know—I was the one who comforted you when Hunter broke your heart a few years ago."

I'm surprised for the second time today. "You and Hunter?"

"She would have slept with Hudson, too, but he didn't want his older brother's leftovers. At least Hunter had the good sense to wear a condom."

Hawk may be onto something. I had no idea Shannon was such a gold digger.

Katie comes over and takes their order. I wander back to the bar. At least Cooper isn't giving me more nervous glances. He's brooding over the fact that a McQuaid is dining here. I join him behind the counter. "Shannon Greer is having Hawk McQuaid's baby?"

"It was all anyone around here could talk about earlier this year. Well, that and Jaxon's little predicament."

"How would you know what everyone was talking about earlier this year? Weren't you off prancing around doing iceboat racing or something?"

His brow arches. "You've watched my YouTube channel?"

I shrug nonchalantly. "I've seen a couple of your videos."

He's surprised. And the look on his face morphs from trepidation into… curiosity? I take this opportunity to walk away, hoping he's watching me as I do. When I glance back just before I reach the kitchen, I catch him staring at my ass. He quickly turns away. I go through to the back thinking how being friendly and not flirty is going to be harder than I thought.

Chapter Seventeen

Cooper

Kelly and I are wiping down the kitchen after the lunch rush when Serenity comes through the back door. Instantly, I feel a surge of longing. But it's mixed with a pang of regret. I watch her as I load a bin into the dishwasher. She slides her sunglasses to the top of her head, and I have the urge to push back a chunk of hair that falls around her face. As she tucks her necklace beneath her shirt, I get a glimpse of it, and I swear I see a ring.

I try to get a look at her hand, but she's too quick for me. She says hello and heads right into the office, leaving the door open as she tends to do these days. I follow, needing to know if I wasn't just seeing things.

"How come you're here so early?" I ask.

She holds up a folder. That's when I see it. Or don't see it. There's no ring on her left hand.

For how long now?

"Thought I'd get a jump on the month-end stuff," she says.

My eyes flit to the wall calendar. "But it's only June eighteenth."

"Thus the jump," she says with a slow and easy smile that has my traitorous heart turning over.

Is she making excuses to be here when I am? It's hard to get a read on Ren lately. Which has made the past few weeks interesting. Or maybe confusing.

Since the day after Tag's wedding, I haven't been able to figure out if she just wants to be friends or if she wants more. One minute she's staring at me like a kid in a candy store—me being the candy. The next, she's flirting with guys at the bar. *Flirting.* Serenity Donovan has taken to flirting with men. Maybe sleeping with me flipped some switch inside her. Then again, maybe she's doing it for the tips. No—she didn't do it before my birthday, only after. Is she trying to make me jealous?

Am I jealous?

The answer comes when I picture her with the guy who was hitting on her last night and my stomach rolls. Damn it.

I don't want to feel this way. I *can't* feel this way.

Come to think of it, she's been acting like a completely different person since the day we were together. Could be I'm onto something, and being with me, hell, being with *anyone*, gave her the courage to move on.

I take a few steps into the office and perch on the arm of the couch. "Need any help?"

"You want to learn the accounting system?"

I shrug. "Sure."

She looks at my cast. "But you're leaving as soon as you get that off."

"I'm not saying I'm going to take over the books, Ren. Who knows, it might be a useful life skill. And I've got an hour or so now that lunch is over."

"I guess pull up a chair, then."

I grab the chair opposite her desk and move it around next to her. Not sure how close to get, I leave a few inches between us. We're close enough, however, that I notice the change in her breathing when I sit.

"Let's start with CoGS. That's the Cost of Goods Sold. It's the total cost of all food and beverage ingredients used during a specific time period. It's the most important thing to measure. To put it simply, it's how much it costs to produce a menu item. It's tied directly to the profit margin, revenue, and inventory. As a general rule, roughly one-third of a restaurant's gross revenue goes toward paying for CoGS. And the CoGS, along with other expenses like labor, utilities, and the lease, is subtracted from your gross revenue to determine your net profit."

My brows dip. "How'd you learn all this?"

"You mean besides growing up in and working at the pub for so long?"

"You learned all this shit by watching your dad?"

"Not all of it. I took classes at CCU, remember? It's why I couldn't go along on many of your excursions. Well, that, and you and Chaz probably didn't want a girl tagging along." She chuckles.

Wait. She laughed? At a memory from before?

I cock my head and study her. A blush crosses her face under my perusal.

Shit. The pink of her cheeks has my dick stirring.

The corner of her lower lip gets bitten by her upper teeth.

Not fucking helping.

She looks away shyly. "Anyway, it's really important to keep track of the CoGS because the cost of produce fluctuates from season to season, sometimes even from week to week. Since we don't like to make a lot of price changes on the menu, we tend to make sure it covers our highest projected CoGS." She pulls up a program on the computer. "Here is the software I use to track it."

As she moves the mouse, her pinky brushes against mine. I don't bother moving my hand, and she doesn't pull away. I'm the one who started this.

I should be paying attention to what she's saying, but damn it, my dick seems to be making other plans. I try my best to focus on the computer screen through a blurry haze of desire.

The vibration of my cell phone in my pocket pulls my mind out of the gutter, and I finally move my hand, albeit not to my phone. *Don't think about her that way.*

I've spent the better part of the past few weeks all up in my head. My siblings won't shut up about it. Addy seems excited even, about the prospect of Ren and me. But I don't get it. How do they not think that makes me a shitty brother? I swore to just let that day go. Pretend it never happened, along with the mind-altering kiss after. I'm half surprised Chaz hasn't killed me in my dreams. He should. I would if I were him.

My phone vibrates again. I ignore it and try to concentrate on what she's telling me. But I already know I'll be researching this CoGS shit on my own, because with her so close, and the way she smells, it's all I can do to keep my burgeoning woody at bay.

For the third time, my phone vibrates.

She stops talking about the computer program. "Cooper, it sounds like someone is really trying to get a hold of you. Don't you think you should answer it?"

I pull out my phone, not recognizing the number. "Hello?"

"Cooper Calloway of Calloway Creek, New York?"

"Yes."

"Oh, wonderful. I'm delighted to reach you. My name is Shawn Waylen. I'm an attorney in New York City, and I was hoping you could meet up with me at my office."

"What's this about?"

"A sensitive matter that can't be discussed over the phone."

My stomach tightens. "Shit. Am I being sued? Is a sponsor pissed? Do they want their money back? Don't they know I'm not trying to pull anything, that I'm out with a broken arm?"

"You're not being sued Mr. Calloway. Nobody is after your money or livelihood here, but I would still very much like it if you could come to my office today. I can text you the address."

"Today?"

Ren eyes me with concern. I shrug.

"Yes, today would be ideal, otherwise… Well, please try your best, and please have a government-issued ID. We'll need to verify your identity."

"Listen, if you want me to come into the city and verify my identity, I'm going to need some more information."

"I'm really not at liberty to say until you produce the identification."

"Then I'm not coming. Goodb—"

"Wait! Mr. Calloway, the only thing I can tell you is that someone you know has passed away. This meeting is in regard to that."

"Who is it?"

"Again, I'm very sorry, but you'll have to meet with me before we go any further."

"Did someone leave me something?" I lift a brow. "Money?"

I chronical everyone I know who might do such a thing and come up with nothing. The only people I know with money are right here in Calloway Creek, and I'd have heard of any of them dying. This whole cloak and dagger scenario does have the adventurous part of me wanting answers, however.

"I'm not at liberty to s—"

"Jesus, fine. Send me your address." I mute him for a second and ask Ren, "Mind if I take off early?" She shakes her head. I unmute. "I can be in the city in about ninety minutes."

"Thank you. Sending the text now."

My phone pings. I open the text and tap on the address. It's in a very prominent location in Manhattan.

"Mr… Waylen was it?"

"Yes."

"You better not be bullshitting me or I'll—"

"Feel free to look me up, Mr. Calloway." He spells his name for me. "I assure you, there's no scam here. See you shortly."

The line goes dead.

"What's all that about?" Ren asks.

"Someone died and they want me to go into the city."

"Oh, gosh." A hand covers her mouth. "Who?"

"He wouldn't say." I google his name and immediately get some hits. "He's an estate attorney. Seems legit, according to this. But I don't know anyone who's died." A thought occurs to me. "Maybe it's one of my sponsors. Some of them are ultrawealthy and own huge corporations. Could be I got named in a will? Who the hell knows."

"Well, go," she says. "I just hope it doesn't turn out to be anyone you were close with."

"Don't see how it could be. I'm not close to many people."

For a moment, our eyes lock. And I could swear we're both thinking the same thing. That once *we* were close—as close as two people could be who shared a common love for a third. I shake off the thought. "I guess I'd better get going."

She stops me before I'm out the door. The smile crinkling the corners of her eyes reminds me how goddamn beautiful she is. "Promise me you'll stop here when you get back. If I have to wait until tomorrow to find out if you've inherited a gazillion dollars, the suspense might kill me."

I laugh. "Yeah, okay."

On the train into the city, I go through my contacts, then I call Mom. "Hey, I know this is a weird question, but do you know anyone who's died recently?"

"Let's see. Murial Peachwood—she was Kurt's grandmother. You went to school with him."

"Anyone else?"

"Roger Dellsbury from church, but I don't think you knew any of his relatives."

"That's it?"

"I think so. Why?"

"I got a strange phone call today from a lawyer in the city. He said someone I know has died. He wasn't able to tell me more. I'm on the way in now."

"To the city? Without any information? Cooper, what if the man is trying to scam you?"

"I thought of that, but I looked him up, and he's an estate attorney in Manhattan."

"Wow, okay. Still, be careful and don't give him any personal information, especially your social security number and bank account."

"I'm not stupid."

"I know you aren't. It's just, in this day and age, people will do anything, and you are kind of a celebrity."

"I'm just a guy who posts crazy stuff on the internet. There's no reason for anyone to target me."

"A guy who posts stuff on the internet with a large bank account."

"Not that large," I say.

"Larger than most, I imagine."

I think of the few hundred thousand in my account. Yeah, it's a lot for a guy my age, but only because I never spend money on anything. My trips are covered by sponsors, who then get a portion of my income generated by my YouTube views. It's not enough to equal what they spent on me. I only have two million subscribers, but they're probably banking on that doubling or tripling in the future.

"You'll call me when you know what this is about?" she asks.

"Sure."

"Better yet, how about your father and I come by Donovan's for dinner? Addy is working so much these days we feel like ships passing in the night."

"That works. I told Ren I'd stop back by. Technically, it's my night to close."

"I guess we'll see you tonight, then."

"Sounds good. Bye, Mom."

I exhaust all possibilities by the time I get to my destination at three thirty. Standing on a very nice street outside a tall building in Manhattan, I surmise that if this is a scam, it's a hell of an elaborate one. Entering, I notice the marble flooring, the statues, the impeccably dressed woman at the reception desk.

I approach. "I'm looking for Shawn Waylen's office."

"Name?"

"Cooper Calloway."

She types something into her iPad. "They are expecting you, Mr. Calloway. The offices for Jones, Waylen, Turk, and Kensington are on the twenty-third floor." She gestures. "You can use those elevators right over there." Handing me a printed sticker with my name on it, she adds, "Please wear this at all times."

I rip off the backing and hand it to her, then stick the name tag on my shirt. "Thanks."

A few other people join me on the elevator. Men in suits wearing power ties. Women in skirts and heels. I look down at my jeans and polo-style shirt and feel a bit out of place. I'm going to a lawyer's office. Maybe I should have changed first.

The doors open on the twenty-third floor, and I'm greeted by an attractive woman in another pencil skirt. "Right this way, Mr. Calloway."

We pass the ostentatious sign behind the reception desk etched with the same names the woman rattled off down in the lobby. We walk by a few conference rooms walled entirely by glass. She leads me into a private room. "You can wait in here. There is water and soda on the side table over there, along with snacks if you so desire. My name is Tina if you require anything else. Mr. Waylen should be in momentarily."

She leaves, shutting the door. I'm alone in a large room with an oblong table and ten chairs around it. Though a private room, it has windows overlooking the city. Art adorning the wall is no doubt meant to impress, along with the high gloss cherrywood conference table. Not to mention the three large-screen televisions built into the far wall, and the various technology that sits on a shelf below. Not knowing if I should sit or stand, I walk over to the windows and gaze out, still trying to guess what this is all about.

Not a minute goes by before someone enters. It's a stout, middle-aged man with salt-and-pepper hair. Cleanly shaven, unlike me. And like the men in the elevator, he's dressed to match the pretentious building. He strides over with confidence, drops a folder onto the table, and holds out his hand. "Mr. Calloway, I'm Shawn Waylen."

"Cooper," I say.

"Well, Cooper, thank you for agreeing to meet on such short notice."

"What's this all about?"

"First things first. Can I please see your government ID to verify your identity?"

I hesitate before retrieving my wallet, remembering what Mom said about my personal information. But then I glance at the impeccable surroundings and think how this has got to be legit. I hand him my driver's license.

He examines it, holding it next to my face. "You've grown out your facial hair quite a bit since this photo was taken."

"Is that a problem?"

"No. Just an observation." He gestures to a seat. "Please, sit."

I do, but irritation is beginning to take hold. "Can we get on with it? I have a job to get back to. Who died?"

He looks sadly at the thick folder. "Jennifer Putnam."

I rack my brain, but the name doesn't ring a bell.

"She went by Jen."

I stare at him blankly.

"It's okay," he says. "After all this time, she wasn't sure you'd remember her. According to her, your, um, *meeting* was a brief encounter."

"According to her? But you just said she's dead."

"Let me start at the beginning. Jennifer Putnam died at 5:38 this morning of Hodgkin's lymphoma. She was diagnosed four years ago, went through chemotherapy, radiation, and a stem cell transplant. She even tried some specialized experimental procedures. But in the end, nothing worked. Jen contacted me about a year ago when she felt she should get her affairs in order."

"What does this have to do with me?"

"She has a child, Mr. Calloway. And she claims you are the father."

I push away from the table, stand, and look at him like he's crazy. "Are you kidding me? So this *is* some sort of scam. You want me to pony up money to support a baby from some woman I don't remember meeting? I haven't even been with a woman in"— Ren's face flashes through my mind—"well, a while. This is impossible."

"Not a baby." He opens the folder, pulls out a photo, and slides it across the table. "His name is Cody. He recently turned five. That would have put your encounter with Ms. Putnam somewhere along the lines of six years ago in August."

Six years ago.

Six years.

Along with ignoring the picture, I try to push all the other crazy shit floating around in my head aside for a moment and think back. I would have been twenty years old. *Fuck.* I pretty much slept with anyone wearing a skirt those first few years of my twenties. "Do you have a photo of her?"

He hands one over. "This was taken before she was very sick."

I study it. Light brown hair, expressive eyes, older than me for sure, but very attractive nonetheless. She could be nobody; she could be anybody. But she does look like someone I might have picked up in a bar. "I'm not giving anyone any money without a paternity test."

"We're prepared to do that now. The results will be back in a few days. But Cooper, this isn't about anyone wanting money from you. That's not why it was imperative you come here today."

I look up at him, my body stiffening as I realize what he's hinting at. I slump back into the chair.

"Cody has no other relatives. The closest is Jen's stepmother, who's not a blood relative."

"But she could still take him, right?"

He shakes his head. "She's older and not willing. She and Jen had a tenuous relationship at best, especially after Jen's father passed away a few years ago."

"I don't get it. Couldn't you have sent someone to Calloway Creek to give me the test?"

"Although we will provide the test, there's really no need for it when it comes to the immediate placement of the child. We brought you here because Jennifer wanted you to raise him after she was gone. We'd like you to take him today."

"Raise him? Fuck no. Do you realize what I do for a living?" I knock my cast against the edge of the table. "As soon as this is removed, I'll be traveling ten months a year. I can't raise a kid. Besides, you can't just give him to me without proof of paternity. I could be anyone. A serial killer. A child molester."

"We understand this comes as a shock. And, yes, changes to your lifestyle may have to be made to accommodate the boy. But to address the legal concerns about you taking him, there are none. Jennifer named you his guardian in her will."

"What the hell? Can she even do that without my consent?"

"She can. It doesn't mean you have to do it. But we're hoping you will." He pushes papers across the table. "Jen had been preparing for this for some time. She created a trust, Cody being the beneficiary. She was the trustee while she was alive, but now it's been turned over to you, with me as co-trustee to keep tabs."

"Trustee? The kid has a trust fund?"

"He does. But we're hoping that's not why you'll take him. There are rules pertaining to what trustees can and can't do with the money. While he's younger, the money can be used to house and clothe him, but if I believe the funds are being misused, I can petition the court to remove you as trustee and even file charges."

My head is swimming. Five-year-old kid, trust fund, guardianship, paternity.

"I don't give a shit about the money."

"Well, that's good to hear."

"Mr. Waylen, I can't have a kid. I don't want one. If he's got money, I'm sure there are plenty of people who can raise him."

"Jennifer wanted you."

"I don't know shit about kids."

"You'll learn."

"I don't want to. Plus, how do you even know he's mine? If it takes days to get the test back, then let's take the damn test and worry about everything else later."

"Jennifer was hoping to avoid putting him in the system, even for only a short time. The boy has just lost his mother." His voice cracks with emotion. "Over the past twelve months, she'd become like a daughter to me, and Cody, a grandson."

"Then you take him."

He smiles sadly. "I'm a sixty-year-old widower with high blood pressure, prediabetes, and stage one prostate cancer, Mr. Calloway. I'm not who that boy needs."

"But if I take him and then you find out I'm not his father, what's the difference? He'll go into the system anyway."

"Ms. Putnam was very insistent that Cody is yours."

"Yeah, well, I'm equally insistent that he's not."

He stands, pushes the folder over to me, and gets me a bottle of water. "Take a minute. Take an hour. But please don't dismiss this until you've read everything. I'll be in my office if you need me. Just press *one* on the phone, and Tina will fetch me."

"What if I leave?"

"That would be your right. We can't force you to stay or even take a paternity test. But I'm hoping you'll do the right thing by that boy. He's a wonderful little kid. Jen did an incredible job with him, even with everything she went through. She even prepared him for this day in ways that amaze me. So, yes, you can walk out of here and not look back. But I can see in your eyes that you're a good man, Cooper. So ask yourself how you might feel a day, a year, or a decade from now if you have a child out there whom you abandoned." He nods to the folder. "Please look at it. I'll be waiting."

He leaves and I sit here, stunned, my life tumbling out of control. I can't have a fucking kid.

Minutes go by as I convince myself the best thing for everyone would be if I left. I'm not father material, not by a long shot. I couldn't save my brother. I sure as hell shouldn't be responsible for a kid.

Ask yourself how you might feel a decade from now.

His words roll through my head, guilt-tripping me at least into looking at the papers. Most of the wording in the will and trust confuses me. But he's right, my name shows up as the guardian. And my name is listed as co-trustee in the case of Jennifer Putnam's death.

There is a listing of assets, not that it matters, but I browse through it to occupy my frazzled brain. She sold her share of an online beauty supply company to her partner eight months ago for half a million dollars. Her bank account and investments total over a million. The proceeds from the sale of her apartment, which are estimated to be around $450,000 after the mortgage is satisfied, would potentially bring the total funds in the trust to over one-point-seven million dollars.

With that kind of money, you'd think she could have found someone to raise him. Why me?

Fuuuuuck.

I lean back in the chair.

I wish Chaz were here. He'd have talked me through this. We always pondered major life decisions together, usually over a joint, sitting on rocks in the clearing along the creek. I pretend to have a conversation with him in my head. He'd tell me to get the paternity test, prove I'm not the dad, and move the hell on with my life. Yeah, that's what I should do. Shawn said the test would take a few days. Surely the kid can stay with the woman's stepmother for that long.

My mind made up, I stand. But on my way around the table, I finally take a glance at the photo of the kid. It looks like a professional took it. He's standing up, wearing jeans and a green sweater, hands casually in his pockets like he's twenty years older than he is. His hair is brown, the top of it haphazard and spiked up in the middle. His smile is a goofy grin if I ever saw one. The kid is cute, I'll give him that.

My mom always said we were lucky Chaz and I were so cute or she'd have taken us out with the garbage with the stress we caused her.

Something occurs to me, and I pull out my phone. Mom always does some stupid social media post with throwback pictures of us kids on our respective birthdays. Before Chaz died, it was always a picture of the two of us every June sixth. Since then, it's just been me. I scroll through until I find this year's photo, which she posted a few weeks ago. My heart slams into my chest wall. Because, holy shit, when I put my phone on the table next to the kid's picture, I realize I don't need a paternity test. The boy is a carbon copy of me.

Mr. Waylen comes into the room. His brows are raised. "Just popping in to see if you had any questions." He walks over to the table to see why I'm silent. To look at what my eyes are glued to. "Wow. The resemblance is amazing. You'll still want a paternity test, though, so you can put your name on his birth certificate."

"I…" My eyes close. "Fuck."

"Tina said you looked like you might walk out."

I glance at a camera mounted in the corner of the room. "You had someone watching me?"

He shrugs. "I wanted to make sure I had another opportunity to convince you."

I sit, a million questions rushing through my head.

"Would you like to meet him?"

My eyes snap to his. "He's here?"

"Yes. As I mentioned, there's really no place for him to go. He doesn't know you're here yet. We didn't want to say anything until you'd agreed."

"If I do this, how would it work? He's not just going to willingly go with a stranger. His mom died. Everything he knows will be turned upside down. He'll lash out. How could I deal with it? What if I can't?"

"I can hook you up with a child psychologist who specializes in treating young people who have lost someone. But you're not a stranger to him."

"How could I not be a stranger? We've never met."

"Jennifer has followed you online for years. Ever since she was diagnosed, she knew this day might come, so she introduced Cody to you through your videos. The boy thinks you're a superhero, Cooper. So while he's hurting, rest assured, you aren't a stranger to him."

"If she knew this day was coming, why didn't she reach out sooner?"

He shakes his head. "I encouraged it, but she was insistent. Honestly, until a few weeks ago, I believe she held out hope that she might recover. And by the time it became evident she wouldn't, she didn't have the strength to make it happen." He claps his hands together. "So, shall we?"

I look down at Cody's picture, wanting so desperately to run in the opposite direction and forget this ever happened, but knowing what a lowlife scumbag that would make me. What choice do I have? I bedded all those women; chances were, this might happen. I guess it's time to man up and face the music. I've already proven myself to be a crappy brother. I don't need lowlife father on my resume too.

Father.

I'm a fucking dad.

"Yeah, okay," I say, my body shaking more than it was when I first jumped out of a plane at 14,000 feet.

"I'll send in the medical technician to swab your cheek for the paternity test, then I'll fetch Cody."

I nod, unable to speak. Because in the last thirty minutes, my life has spiraled out of control.

A lady comes in with a medical kit, swabs my cheek, checks my ID, and has me sign some papers. "The results will be delivered to you via email in two or three days. Mr. Waylen will also get a copy of the results according to the agreement you just signed."

The woman leaves and I nervously pace the length of the room, waiting for what comes next. The door opens and Shawn appears with another woman and the kid. He looks like the picture, only sadder and without the spike in his hair. His eyes are red and sunken, his shoulders slumped. He looks like how I felt the day Chaz died… and every day after.

"Cody," Shawn says. "I'd like you to meet someone."

The boy looks up at me, and his whole demeanor changes. His face brightens in surprise. His mouth opens. His spine straightens. "Daddy?" he asks, his voice cracking with emotion.

I can't say a word. I can't get one out. I swallow. And I think I might nod.

He runs over and barrels into me, grasping onto my hips as if I might disappear into thin air. His body starts shaking with sobs. Not knowing what to do, I pat his head.

"She said I'd meet you someday." His muffled words tumble into my shirt.

My heart pounds. My mind races. My body slowly softens.

"Hey there, uh…" *Buddy? Sport? What is it Donny calls Ren— pumpkin?* I settle on his given name. "Cody."

He loosens his death grip on me and stares up. "Mommy and I watch you on her computer."

"Yeah? Hey, about your mom, I'm really sorry."

He sniffs and nods.

Maybe I shouldn't have brought it up. I have no clue what I'm doing.

"This is Tilly Putnam," Shawn says, introducing the older woman in the room.

I raise my chin. "Hello." I motion to the window. "Can I have a word?"

"Cody," Shawn says, "you must be hungry. Let's go check out the snacks."

Cody looks at me like he doesn't want to leave my side.

Shawn holds out his hand. "It's okay. They'll just be right over there."

Cody's eyes stray from me only long enough to pick out a candy bar, then he watches me as he eats.

"Mrs. Putnam," I say, out of Cody's earshot. "While I'm sorry for the loss of your stepdaughter, I'm confused as to why you think placing him with me is the best option. Wouldn't he be more comfortable with you?"

"Believe me," she rasps with the rough voice of a two-pack-a-day smoker. "That boy is more attached to you than he is me. I show up maybe once a month for dinner, more out of obligation than affection. And during those dinners, especially as of late, all Cody can talk about is his father who climbs rocks like Spiderman and flies through the air like Superman. Jennifer and I had a falling out years ago. I'm not a horrible person, Mr. Calloway. I just travel a lot. And I'm seventy-one, too old to be raising a child. Heck, I have great-grandchildren from my first marriage. You're the best option to give that boy the life she dreamed for him."

She has no idea how wrong she is. Some days I feel I can barely take care of myself. How can I be expected to be responsible for another human?

Her brow line lifts. "And don't forget, he comes with a pretty sizable trust fund."

"I couldn't give a shit about that."

She nods and smiles softly. "Maybe that makes you the best one for the job."

"Even if I'm not father material?"

"No man is a father until the day he becomes one, Mr. Calloway."

Is she quoting proverbs?

"I'm just not sure I can."

"You'll never know until you try." She glances at the clock on the wall. "I have an eight o'clock flight out of LaGuardia. I'm going down to Boca for my fiftieth reunion with my sorority sisters. Then I'm off on a cruise out of Miami."

"You're just going to leave him? *Now?*"

"Like I said, Cody isn't attached to me. My being gone won't affect him. I'm only here today because Jennifer's home hospice nurse called me early this morning. If I'd already been in Boca, I wouldn't have bothered returning."

I try not to let my disgust get the better of me.

She motions to Cody. "Cody, dear, I have to be off now. You listen to this nice man and be a good boy."

He nods. "Okay, Tilly."

Tilly? He doesn't call her *Grandma?*

Tilly doesn't even hug him. She goes for the door and turns back. "With all the commotion of the day, I completely forgot the letter."

"Letter?"

"Jennifer wrote a letter to you recently. She wanted me to bring it to Mr. Waylen to give to you. I'll have it sent over when I return."

She leaves and the three of us stare at each other.

"So?" Shawn asks.

I shrug, crack my neck, and nod.

Shawn gets down on Cody's level. "Cody, do you want to go stay with your, uh… Mr. Calloway?"

Cody's eyes go wide. "Like at his house?"

"Yes. We've packed some of your things in a suitcase right outside. You'll be able to come back for the rest of your belongings soon." He looks up at me. "This weekend maybe?"

I hold up my hands, shrugging once again, because my brain can't even get past the next two minutes.

Cody looks at me like he can't believe it. He's five. I wonder if he had any thoughts today about what would happen to him now that his mom is gone. Hell, I don't know if he's even capable of understanding what death is. I am *so* the wrong person for this.

"Do you have a 'partment?" Cody asks.

"Not exactly. I have a cabin in the woods."

A one-room cabin.

"A cabin? Like a bat cave?"

I laugh. "Not exactly."

"Do you have Xbox?" he asks. "Mommy doesn't let me do Xbox, but the kids at camp play it."

"I guess we'll have to pick one up," I say.

Along with the TV I don't own, the toys I don't have, not to mention the wherewithal to do any of this shit.

His eyes light up. "Really?"

"Sure. Why not?"

Shawn produces another folder. "If you can just fill out this paperwork, we can get the ball rolling on being able to release funds to you."

While I do that, Cody munches on a bag of potato chips, gazing out the window. How much of a culture shock will it be for him to go from living in a Manhattan apartment to a cabin in a small town?

A third folder is placed in front of me. "This is all the paperwork you'll need to enroll him in school. Guardianship papers. His birth certificate. And a few pamphlets I found on helping kids deal with death."

"School?" I look up and scrub a hand across my jaw. "Jesus."

"He'll need to start kindergarten this fall."

Reality punches me in the face. *School. Xbox. Kid.*

I put down the pen and hand Shawn the papers.

"Well, that about does it," he says. He hands me his card. "Call me anytime. Take a day or two and get settled in. Get acquainted with each other. We'll touch base about the trust and getting the rest of his things after the results come back." He glances between Cody and me and then looks at the photo still on the table. "But I'm guessing you already know how that will go."

"So that's it? I can just take him?"

"That's it."

I half expect him to hand me another folder, binder, or book. A guide for someone who's just inherited a kid they didn't know they had. I mean, shit, I don't even know if the kid is potty trained.

I turn to Cody. "I guess, let's go."

He trots over, looking excited. "To the cabin?"

"Yeah, only we have a stop to make first."

Outside the conference room are a large suitcase and a small backpack. Shawn puts the pack on Cody. "Tilly packed what she thought he'd need, but I can't guarantee anything."

"We'll manage."

Maybe.

I pull the suitcase behind me to the elevator. Shawn follows. Then he gets down on his knees. "You take care, Cody." He pulls him in for a hug. "I'll see you soon, okay?"

"Okay."

On the way to the lobby, Cody asks, "Where is your cabin?"

"Like I said, in the woods."

"Do we have to fly to get there? I like planes."

"No, we'll take the train."

"I like trains, too."

"Good."

Cody bombards me with questions along the way. Is the cabin made out of logs? Are there bears? Do I have a dog? What Xbox games can he get? Do I have other kids?

By the time we're on the train, he looks exhausted. I give him the window seat, and he almost immediately falls asleep. I watch him, wondering what's been going through his head all day.

I pull out the pamphlet Shawn gave me. It describes all the ways children might deal with the death of a parent. Some cry, some ask questions, some lash out, some seem to have no reaction at all. It says to just be there. Answer questions truthfully, offer comfort, and explain what is happening. And give them a role. Playing an active role can help them cope.

The problem is, how can I answer questions? I don't know him. I don't know his mother. I know exactly squat about his life.

I text the one person I know who may be able to help. Mom raised five kids. If anyone will know what to do, it's her.

**Me: On my way back. Meet me at Donovan's
in an hour. And bring the troops.**

Chapter Eighteen

Serenity

"He's almost here?" I ask Cooper's mom.

"He just texted me. He'll be coming through the back. Wants all of us to meet him in the kitchen."

I haven't heard from him in five hours. Whatever it is the lawyer wanted to talk to him about must be significant if he's gathered his family here.

"Did he say anything?"

"Just that I should call Tag, Jaxon, and Addy and meet him here."

I glance at the door to the kitchen. "Maybe I should stay out front."

Libby puts an arm around me. "You're family, too, Serenity. Besides, this is your restaurant. If he had anything to hide from you, he wouldn't be coming here at all."

Cooper's mom corrals her husband and kids into the kitchen. I stand off to the side, not really knowing where I fit in.

"Anyone have any idea what's going on here?" Jaxon asks.

Tag glowers. "This better be important to have dragged me away from Gigi after having been gone to Barbados for ten days."

Everyone stares at Libby.

"I don't know anything," she says. "Except that he said what happened is quite unbelievable."

Addy turns to me. "You said a lawyer called him and someone died. Maybe some old fart left him money and he's a millionaire."

"My guess is that he's taking off again," Jaxon says.

A gush of air escapes my lungs at the thought of him leaving. "But he's still got a broken arm."

"As if that would ever stop him from doing something idiotic."

The back door opens. Cooper walks through with a suitcase. Followed by... *a kid?*

Libby gasps and her hand flies to her mouth.

Cooper glances around. "Hey, everyone." He looks at the boy. "This is…" He hesitates.

"Your son," Libby says.

All eyes in the room widen. Jaws drop. More surprised gasps echo off the walls. Tag chuckles.

"Cooper, he's the spitting image of you when you were that age," his mom adds.

"Holy shit," Tag says, earning him a punch in the arm from Libby.

"What the…" Addy muses.

"How?" Jaxon adds. "Why didn't you tell us?"

"Just found out," Cooper says.

Libby walks over and leans down. "What's your name, young man?"

"Cody."

Tears fall down her face. "Cody, it's so very nice to meet you. I'm your grandmother. Can I give you a hug?"

"Okay," the boy says.

Libby's smile is a mile wide. The rest of us are stunned into silence watching grandmother and grandson bond.

"What exactly is going on here?" Cooper's father asks.

Libby takes the boy's hand. "Cody and I are going to go out front and order a bite to eat." She studies him thoughtfully. "Let me see, I'm guessing you like chicken tenders and French fries, and maybe a cookie or brownie for dessert. We'll save the vegetables for tomorrow. How does that sound?"

Kelly, who's been quietly watching from a distance, holds up a platter of desserts. Cody grins shyly.

Libby turns to Cooper. "Is he allergic to anything?"

Cooper shrugs helplessly.

"Better make it a dessert without nuts," she says to Kelly.

"I'm on it."

Cody and Libby leave the kitchen. All eyes are on Cooper. He shakes his head as if he still can't believe what has happened. He walks into the office, and the five of us follow. Although it's my office, I hang back and lean against the doorjamb.

"Son," his dad says, "start from the beginning."

Cooper sits on the couch, slumped in his normal fashion, with elbows on his knees. "The *beginning* was about five hours ago when I got a phone call from a lawyer." He explains everything that happened since, leaving us all astonished.

"So you don't really know he's yours," Tag says.

"He's his," Johnathan says. "Your mother is right. He looks just like you."

Cooper pulls out a photo. "This is a picture of Cody." He holds up his phone. "This is a picture of me when I was six."

I take a step closer, as stunned as the rest of them to see that Libby was spot-on.

"Who exactly was this Jennifer person?" Jaxon asks.

Cooper looks ashamed. "I'm not going to lie and tell you I remember every woman I ever hooked up with." He looks up at Johnathan. "Sorry, Dad. This isn't exactly how I wanted you to find out your son was a womanizer."

"What's done is done," he says. "You have more important things to worry about."

I'm learning a thing or two about Cooper myself. I knew he had his share of one-nighters back then, but I had no idea he was a playboy like Tag. Then again, the woman was from the city, where he must have done most of his canoodling.

"You're really going to do this?" I ask, suddenly curious how a guy who lives his life on the edge, mostly out of a converted van, could take on a child.

He shoves a hand through his hair. "Doesn't look like I have much of a choice."

"There's always a choice," Jonathan says. "I'm glad you had the good sense to make the right one."

After his family asks a barrage of questions Cooper doesn't know how to answer, he addresses me. "Ren, I'm sorry to leave you in a lurch, but I have to quit."

My gaze meets the floor. His announcement makes me sadder than I've been in weeks. The thought of not seeing him on a daily basis rips at my insides. And it occurs to me that him having a child and stepping up to take care of the boy somehow makes him… *sexier?*

"Wait, no," I say hastily. "You're just starting to learn the business. My dad was right, I can't do it alone, and we still have at least another month before he's back. Maybe more." I motion to the corner of the room. "We can put a table here. Cody can do crafts or homework or play games. There are plenty of people here to keep an eye on him. Heck, when I was his age, I was folding napkins and filling salt containers."

"I'll help," Addy says. "I'll even babysit whenever you need me."

"I know your mom and I would be delighted to pitch in," Jonathan says.

Tag adds, "You know Sophie, right? I'll bet she would help, too. And Josie would probably love to have a playmate. As would Gigi. She's around Cody's age. They could have play dates."

Cooper's taking it all in, but I can tell he's completely frazzled.

"I know this seems daunting right now, son," Johnathan says. "But we're all here to help. What's that saying, it takes a village to raise a child?"

"Or maybe it takes a creek," Addy says with a laugh.

Cooper looks at me. "Are you sure? I don't even know if he's a good kid. We had like one conversation on the train. He could run into the kitchen and play with knives. He could help himself to the food. He could run out the back door."

"I'm sure," I say with an inviting smile. "Just try it. Take a few days off to get to know him. Bring him by for lunch to get him used to being here. It'll be fine. You'll see."

"Okay. Maybe it's not such a bad idea. The two of us being in my cabin day and night doesn't exactly seem like the best option."

"You'll have to think about getting something bigger," his dad says.

"One thing at a time, eh, Pop?"

"Yeah, of course."

Johnathan gestures out the door. "Now, if you don't mind, I'd like to go greet my grandson." He looks at Cooper. "You coming?"

Cooper exhales a slow breath. "Sure."

As he walks by, I put my hand on his arm. "You can do this, Cooper."

"I guess we'll see."

The four of them join Cody and Libby in a booth. I watch from behind the bar, still in disbelief, trying to imagine what a shock it was for him to walk into the lawyer's office and find out he has a child.

Selfishly, I wonder what this means for us. I felt like maybe we had a moment earlier today. And having a child probably means he can't go off on his daredevil adventures anymore, or at least as much. So maybe he'll be around. And maybe I need to give him space to find out how he feels about his son before he can decide how he feels about me.

I study the two of them, father and son, strangers to each other, yet somehow, family. And I realize I'm longing for the same thing. Dad and I are close, and I love him dearly, but something is missing. Something's been missing for a long time now. I look at Cooper. I stare at Cody. And somehow, I know what's missing is them.

Chapter Nineteen

Cooper

Tag gives Cody and me a ride back to my cabin. It's dark out, the only light coming from the peek-a-boo moon behind some clouds.

"Wait here," I say, leaving Cody in the car with Tag while I go inside and turn on the lights. Because aren't kids afraid of the dark?

I run back out and get Cody's suitcase out of the trunk.

"Thanks for the ride," I say.

"Anytime. Call if you need anything."

Cody stands, holding his backpack, watching Tag drive away. "Don't you have a car?"

I nod to my van parked off to the side of the cabin, barely visible by the light from the porch. "I have a van. But I pretty much walk everywhere in town. The van has been converted so I can live in it. I can drive across the country and go anywhere I want."

He looks up at me, a question looming in his sad, innocent eyes. "Are you going to leave?"

"Right now, I'm going inside," I say. "It's been a long day, and you must be tired."

I carry his suitcase up the front steps, through the door, and set it down. Cody looks around the place. "Is this it?"

I laugh. "Yeah. I wasn't exactly expecting to have company. You can take the bed. I'll sleep on the couch. It'll do for now."

He takes his backpack over to the bed and sets it down. "It's like camping. Mommy took me camping once. We slept in a big tent."

He yawns. It's late. He should probably go to bed. But I realize I have no idea what's supposed to happen.

"Listen, Cody. You have to bear with me here. I have no clue what I'm doing. I've never done this before."

He looks confused. "But don't you live here?"

I remind myself that he's only five. "What I mean is I'm not around kids much. I don't know what you need or how to take care of you. You may have to help me out. Like, I assume you brush your teeth before bed. Do you have pajamas? Do you need to, uh, wear a diaper or anything?"

"I'm not a baby. I don't wear diapers."

"Okay, good. See, now I know one more thing about you. So the teeth and the pajamas?"

"Mommy makes me brush my teeth. She helps sometimes. And my pajamas have SpongeBob on them."

"Now we're getting somewhere." I open his suitcase and sift through his clothes until I find the pajamas, but I don't find a toothbrush. "You can change in the bathroom. It's through that door. I'll see if I can find your toothbrush."

He looks at the pajamas but doesn't take them.

"Do you need help changing your clothes?" I ask.

He shakes his head.

"Great." I hold them up.

He shuffles over morosely and takes them from me. But the look on his face makes me wonder if Jen used to help him change. Knowing exactly squat about children, it's hard for me to figure out what's going through his mind. Does he think this is temporary? That she's gone away on vacation and will return? Even though I read through the pamphlet, I'm still unsure of what to do. I hesitate to bring her up. I don't want to upset him. Especially after what must have been an overwhelming day.

I go through his backpack when he's in the bathroom. I find a plastic bag filled with toiletries—a toothbrush, shampoo, body wash, and hair product that's probably used to spike up his hair like in the photo. I pull out some books, a set of Legos, a framed 5 x 7 photo of his mom, a deck of cards, and a stuffed bear.

"That's Ozzy," Cody says from the doorway.

"Ozzy. Cool name. Did you come up with it?"

He shakes his head in silence.

I hold up his toothbrush. "Found it. No toothpaste, though. I hope you don't mind the kind I use. We can go to the store tomorrow and get whatever you need."

His eyes light up. "Can we go in your van?"

"Sure. Especially since we have to get an Xbox and a television. We can't carry those home on our backs."

The goofy grin from the photo appears on his face. Then he glances around. "You don't have a TV? What do you do here?"

"Eat. Sleep. Hike."

"Hike?"

"Yeah, you know, walk the trails. There are a lot of trails around Calloway Creek."

He studies me. "Are you the president?"

I realize he may have just made the connection between my name and the town. "No. I don't have anything to do with the name of the town except that one of my ancestors won a bet."

He stares blankly. He obviously has no idea what I just said.

"Anyway, let's go brush your teeth."

On the way, he asks. "Can I hike too?"

"I don't see why not."

"Do you have Cheerios?"

"Nope."

"What do you eat for breakfast?"

"Coffee."

"Gross."

I chuckle. "You won't think so in about fifteen years."

~ ~ ~

A noise awakens me from a dead sleep. Outside, it's pitch black. It sounds like a baby bird fell out of a nest or something. I stretch out and my leg flops off the couch. I realize two things simultaneously. One, I'm not in my bed because Cody is; and two, he's crying.

I lie here and try to think of what to do. The kid just lost his mother. He's in a strange place with a strange man. A man who knows literally nothing about him except his preference of breakfast cereal and nighttime clothing choices.

Maybe he had a bad dream or is scared of the dark. I turned off all the lights after he fell asleep. I cross the room, flip on the bathroom light, and sit back down. He's still crying.

"You okay, kid?" I ask.

My question only makes him cry harder. *Shit.*

I go over and sit on the edge of the bed. "I'm really sorry about your mom. I know how hard it must be. Someone close to me died a few years ago. My brother. I guess he would have been your uncle."

He hiccups a few times and settles a bit. "Gage from day camp has five uncles. I always wanted to have uncles."

"Well, it appears you might have two. My brother Tag, who drove us here, and my other brother Jaxon, who you met at the restaurant. And my sister, Addy—I guess she could be your aunt. And Tag and Jaxon have kids, so they could be your cousins."

He turns, wipes his eyes, and looks up at me. "Are you really my dad?"

"I don't know. But I think so. We'll know for sure in a day or two. Remember when they wiped the inside of your mouth? They did it to mine, too. And they will take those swabs and compare them to see if we're a match."

"A match?"

"A match would mean I'm your father."

"What if we're not a match?"

"I'd say the chances of that are pretty low. Everyone says we look alike."

"We do?"

"Well, not right now, but if you look at a picture of me when I was your age, I looked like you do now."

"Oh." He pulls Ozzy close and sniffs. "He smells like Mommy."

"Do you want me to put him away?"

He shakes his head.

"Okay, I'm going back to bed. Do you want me to leave on the light?"

He nods.

"Try to get some sleep. Tomorrow, I'll teach you how to play Mario Kart."

"I know how."

"I thought you said you didn't have an Xbox."

"Mario isn't on Xbox. Sonic is on Xbox. Gage has all the games. We have play dates."

"You *are* only five, aren't you? I mean, you seem to be pretty smart for a five-year-old."

"That's what Mommy says."

"I think your mom was right. Now get some sleep, sport. You're going to need it if we're going hiking tomorrow."

The goofy grin is back. "Gage's daddy calls him sport."

"Eyes closed. Now."

He snuggles Ozzy and does what I ask.

Chapter Twenty

Serenity

What am I doing?

I stare at the Mustang, then at the keys in my hand, wondering if this is a terrible idea. I rub the ring on my necklace between my fingers, inhale, then step over to the driver's side door. I swear I can see Chaz inside. *"Get in,"* I can almost hear him say, remembering the first time he picked me up for a date.

It was cold outside. He was wearing a bomber jacket and dark jeans. And flowers sat on the passenger seat, waiting for me as if he were embarrassed to bring them to the front door.

I remember hesitating. I knew if I got in, I'd probably never look back. I had been infatuated with him since the first moment he walked into my geometry class.

"Come on," he said. *"What are you waiting for?"*

I smile. It's almost like he's daring me to do it right now.

"Fine."

I open the door and slide into the driver's seat. I expect the smell to overcome me. *His* smell. But it doesn't. The car just smells like the rest of Dad's garage, musty.

"It probably won't even start," I say to no one as I insert the key. I'm surprised to learn that it does.

"Well, I guess that's that."

I back out of the driveway, stop at the bakery on McQuaid Circle, then head out, turning left onto the dirt road that leads to practically nowhere. I'm relieved the road isn't muddy; this old car definitely doesn't have four-wheel drive. Again, I ask myself what I'm doing as I pull up behind Cooper's van.

I contemplate turning around, but then I see movement on the front porch. It's him. He's sitting on the bench sipping coffee. I turn off the engine, grab the food, and join him.

He nods to the Mustang. "Nice car." He stares at it. "I was always jealous of that thing. Chaz had the good sense to save all his money when we were kids, whereas I spent every nickel I ever had."

I hold out the keys. "You should have it."

"What? No."

"Cooper, you'll need a car. You can't drive Cody around in *that* big thing." I gesture to his van.

"I'll have you know he was excited about the van."

"Even so, the car is yours now. I don't want it. I don't"—I glance over at it—"need it."

He regards the car, then me. "At least let me pay you for it."

"It was never mine, Cooper. Besides, you need to save your money. Raising a kid can be expensive."

"Not when said kid comes with a trust fund."

My eyes widen. "Seriously?"

"I didn't say anything yesterday because I thought everyone might believe I only agreed to this for the money."

"Why did you agree?"

"He has no one. A step-grandmother who would rather be on a cruise than with him."

"And if he turns out not to be yours?"

"I don't think that's going to happen."

"So you're really going all in on this?"

He shrugs noncommittally. Then he looks at my bags. "What's with those?"

I pull out the drink containers. "I brought coffee. But it looks like you beat me to it." I hold up the other bag. "And muffins for Cody. I wasn't sure you had time to shop for food, and I know you don't eat breakfast. At least you and Chaz never did before."

"You're right, I don't." He sighs and looks away. "Does it feel strange when you talk about him?"

"Chaz?" I nod. "It did. For a long time, I wouldn't even mention his name. A month ago, I wouldn't have dreamed of getting into his car. But now… How about you, do you find it strange?"

"It's weird as shit when I talk about him with you of all people."

"Why?"

"Isn't it obvious, Ren? You were his girl."

"And?"

I hold my breath, waiting for him to answer.

"And the thoughts I'm having about my brother's girl should have me arrested." His face contours with a mixture of embarrassment and misery.

I try not to smile. Because I've been having thoughts about him too. Lots and lots of thoughts.

The front door opens, and Cody appears wearing SpongeBob SquarePants pajamas.

"Hi, Cody. I'm Serenity. We met last night. I really like your pajamas." I tug on the hem. "I know most people love SpongeBob, but Squidward is my favorite."

He grins, and I swear it's the same roguish grin Cooper has. "Squidward is my favorite too."

"Wow, that's pretty cool." I hold out the bag of food. "I brought muffins. I didn't know if your…" I suddenly realize I'm not sure what Cody is calling Cooper. "Uh, I didn't know if you had any breakfast food here. I brought chocolate chip and blueberry."

He takes the bag and looks inside. "Which is *your* favorite?" he asks.

I ponder it like it's the million-dollar question. "I like them both, but I guess blueberry."

He reaches in, comes out with the blueberry muffin and hands it to me.

"Thank you," I say. "But are you sure you don't want this one?"

"Mommy said I should be curt-is to others, 'specially girls."

"Well, that *is* very courteous of you, Cody. Your mother sounds like she was one special woman."

He nods, sits on the bench, and digs into the chocolate chip muffin.

"I brought hot chocolate too, if you like it."

"Yes, ma'am. Thank you."

"Cody?"

He looks up.

"You can call me Ren. All my friends do."

"Ren?" He takes a big bite and then asks around his food, "Do you go hiking?"

"I love hiking."

He turns to Cooper. "Can she come?"

Cooper takes in my yoga pants, tank top, and running shoes. "I don't know, can she?"

I smile. "She can."

A half hour later, we're on the hiking trail to the east of his cabin. I'm learning what a chatterbox Cody is. He talks even more than Maddie's daughter, Gigi, and I thought *she* talked a lot. It's evident he's a very intelligent child. He tells us about his friend, Gage, and the day camp he goes to. He talks about his 'partment,' saying how it's up high and how he likes to watch the tiny people and little cars that look like toys from the window.

We come across a tree that's fallen over the creek. Cody runs ahead and starts climbing out onto it.

"Whoa, whoa, whoa!" Cooper yells. "Easy there, sport. That's dangerous."

I cover my mouth and laugh.

"What's so funny?" Cooper asks.

"Now you know how the rest of us feel."

He cocks his head. "Feel?"

"You know, watching your videos. Seeing the risks you take."

"I can be like you," Cody says, standing at the edge of the tree.

"Someday, yeah," Cooper says. "Not today."

"Will you teach me to do the stuff you do?"

"That's kind of a tall order, kid."

Cody's nose scrunches. "What's a tall order?"

"It's something that's hard to do."

"Can we get my Xbox now?"

"Sure, kid."

"How come you call me kid?" Cody asks.

"You are a kid, no?"

Cody shrugs. "Yeah, but…"

"But what?"

"I kind of like the other name."

Cooper's face softens, and he grips Cody's shoulder. "Sure thing, sport. Let's go."

"Can we hike every day?" Cody asks on our way back.

"Not *every* day, but some days."

"Can Ren go with us again?"

Cooper looks at me. Cody looks at me. "I'd love to," I say.

"Tomorrow?" Cody asks.

"Serenity has to work," Cooper says. He looks at his phone. "In fact, she'd better get going or she'll be late."

"Trying to get rid of me?" I joke, jogging ahead.

He blows out a breath. "Like you wouldn't believe," he mumbles just loud enough for me to hear.

I'm not exactly sure how he meant it, but when I turn and see him watching me, I'm pretty sure I have my answer. "I'll be here," I shout. "Be ready at eight. I'll bring muffins."

"Bring Cheerios!" Cody calls out.

I give him a thumbs-up and jog around the corner.

Chapter Twenty-one

Cooper

After going into town for electronics, we stop at Donovan's for lunch. Ren isn't anywhere to be seen. She must be either helping in the kitchen or doing paperwork in the office.

"Cooper, over here," Sophie says, sitting in a booth with two-year-old Josie.

Cody and I walk over.

"Would you like to sit with us?" she asks. "We just ordered."

"That would be nice." I sit and Cody scoots into the booth next to me.

"I've heard so much about you, Cody," she says. "This is Josie and I'm her nanny."

"You're her grandma?" he asks innocently.

Sophie chuckles. "No, a nanny is like a babysitter. Do you know what a babysitter is?"

Cody nods. "Mora is a girl across the hall at my 'partment. She goes to high school. She's my babysitter."

"Well, a nanny is a babysitter who is with you a lot more than a night or two a week. I've been helping out with Josie since she was a little baby." She turns to me. "I'd be totally willing to babysit him whenever you need me to. Amber and Quinn already said they wouldn't mind." Back to Cody. "Would you like to play with Josie and me sometime?"

"Do you have Xbox?" Cody asks.

"No. But my apartment complex has the best playground in all of Calloway Creek."

Cody looks at me and I nod. "Okay," he says.

"Thanks," I tell her. "That would be great."

Addy comes over and scoots in next to Cody, squishing him between us. "Hey, little dude."

"Do you remember Addison?" I ask.

Cody asks, "Is she my aunt?"

"I guess she might be, sport."

"Heck yeah, I am," Addy says. "And I'm going to be the coolest aunt ever. I always wanted a nephew. I have three nieces already, so having a nephew is going to be awesome. I know your dad here isn't going to be as strict as a lot of dads, but if he does turn out to be some lame-o dad, you can count on me to set him straight."

My pulse races each time she says the word *dad*. I know that's most likely what I am to him, but we haven't really had a conversation about it, and he hasn't called me dad since the moment we met yesterday.

"We should order," I say. I look at Addy over Cody's head. "And *you* should get back to work."

"Jeez, I hope you're not a drillmaster at home, too." She giggles. "Just kidding, Cody. I'm sure he'll be great. Of all my brothers, he's definitely the most fun. Even if he is dim-witted half the time." She stands and gets out her order pad. "What sounds good? A delicious, greasy-as-sin burger?"

Cody nods.

"Make it two," I say.

Someone comes out from the back, but it's Gino, not Ren.

Addy follows my gaze, then says, "She's in the office."

I play it off like I don't know what she's talking about.

"Oh, come on," she says. "Like you haven't been sitting here waiting for her to come out."

"You think about things way too much, little sister."

"Who's in the office?" Cody asks.

"Ren," Addy says. "Your dad here is smitten with her."

"What's smitten?"

"He wants her to be his girlfriend."

"Dang, Addy. How about you keep your mouth shut and do your job."

"You like Ren?" Cody asks.

"I think I'll take a chocolate milkshake with lunch. How about you, Cody?"

He nods emphatically.

Addy laughs. "Coming right up."

I look awkwardly at Sophie. "Sorry about that."

"About what? I didn't hear a thing," she says with a wink.

Sophie is very attractive. Nice. A few years younger than me. Exactly the kind of woman that would give me a stiffy back in my womanizing days. But as we sit three feet across from each other, my dick is completely flaccid.

Then Ren walks up, and I swear the little general tries to salute her.

"Hey, you guys." She greets Sophie, kisses Josie's head and turns to Cody. "I have something to show you. Want to come in the back and see?"

"Can I?" he asks me.

I nudge him out. "I want to see too."

In the back, I'm surprised by what Ren has done to the office. She talked about it last night, but I wasn't sure she really meant it. The bookshelf has been moved and a card table is in the corner. On it is a pile of games, puzzles, and books. Even an old handheld gaming device.

"A Game Boy?" I pick it up. "Where did you get all this stuff?"

"Went through some boxes in our storage closet." She nods to the game in my hand. "Can you believe I even had the charging cord for that? Cody, back when I was a little older than you are now, I played with this."

I hand it to him, and he examines it. "Cool."

"Do you think you'd like to hang out in here when I come back to work tomorrow?" I ask.

He looks at everything on the table. "All this is for me?"

Serenity pulls a game out of the pile. *Hungry Hippo.* "I used to play back here when my dad was working. He'd sneak in here and play this one with me. It's a lot more fun if you have two or more players."

"Can we play it now?"

"Sure." She unboxes it. "You put all the marbles in the middle and then push down on these levers really fast and see whose hippo can eat the most."

The two of them put their hands on the levers. Cody looks at me. "You too."

I step up to the table. Then the three of us play the stupid game until Addy pokes her head in and tells us our food is ready.

"Ah, man," Cody says, disappointed that the fun has ended.

Fun. It's now that I realize that for the past ten minutes he'd been having fun. And he was laughing. Kid has one hell of a contagious laugh, too. Because Ren was laughing. I couldn't laugh, though. All I could do was stare at the two of them, something unfamiliar stirring deep inside.

"I have to use the bathroom," he says.

"Okay, it's right out here."

He looks up at me. "I have to do number two."

"Uh…" I stand here like a deer in headlights. I know the kid is human. He eats and drinks, but I guess I didn't really think about him taking a shit. He hasn't since yesterday—that I'm aware of.

Ren steps forward. "I'll take him."

Relief surges through me. There are so many things about this I hadn't considered. "I'll wait at the table."

A few minutes later, Ren walks him back to the booth, and Cody's eyes bulge when he sees our giant burgers.

"He did wash up, right?" I ask.

"Like a pro," Ren says. Then she laughs. "Cody, tell him what you say when you wipe."

"Wipe and fold, wipe and fold, 'til the poopy's all controlled." He turns to me. "Controlled means until it's all gone. Mommy likes to rhyme."

It's not lost on me that Cody still refers to his mom in the present tense. It makes me wonder if he really does grasp the whole concept of death.

Sophie is cracking up. "I'm definitely going to use that one when potty training Josie."

"I'll leave you to eat your lunch," Ren says.

"Bye, Ren," Cody calls out after her. "Don't forget about hiking."

"I won't."

When she looks back, she glances at him sweetly, then her eyes capture mine. She smiles. I smile back. The general really likes her smile. But I turn away, realizing how wrong it is that he does.

~ ~ ~

After another long day, Cody is getting ready for bed. I turn off the television, put away the toys my mom brought over earlier, and switch off the kitchen light. It's strange having to go to bed when he does, but with only one room, it's not like I can stay up, watch baseball, and drink a couple of cold beers.

If the paternity test comes back positive, I'll have to think about getting a bigger place.

What are you talking about if?

He comes out of the bathroom wearing his pajamas, races across the room in bare feet, and torpedoes himself onto the bed. He reaches into his backpack and pulls out a book before holding it out to me.

"You want me to read?"

"A book a night makes Cody bright."

I snicker.

"Do *you* know what bright means?" he asks.

"In this case, it means smart."

"Mommy says I'm bright for my age."

"I think I'd have to agree. Can you read?"

He shakes his head. "I know letters. Mommy says I'll learn reading in school."

I take a seat next to him on the bed and read his book. By the end, he's having a hard time keeping his eyes open. When I close the book and pull away, his little hand holds on tight. "Will you go anywhere?"

"I'll be right over there on the couch, sport."

"Will you get sick and go away like she did?"

Fuck. "No, Cody. I'm not going to get sick."

"Promise?"

I close my eyes and lie, knowing I'm the last person who should ever make promises. "Promise."

~ ~ ~

"Chaz?" I can see his head when I sit up. I think we're pinned by the same boulder. It's the size of a small refrigerator, but it still must weigh over a ton.

The rock has me trapped just above my ankle. My ankle hurts like's it's twisted, but I can wiggle my toes.

"Yeah?"

"How bad is it? Can you move? Can you feel your toes?" I wipe blood off my forehead. "Are you bleeding?"

"Dude, I can't feel shit. This rock is heavy as fuck." He coughs, then groans. "The damn thing is crushing my entire lower half and my left side up to my armpit. My arm is cut."

He holds his arms over his head. One of them has a trickle of blood running down the side. At least they're free. We may be able to get some leverage.

"Damn it, brother. Why in the hell did you make us go up there?"

"You didn't have to go, Coop. Last I checked, we do have separate brains."

"And your shit for brains may have ruined everything. What if you're paralyzed?"

"I'm not paralyzed."

"You can't feel anything."

"Because this rock is crushing me, not because my neck is broken. Can you get to your phone? I don't suppose you can call someone to help us out of here."

I pull my phone out of my pocket. The screen is cracked, but it still works, although I don't have service. I slide my backpack off and get his phone out. It's totally destroyed. I must have fallen on it when I hit the ground. I go back to mine and hold it up as far as I can. Still nothing.

"No service," I say. "Any more bright ideas?"

"Sit and wait for other hikers to come?"

I don't mention that we passed no one on the trail up. Not a single soul. This isn't a well-traveled trail. Still, someone is bound to come sooner or later. I quickly calculate how long we could be here before things get dicey. I have my water bottle. It probably has at least fifty ounces left. And Chaz has his. And we each have protein bars and snack mix. We're fine.

"Motherfucker," Chaz says. "I think I peed myself. Wait, ah shit... my water bottle exploded."

I pull mine out, thankful it's still intact. "It's okay. Mine's good."

"How long do you think it will take before someone finds us?"

"Hell if I know." I take in my surroundings. Rocks of various sizes landed all over. There are a few tree branches as well. "Maybe we don't need to wait." I can just reach one of the large branches. I thwap it against the ground. "This branch here looks sturdy. If I can use one of these smaller rocks as a fulcrum, I might be able to lift the boulder a few inches to pull my leg out. Then I can come do the same on your side."

"Sweet, because I don't feel so good."

"You probably gave yourself a concussion."

I pick up a heavy rock about eight inches in diameter. Damn, with as heavy as this one is, I can't even imagine how much the one sitting on us weighs. I question the branch's ability to lift it without snapping. But I put the rock in place and maneuver the branch under the boulder as far as it will go. "Ready?"

"Go for it."

I sit up as tall as I can and push down with as much of my body weight as possible. I feel it start to budge, but just barely.

"Stop! Stop!" he yells.

"Jesus, what?"

"When you do that, I feel like the boulder is cutting me in half."

I look over. His face has gone pale.

"Oh shit," he says, showing me his hand smeared with blood.

My heart stops. "Whoa, where did that come from?"

"I don't know. Underneath me, I guess. It feels better now that you stopped."

"We sure as hell aren't doing that again. We'll just have to wait."

We spend hours talking about our business. How we'll get it up and running. Where home base will be. How we'll definitely be purchasing a satellite phone in case anything like this happens again.

The sun goes down with no sign of hikers. Nobody is coming today, and we both know it.

"I think we'll just camp here for the night," I joke.

He laughs, then coughs.

"You okay?"

"Yeah. I just hope someone comes tomorrow."

"Someone will. Get some sleep. We're going to need our strength."

As the stars come out, I stare up, looking for constellations as I drift off.

Warmth spreads across my face. I open my eyes and realize it's morning. Then yesterday's events come rushing back. "Chaz?"

I reach over and touch his head. He groans. "It's still so goddamn cold," Chaz says.

It's July. And yeah, we're up high, but I'm not cold at all. And I realize that's a bad sign. He may have lost a lot of blood. I pull a protein bar from my pack and hand it to him. "You need to eat."

"I'm not hungry."

"Eat anyway."

"You're not the boss of me."

"You got us into this, Chaz. Just eat the fucking protein bar."

He tears the wrapper off and takes a bite, choking it down like he's eating bear shit. I hand him my water bottle. "Drink."

He takes two sips and hands it back. "You need to eat and drink too."

"I already did."

It's a lie. I didn't. I'll drink when I have to, but he's still pale; he needs it more. I wiggle my toes just to make sure I can.

A retching noise comes from the other side of the rock. I stretch up and see Chaz vomiting. He wipes his mouth. "Told you I didn't want to eat."

Damn it. If he can't keep food down, his crush injury may be worse than we thought. "Maybe you should stick to water," I say.

"Ya think?"

In a heightened state of panic, I use my fingers to dig into the dirt, hoping if I dig down far enough, I can make space to pull my leg out. They become bloody and raw. Then I pick up the branch but make no headway when I realize my leg is pinned between the boulder and another rock, not the boulder and the ground. Digging myself out isn't an option.

The day goes by at a snail's pace without any hint of other life with the exception of a family of squirrels and the occasional bird. By the afternoon, I'm yelling for help. I figure if someone is hiking nearby, they could hear. But my voice only holds out for so long. I unzip my pants and take a whiz off to the side, noting how dark my urine is. "I can't believe we're going to have to spend another night here."

When I wake the next morning, Chaz doesn't wake with me. Terror like I've never felt consumes me. I lean over and shake him. "Chaz, wake up. Wake up, brother."

"Stop it," he finally says, to my relief. He looks at me, eyes fuzzy. "How long have we been here?"

"Almost two full days. Listen, I'm thinking we should try again," I say. "If I'm really quick, maybe I can lift it off me without hurting you."

His lips are dry and peeling. He shakes his head. "Cooper." His voice is ridden with hopelessness. "I'm pretty sure this rock is the only thing holding me together. I think if you move it I might die."

My throat thickens. "Well, shit." I search my pack for something—anything that could help. I hold the pocketknife in my hand and put the length of rope to one side.

"What are you doing?" he asks.

"Thinking," I say curtly. "Would you let me think for a goddamn minute?"

"Cooper, what is it?"

"We're almost out of food and water. If someone doesn't come soon..."

"If someone doesn't come soon, what?"

I eye the supplies, not quite believing what I'm about to say. "If someone doesn't come soon, tomorrow maybe, or the next day at the latest, I'll cut it off."

"Cut what off?"

"My leg."

"The fuck you will." His words come out stronger than any of his words over the past twenty-four hours.

"Chaz, it may be our only hope."

"I'm not letting you cut off your leg."

"Think about it. If I use the lever to push the rock off my leg, you'll die. If I don't, we both die. Remember the movie about the guy trapped in a canyon or whatever? He cut off his arm to save his life. I have rope. I could tie it off. I wouldn't bleed out."

"That's ridiculous."

"It might become necessary."

"Jesus Christ, Coop. You're not cutting off your leg."

I look down the mountain, willing to see hikers come our way. "Maybe it won't come to that."

He holds out his arm, resting it on the rock because he doesn't have enough strength to keep it up. "Give me the knife."

"Like hell."

"Give it to me. I'm not going to sit here and watch you amputate your leg."

"Come and get it if you want it."

"Screw you." He coughs twice and clears his throat. "Someone will come along. They'll get help. Emergency services will figure out a way to get this off us."

"Yeah," I say, more confidently than I mean it.

I wake the next day, a massive cramp in my hamstring. It's a sign of dehydration. Someone has to come today. My eyes close and I do something I've never done before. I pray.

"Chaz?"

He doesn't answer. I reach over and press my hand to his neck. I'm relieved to feel a pulse. I eat the last of the snack mix, feeling guilty that he can't keep food down. Hell, he can barely stomach water at this point. I check my bottle. Just under ten ounces left. I figure that could last us today. But then... I wiggle the toes on my right foot, wondering if after tomorrow I won't have them anymore.

"Ren?" Chaz says. "Ren, where are you?"

He's confused again—another sign of dehydration.

I hand him the water bottle. "Chaz, drink this. Drink all of it."

"Cooper? What happened?"

It takes him a minute to get his bearings. He curses and drinks a few sips of the water.

"I said all of it."

He hands it back. "You need it too."

"Not as much as you do."

"I'm not drinking all of it. Listen, you know as well as I do that you have a much better chance." His voice is weak and strained, as if talking is exhausting for him. "Use the lever. Get out of here. Maybe I'll be okay. You can make it to the road and send help."

"I'm not going to do anything that will kill you."

"You might have to, Coop. It's better than both of us dying."

"Would you do it if the tables were turned?"

His silence is my answer.

"I need you to do something for me," he says sometime later.

"What?"

"Take care of Ren. If I die, she'll be torn up. I need to know she'll be taken care of."

"Take care of her yourself."

"I need you to promise, Coop. Promise me you'll take care of her. She deserves... so much better."

"Fine. I promise. But it's not going to come to that. We're both getting out of here. One way or another, I promise you."

He falls asleep. I start yelling for help. Someone has to come. They have to.

Arms come around me. "Wake up!"

I jolt awake, still screaming in my sleep. I look at Cody by the dim light coming from the bathroom. He's terrified. "Hey, little man. It's okay. Just a bad dream."

He crawls up on the couch with me and snuggles under my arm. "Mommy gets into bed with me when I have a bad dream. Was it a monster?"

"I was dreaming about my brother, Chaz. He died too, like your mom."

"So he's never coming back?"

"No."

He's silent for a beat. "Is my mom ever coming back?"

I sigh and shake my head. "No."

"So we're alike."

"Yes."

"Can I sleep here?"

I sit up. "No, but we can move to the bed."

I climb into bed, and he gets in next to me, pulling Ozzy close. But he doesn't shut his eyes. He stares.

"What is it?" I ask.

"If that test says we match, will I get to call you Dad?"

"I guess you will, sport." I reach out and straighten Ozzy's bowtie. "I guess you will."

~ ~ ~

After a fitful night of sleep, I wake before Cody, wondering which one of us will stop having bad dreams first. I quietly make my way to the shower, and after, I stare in the mirror for a long time, reliving last night's dream yet again.

My phone alarm chimes. It's almost eight. I leave the bathroom to wake him up, but the bed is empty. "Cody?"

I look around, but I just came from the bathroom. There's nowhere else he could be. I race to the front door, collecting my shoes along the way. On the other side, Ren is coming up the porch steps with more coffee and breakfast.

"Everything okay?" she asks after seeing me rip the door open.

I quickly glance around the porch and yard. "Did you see Cody?"

Her smile falls and worry darkens her expression. "He's not inside?"

I slip on my shoes. "He was sleeping. I took a shower. When I came out of the bathroom, he was gone."

She looks out into the woods and drops everything in her arms. "Let's go."

We run out, taking opposite directions. "Cody!" we both shout, her voice getting more distant the further apart we get.

"Cody, where are you?"

I run through the tree tunnel, checking the clearing. He's not there. I run down along the creek, praying he didn't fall in. I don't even know if he can swim—it's a thought that terrifies me to my core.

A feeling of complete powerlessness comes over me. It's exactly how I felt up on that mountain. Pain, sharp and jagged, spears my insides as my thoughts leap fervently from one horrible scenario to the next. He's five. Only five fucking years old. I scramble through the woods, in and around trees, looking for any trace of him as brittle pieces of my nightmare slice through my brain.

"Cody!" I yell.

In the distance, there's a flash of yellow pajamas, then he comes around a tree, running toward me. Relief hits me square in the chest, taking my breath away. I race forward. He slams into me, gripping my hips tightly.

"Jesus, why are you out here?"

He squeezes. "You were gone. I thought you left." His voice fades to a whisper as his body trembles against mine.

"Hey." I get down on my knees to see he's utterly frightened. "It's okay. I was in the bathroom. Next time check there first, okay?"

He nods and latches onto me again. "Okay. Because you promised, right?"

"Yeah, I promised."

He loosens his grip and looks up at me. And I swear to God, I look down into my own eyes. Suddenly, my whole life changes. I don't want to jump out of planes, rappel off buildings, or swim with sharks. I don't want to do any of that.

Because in the last thirty-six hours, I've been given something I haven't had in four years.

Purpose.

Chapter Twenty-two

Serenity

I walk through the back door and into the office.

"Isn't it my day to open?" Cooper asks, looking up from behind the desk.

"I thought you could use a hand today."

Cody is already digging through the games and puzzles. I hand him a stack of coloring books. Then I pull out a lined notepad filled with traceable letters. "Thought you might want to start practicing for kindergarten." I get out a crayon. "Look here. You just follow the lines of the letters." I trace the letter *A* as he watches.

He gets a green crayon and expertly traces the *B*.

"I can see you're already ahead of the game. Have you done this before?"

He nods as he uses the blank space next to the letters to write his own. "I know the letters. Mommy taught me the song. And I can write my name."

"No way," I say dramatically. "Let's see."

Proudly, he spells out a messy *C O D Y*. He holds it up and I clap.

"Wow," Cooper says. "Impressive."

Cody smiles from ear to ear. He pushes the pad to me. "What letters are in your name?"

I write out my full name and then circle the Ren part.

"It's neat that you have two names," he says.

"Hey, everyone," Gino says, walking past the office.

"Ren and I have to go to work now," Cooper says. "I'll check on you every so often. Other people have promised to stop by, too. My mother, and Tag and his daughter Gigi. If you need me, I'll either be in the kitchen or out front. But try to stay in here most of the time, okay?"

"Can I come out for lunch?"

"Of course. We'll eat together. But I'm going to have Kelly make you some vegetables today."

"Can I still eat a hamburger?"

"Sure."

"Can Ren eat with us?"

"I'm not sure she—"

"I'd be happy to," I say.

Cooper and I back out of the office, neither of us quite ready to leave him on his own.

"The boy will be fine," Kelly says. "Allen and I will keep an ear out. And don't worry, we won't leave any knives lying around."

Cooper starts opening duties. I hang back, not going far from the office. I don't miss how he keeps making excuses to go back in there as well.

Just after I unlock the doors and turn on the OPEN sign at eleven o'clock, Cooper looks down at his phone as if it might combust.

"What is it?"

"A text," he says. "The results are in." He pulls out a barstool and scrubs a hand across his jaw. "Shit. Forty-eight hours ago, I knew what result I would have wished for. Now… well, let's just say the kid has kind of grown on me."

Not to mention he has no one else.

"I'll leave you alone."

He reaches out and puts a hand on my arm. "That's okay, you can stay."

I sit, happy he wants me here. And maybe wondering what it means that he does. "I hope it turns out the way you want it to."

He nods, and it occurs to me that at this point, it's hard to say exactly what he's hoping for.

He taps the link and enters his credentials. It pulls up a lab report. I try to read over his shoulder, but it just shows a bunch of numbers on it that mean nothing to me. Then he scrolls to the note on the bottom.

The alleged father is not excluded as the biological father of the tested child. Based on testing results obtained from analysis of the DNA loci listed, the probability of paternity is 99.9998%.

He gasps once. Then again. A third time even. Is he hyperventilating?

His head slumps forward into his hands as he tries to control his breathing. The reaction gives nothing away, and I'm left wondering if I should comfort or congratulate him.

Then a sudden gush of soul-cleansing air is released from his lungs. He looks up with quiet determination. Acceptance. Pride.

I think I have my answer. I take the phone from him and reread the results. Then I joke, "Well, this is totally inconclusive. There's a .0002% chance the test is wrong."

We both laugh. Then he stiffens. "Oh my god, Ren. I'm a fucking dad."

I smile. "Congratulations."

"I mean, I thought it was going to come back this way, but thinking it and knowing it for sure are two different things. This is…"

"Pretty huge."

"Yeah."

His phone rings. "It's the lawyer." He answers and puts him on speaker. "Hello?"

"Cooper, it's Shawn Waylen. Have you seen the results?"

"I have."

"And how are you feeling about it?"

"I'm, uh, a little overwhelmed, I guess. But it wasn't unexpected."

"How's Cody doing?"

"He's fine. Settling in."

"Glad to hear it. And how are you holding up?"

"As good as anyone could be under the circumstances."

"Am I to take that as affirmation of you being on board with this?"

"I suppose you can."

"Excellent. I'd like to set a time for you to come back to the city. We can meet up at Jennifer's apartment, and you can collect the rest of his things. There are still a few decisions to be made."

"When?"

"I'll make time whenever you can get here."

"Hold on a sec." He mutes the phone.

"I'll help," I say. "If you need it, that is."

"We can't both be away."

"How about tomorrow morning? We'll go early, say eight o'clock? I'll call in an extra server to oversee front of house until one of us can get back."

He unmutes the call. "How's tomorrow morning around nine?"

"I'll text you the address."

"See you then."

He thumbs to the back. "I suppose I should go tell him."

"He's going to be ecstatic."

"You think so?"

"Cooper, the boy worships you. I saw you together this morning after you found him on the trail. Believe me, he wants this." I hold his stare. "And based on what *you* looked like, I'd say you want this too."

He takes a deep breath and heads to the back.

I should stay out here. Give him space. But my need to witness the moment overtakes any moral obligation to honor their privacy. So I follow, but I hang back in the kitchen, shushing Kelly and Allen so I can hear.

"Hey, sport," Cooper says from the doorway.

Cody barely looks up, engrossed in his coloring book. "Hi."

"So, uh, remember the test I told you about? The one we took to see if we're a match?"

Cody nods, still coloring.

"Well, it came back. And it looks like..." He looks over his shoulder at me. I give him an encouraging smile. "It looks like we're a match."

I can see the moment Cody realizes what Cooper has said. Tears come to the boy's eyes. "Does that mean I can call you Dad now?"

Even from behind, I can see Cooper's body heave an exaggerated breath. "Yeah. Yeah, it does." He falls to his knees, and Cody runs into his arms.

Chapter Twenty-three

Cooper

As I walk through Jennifer Putnam's apartment, bits and pieces of Cody's life are revealed. A large picture of them at the beach in front of the sunset is displayed proudly above the couch. A collage of photos from Disney World is in the hallway. And in Jen's room, on the wall next to her bed, is a line of six photos of Cody—the first one is of him wrapped in a hospital blanket with a little beanie on his head. Each of the other five have him smiling in front of a birthday cake.

"Looks like chocolate is his favorite," Ren says, studying the pictures alongside me.

I sit on a chair by the bed and rest my elbows on my knees. "There's so much I don't know about him."

"You have a lot of time to find out."

"Yesterday, when we couldn't find him, all I could think about was what if he didn't know how to swim? He's my kid and I don't have a clue about what his favorite food is."

"So ask him."

Shawn enters the room. He nods to the wall. "These will have to come down for staging, but I didn't want to remove them before Cody came back."

"Is he still in his room?"

"He's playing with his dinosaur collection," Shawn says.

"What's going to be done with all her stuff?" Ren asks.

"Anything Cooper doesn't want can be sold at auction if that's what he decides."

"What do you mean if that's what I decide?"

He waves his arm around. "Everything here, including the apartment itself, was put into the trust. In fact, if you wanted to keep this place, you could. The trust is paying for it for now. And as co-trustee, I'm managing the bills, and I'll oversee the sale if you choose to sell."

"I can't stay in the city." I glance into the hallway. "Unless you think it's what's best for him."

"I think what's best for him is to be surrounded by people who love him. Serenity tells me you have a large family that has welcomed him with open arms."

"They're planning a party for him," I say. "An official welcome to the family shindig. My mom cried when I told her the news yesterday."

"Then it sounds like he's right where he needs to be." He hands me a folder. "Everything you need to know about the contents of the trust is in here. Valuations, rules, instructions on how to link it to your bank account so you can withdraw funds."

"I won't be taking any funds."

Shawn cocks his head. "No?"

"The money doesn't belong to me. I have no right to it."

"It'll help make his life easier, Cooper."

"I have some money. And I'm perfectly capable of making more. The trust is for Cody, when he gets older."

"Well, then, he's going to have one hell of a twenty-fifth birthday."

I get up and stand in front of his baby picture. "I just wish she would have told me about him sooner. Things could have been different. I would have known him. Do you realize I don't even have a clue what his favorite color is?"

"Are you sure things would have been different?" Ren asks. "You were twenty years old, Cooper. And you and Chaz were always plotting how to start your adventure guide business. Do you honestly think you would have dropped all that to become his father?"

My eyes follow the progression of his birthdays on the wall. "I don't know. But I would have liked to have been given the option."

"I may not have agreed with every decision she made," Shawn says. "But she loved that boy fiercely and did everything she could to ensure his future."

"We'd better get started packing his things," I say.

Ren and I go down the hall to Cody's bedroom. I stop in the doorway when I see him crying on his bed, my heart breaking for the kid. His world has been turned upside down. I go over and sit on one side of the bed. Ren sits on the other.

"You okay, sport?"

He's clutching a book. I look at the title. *Are You My Mother?*

Ren and I share a look. Then she rubs his back. "That was always one of my favorite books," she says.

He sniffs and hiccups. "Mommy read it to me every night."

"And now every time you read it, you'll think of her. You might cry at first. But someday when you're reading it, you might smile at the memory of her reading it to you." She leans against the headboard, still rubbing his back. "My mom died too."

He looks up at her. "She did?"

She nods. "Unlike you, I never got to know my mom. She died when I was a tiny baby. But my dad showed me all kinds of pictures of her and told me stories about her, so I felt like I knew her. From what Shawn tells me, your mom was a very special lady, and I think you were lucky to have her."

"She was pretty."

"I can see that from all the photos. Cody, would you mind if I did something for you? I'd like to take the pictures and make them into a photo album. You could keep it right next to your bed and look through it anytime you wanted. That way, she'll always be with you."

"Because we can't stay here, right?"

"That's right."

"Because I'm going back to Calloway Creek to live with my dad."

Ren glances at me and smiles. "Yes, you're going to live with your dad."

"You can do the thing with the pictures."

"Thank you. I promise to be very careful and get them back to you really soon."

He sits up next to her, handing her the book. "Can you read it?"

She looks at me guiltily. "Maybe your dad should read it."

Cody looks sad. "I thought you could… do the voices like Mommy did."

"You should do it," I say to Ren.

She raises a brow at me as if asking if I'm sure. I lift my chin and smile. Then she reads.

Tears coat Cody's lashes as he listens to the story. He's sad, that much is obvious, but it's almost like he needs this to help him. Help him remember. Help him let go. Maybe a little of both.

As she reads, I look around his room. There's a lot of stuff here. Toy bins filled with cars, army figures, superheroes, and Nerf guns. Tonka trucks line the baseboard near the door. A basketball hoop is attached to one wall, posters of Spiderman, Iron Man, and The Hulk are pinned to another. Toy airplanes hang on strings from the ceiling. And large letters spelling his name are painted above his bed.

"You have a cool room, little man," I say when they're done reading.

He glances around morosely and nods.

"What do you say we take it all with us?"

"*All* of it?" Cody asks, seeming excited for the first time today.

"We've got Uncle Tag's SUV. We should be able to fit everything but your bed. And we'll buy you a new bed. You can even pick it out. Don't they make superhero beds?"

"Gage has a Hulk bed. The posts are Hulk hands."

"If you want a Hulk bed, we'll get you one."

He thinks on it. "Or maybe Spiderman. Where will we put it?"

"I've been wanting to talk to you about that. What if we just keep the cabin for weekends, but get an apartment or a house for the rest of the time? That way, we can set up a room for you just like this one."

"A house? Like the ones on TV?"

I laugh. I suppose living in the city, he's only ever known apartments.

"Maybe like the ones on TV. Also like the houses we passed in Calloway Creek."

"A house would be neat."

"Then it's settled. We'll get a house."

"Can Ren live there too?"

My eyes snap to hers. She blushes. "Well, uh, no. Ren has her own house, sport."

"Oh."

"Come on, let's get started packing while Ren collects those pictures."

An hour later, the car packed, we're heading back to Calloway Creek.

"I think we should play a game," Ren says.

"Here in the car?" Cody asks.

"It's a question game."

"How do we play it?"

"It's simple. We ask one another questions. Anything you want."

"Like what?" he asks.

"I'll start," she says. "Cody, what's your favorite color?"

"Blue."

"Now it's your dad's turn."

Ren grins at me. I roll my eyes. She's way too good at this parenting thing. "Okay, how high can you count?"

"I can count to one-zero-zero."

I eye him in the rearview, surprised. "You can count to a hundred?"

"Want to hear me?"

I laugh. "Sure."

He gets to thirty-eight and forgets where he was. "Can I ask a question now?"

"Yes."

"Do you like pizza?"

"I *love* pizza," I say overdramatically. "My turn. Do you like pepperoni?"

"Pepperoni is my favorite."

"Should we have Kelly make pepperoni pizzas for your party?"

He claps. "Yes!"

"Pepperoni pizzas and chocolate cake," Ren says.

"Yummy! Now you go, Ren."

"I have one for your dad. What's your favorite thing of all the things you've done in your videos?"

I don't hesitate. "Skydiving."

"Why skydiving?"

"It's hard to explain. I guess because it gives an incredible perspective of the world. Even when I'm descending at 120 miles per hour, I don't have the sensation of plummeting to earth. It's more like flying. Your adrenaline is pumping, and all your senses come alive. It's windy. Loud. Intense. But at the same time, the most serene thing I've ever done."

"Can I skydive?" Cody asks.

"No!" Ren and I say at the same time. Then we glance at each other and laugh. "At least not until you're a lot older. Now me. My question is for Serenity."

In my periphery, I see her brows lift.

"Do you have any plans to go back to Alaska?"

"Where's Alaska?" Cody asks.

"All the way on the other side of the country and up near Canada." I turn to her. "So?"

"I guess I haven't given it much thought," she says. The way she says it though makes me think she has.

"But your reason for being there, is it…?" *Shut the hell up*, I tell myself. I shouldn't be so interested in where she's going to end up.

"My reason for being there doesn't apply anymore. So, I don't know. I guess maybe I'll stay." She shrugs and turns to Cody. "My turn. What do you want to be when you grow up?"

"My dad."

Emotions I've never felt before surge through me. Ren reaches over and puts a hand on mine. When I look at it, she pulls it away. "Sorry," she says.

"It's, uh, fine."

It's not fine. Nothing about her touching me is fine. Because every time she does, it's a sobering reminder of what we did in the clearing. A powerful realization of how her touch makes my body hum. How each heated gaze sparks my desire. How every whispered word sends liquid heat straight to my core.

And most of all, a painful sign of what a shitty brother I am.

"What do you want to be, Ren?" Cody asks.

"I want to own a restaurant."

"Like Donovan's?" he asks.

Ren smiles. "Exactly like Donovan's."

Then Cody blurts, "Do you want to be Dad's girlfriend?"

I clear my throat. "Mmmkay, maybe enough of this game for now. How about we play *I Spy* instead?" I spare a glance at Ren, whose face has turned three shades of pink for the second time today. And, damn it, parts of me really like it when she blushes. I concentrate on the road in front of me, even though my mind is anywhere but. My traitorous brain is too busy wondering what the answer was to Cody's question.

Chapter Twenty-four

Serenity

Cooper goes behind the bar and pours himself another beer. I've lost count. I'm pretty sure he has, too. It's the first time I've seen him let his hair down since I've been back.

"I still can't believe it," Allie says. "Cooper Calloway is a dad?"

My friends sit at the bar and keep me company while I work serving all the Calloway relatives who are here to welcome Cody to the family. It's all the same people who showed up for Addy's graduation last month, only this time, I don't feel the need to hide from all of them. Even my dad is here with Patricia to commemorate the occasion.

"Look at those brothers," Mia says. "A year ago, none of them had kids, and now they have four between them. Who'd have thought?"

Allie laughs. "Well, with as much as Tag and Cooper used to bed anything in a skirt, it's no surprise one of them ended up with a kid they didn't know about."

I look at her sideways. "What do you mean *used* to?"

"We all know Tag had a gaggle of women lined up to be with him, right up until the day he got with Maddie. And Cooper, I can't be sure what he does when he's off daredeviling around the world, but rumor has it that after Chaz died, he quit his womanizing days."

I glance across the room at him. For weeks now, I've wondered about him. I've thought—no, *tortured* myself with pictures in my head of him with other women. The other day when his old girlfriend Missy came into the pub, I couldn't help but feel jealous. I put it out of my mind as I fill a few drink orders and try not to stare at Cooper.

"Oh my god, you *like* him," Mia says.

Allie's mouth opens. *'That's* what's different tonight. I couldn't put my finger on it, but it makes sense now. At Addy's graduation, you couldn't keep your eyes off him either, but in a different kind of way."

"I… no."

Totally yes.

"Admit it, Ren," Mia says. "And really, what's not to like?"

Allie gives me the stink eye. "Wait, do you really think you could, like, do stuff with him? Wouldn't that be creepy considering he looks just like Chaz? It might even feel like it *is* Chaz."

Across the room, I watch him laugh at something Jaxon says. His eyes crinkle at the corners. He catches me staring and lifts his chin.

"It doesn't."

Allie and Mia both spit out their drinks in surprise. *Did I say that out loud?*

"You've done things?" Allie says.

I should tell them. The three of us have become close again since my return. It's been so long since I've been close with anyone. Besides, it's killing me not to talk about this with someone. "Okay, yeah, but nothing that really meant anything. It was on their birthday. We were both incredibly sad. And then I might have kissed him the next day."

"Didn't mean anything, huh?" Mia says. "Based on the way you keep glancing at each other, I'd say it means a hell of a lot more than you think it does."

"He feels guilty, like he's betraying Chaz."

Allie does a head bob. "You were his brother's fiancée. Hell, you still wear his ring." She nods to the necklace. "Even if it is only around your neck."

"Could be the ring is some kind of barrier," Mia says. "A force field keeping him away."

"Force field?" Allie scoffs. "I doubt it. Ring or no ring, maybe he's just trying to respect his dead brother."

"He thinks I can't separate him from Chaz. He even made a comment afterward that I was fucking his brother."

The jaws of my two friends are resting on the bar.

"You *fucked* him?" Allie says boisterously.

Heat crosses my face as I quickly glance around to see if anyone heard. "Shhh!"

"You fucked him?" she repeats, in a whisper this time.

"I told you, we were both… dealing."

Mia laughs. "That's my kind of dealing."

"Ren!" Cody calls from across the room. He scoots out of the booth, trots over, and takes my hand. "Come have cake."

"I'd love to, bud."

As I walk away, I hear Allie say to Mia, "Looks like the father isn't the only one she's infatuated with."

I toss them a look over my shoulder.

~ ~ ~

Later on, Cooper stumbles to the bar for yet another drink. Jaxon comes up behind him. "You think that's wise, brother? You do have a kid you're responsible for. Good luck getting him home if you can't even walk."

Tag overhears on his way to the bathroom. He comes over. "Everything okay?"

"Cooper's sloshed."

Tag laughs. Then he cups Cooper's shoulder. "Way to step up, man."

"I'm fine," Cooper slurs. "Jeez, people, cut me a break. A lot has happened this week." He looks back at Cody, who's happily playing at the table with Gigi and Josie. "It's just, tonight made everything so real. Do you know how many people have congratulated me on becoming a father?" He shakes his head as if he's still coming to terms himself. "I'm a fucking father. I'm looking at a goddamn house tomorrow, where my kid might grow up. I've had to pretty much give up my life, not to mention the fifty grand I have to give back to my sponsors. And then there's…"

He glances at me.

"Then there's what?" Tag asks in a challenging manner, looking between us as if he knows something. *Does he?*

"Nothing."

"I'll admit it's a lot to digest in one week. You're due a night off, brother. How about we take Cody for the night? He's been getting along great with Gigi."

"I don't know," Cooper says. "I mean, he's still getting used to *me.*"

"Which is precisely why he shouldn't have to be with you when you're drunk off your ass." Tag calls Cody over. "Hey, little man, what do you say you come back to my house for a sleepover with Gigi? We'll build a tent under the dining room table."

Cody looks up at Cooper. "Can I?"

"We'll drive you home and pick up his things," Tag says.

"Fine." Cooper walks behind the bar and gets a drink. He holds up a bottle of beer. "Looks like I'm good to have this, then."

"Come on, Cody," Tag says. "Let's go say goodbye to everyone. It's getting late."

"Bye, Cody," I say. "I'm glad you enjoyed the party."

He runs back and hugs me before walking off with Tag. My heart soars and hurts at the same time.

I go back to the office and lean against the wall, wondering how I've become so attached to a five-year-old over the course of one week.

Cooper walks in.

"You forget something?" I ask.

"Gotta hit the head."

I chuckle, grab his shoulders, and turn him around. "You're in the wrong place, soldier."

He spins, pulls me into his arms, and kisses me. I want his lips on me. God knows I do. But I push him away knowing he's drunk.

He blows out a long breath. "What the hell are you doing to me, Ren?"

"Everything okay in here?" Dad asks.

I take a step back, putting distance between Cooper and me. "Everything is fine." I point. "The bathroom is that way."

Dad takes Cooper's elbow. "I'll make sure he gets there."

I'm leaning against the wall when Dad returns. He closes the office door. "Want to tell me what that was all about?"

"Not really."

He thumbs to the front. "Everyone's leaving. Katie and Gino are cleaning up. I doubt we'll have too many other customers coming in. Why don't you head out?"

"I have to close."

"I'll do it."

"Patricia is out there."

"She'll help."

"Your hip."

"Pumpkin, stop making excuses. I can be here for a few hours. My hip is healing splendidly. Patricia will sip a glass of wine and keep me company. And it's pretty evident that you have some things that need to be taken care of."

"Dad, it can wait."

"Serenity, I saw what happened. And I've seen big changes in you this past month. If he has anything to do with those changes, I'd say it absolutely cannot wait. Take it from a man who waited decades to jump at the opportunity for happiness."

Like I did with Cooper, he takes me by the shoulders, turns me, and pushes me toward the door. He doesn't stop until I'm standing outside. "I love you, pumpkin."

My father is stubborn, if nothing else. "Love you too, Dad."

~ ~ ~

Two hours later, I'm sitting on a bench in the park, staring at the full moon, pondering life. I watch as couples stroll by, hand in hand. Some stop along the paved walkway and kiss. Some laugh with each other. I'm pretty sure I even see a proposal happen on the footbridge going over the creek.

Romance is all around me, suffocating me. Taunting me.

Even in the dark, I know the way, and twenty minutes later, I'm turning the corner on the trail, looking over at his cabin. I stop when I see him on the front porch. He's on the top step, drinking something from a coffee cup. I'm hoping it's coffee.

I approach. He looks up. I walk over, climb the porch steps, and sit next to him. "Have you ever heard about the grief box?"

He shakes his head.

"Hilda, that's my old boss back in Sitka, she told me about the box and the ball. So there's this box with a huge ball inside that's almost as big as the box. Also on the inside of the box is a button on one side. The button is pain. And at first, since the ball is so big, it can't move around at all without hitting the button over and over. But through time, the ball gets smaller and hits the button less. When it hits it, however, it hurts just as much. Sometimes it randomly hits the button when you least expect it. Since the box is sealed, the ball can never escape, but it does continue to get smaller."

"And you're telling me this why?"

"When I first got here, my ball was massive, and it was pounding the button incessantly. Then something happened." I swallow as I prepare to rip myself open and lay my feelings on the table. "You happened, Cooper. And suddenly, the ball began to deflate." I pull the necklace out from under my shirt. "I'm not sure I'll ever get over losing him. Just as my dad will never get over losing my mom. Just like you'll never get over losing your brother. But that doesn't mean we shouldn't move on. They would want us to."

He sighs through his nose. "You think Chaz would want me to move on—with you?"

"I think he would want you to be happy. I think he would want both of us to be happy."

"Not together, he wouldn't." He stands and paces a tight circle on the dirt. Then he looks over. "You're fucking gorgeous, do you know that?"

My heart pounds.

He looks away. "But every time I look at you and think it, it's a betrayal."

"I admit I left Calloway Creek because of you. I used to look at you and see him. But I don't anymore. You know why? Because although you are identical, there are so many things that set you apart. You don't do it much, but when you laugh, it's different from his. He was a snorter. You're not. And the way you say my name, it's… softer somehow." I hop off the steps and walk over to him and touch his beard. "This—he never had facial hair this long." I run my finger across his flawless brow. "You don't have a scar." I touch his lips. "And here, the way you kiss."

I try to surmise if his heart is beating as fast as mine. Because mine is ready to pound out of my chest.

"That day after the speech, I knew it was you and not Chaz. I knew it as soon as we kissed."

Instantly, my thoughts are back on that day. The way he held me in that moment. The way his lips teased mine. It wasn't any better or worse than how Chaz kissed me. It was just… different.

I see the question on his face in the moonlight even before he asks it. "Why didn't you say anything?"

"For the same reason you didn't. I didn't want to hurt him."

He turns away. "Yet you're willing to hurt him now."

"He's not here, Cooper."

"That kiss stopped my fucking heart, Ren. And it's a guilt I lived with for years. He'll *always* be here." He stares at my necklace. "He'll always be between us."

I embolden myself to remove it. Then I hold it up. "Is this what you want? Fine, it's gone. Are you happy now?"

He takes it from me and puts it back around my neck. "You don't get it, do you? I *did* hurt him. I hurt him in the worst way because I didn't save him. It's my fault he's dead. I have no right to be here without him. Especially not with you."

"It's not your fault, Cooper."

He shakes his head with a sharp jerk. "You don't know what happened on that mountain."

"Yes, I do. The boulders fell. Your leg was trapped. He was pinned. There was nothing anyone could do."

"There was something I could have done. I was too goddamn chicken."

"I don't understand." I step back. "What aren't you telling me?"

"Fuck." He leaps up on the porch and goes inside.

I follow. "Cooper, I deserve to know what happened. And quite frankly, you're scaring me."

He goes for a bottle of whiskey. I stop him. "Haven't you had enough?"

"Not nearly," he says. "Not if I'm going to tell you what you want to know."

I back off and let him pour himself a glass. I eye the large pile of boxes in the corner. Cody's things. They take up a good portion of the room. But the couch is empty, pillows and sheets neatly folded off to one side. Cody's bear sits on the bed, so I surmise Cooper is the one sleeping on the couch. I walk over and sit, trepidation eating away at my insides.

He downs a shot and adds more to his glass, then he sits on the opposite end of the couch, as far away from me as he can get. "It was a family decision not to tell you."

My insides clench into a ball. "Not to tell me what?"

"Ren, you have to just shut up and listen. If you talk, if I even look at you, I'm not sure I'll get through it."

I sit silently, fear climbing my spine inch by torturous inch. He turns away, takes another sip, then slumps, forearms on his knees. "It had been days, and nobody had come. There was a branch I could have used as a lever to lift the boulder off my ankle, but it would have killed him. He said the rock was the only thing holding him together. He was so pale. His pulse had become thready. At night, sometimes I'd lie there with my fingers on his wrist just to make sure he was still alive. Nobody was going to save us. It was up to me. I had a pocketknife. Rope. I was trapped at the ankle. How hard could it have been? I'd seen it done in a movie. I had everything I needed to free myself."

I gasp. "By cut—"

"Ren, don't. I'm fucking serious."

Keeping my mouth shut is the worst form of torture. My throat is thick with fear, my thoughts churning with what might come next.

"He kept talking me out of it. Saying someone would come eventually. But after three days, I wasn't so sure. And he was getting worse. So much worse. He hadn't eaten in days, couldn't keep anything down. I made a promise to myself that if nobody found us by noon the next day, I'd do it. Even if I had to hobble down to the road on one leg, I'd do it to save us."

Hot tears are flowing down my face as I hear him recount the worst day of his life. His voice is shaky and hesitant. I don't try to stop him when he refills his drink a third time.

But he doesn't come back to the couch. In fact, he stays all the way across the room, as if he thinks telling me what he's going to tell me will wreck me. I'm beginning to think it might.

"I woke up the next day." His voice cracks. "But he didn't. He… *fuck!*" He paces over by the kitchen. He wipes his nose on his sleeve. "There was so much blood. I could see it from where I sat. I yelled. I shook him. He wouldn't wake up. There was no time to use the knife. So I used the branch to free myself. And I knew it was bad when he didn't yell like he had the first time I tried it."

I can barely see him through my tears. My throat burns badly as I try my hardest to remain quiet and not fall down sobbing.

"There was so much blood. It was still trickling out of his arm when I got to him. I took off my shirt and wrapped it around the gash. I couldn't find a pulse on his neck, so I did CPR. But my shirt around his wrist became soaked with blood. Still, I pumped on him for what must have been an hour before my body gave out and I collapsed next to him. When I looked over at the rock, I saw it. A sharp edge jutting out. It was covered in blood. He'd used it to slit his wrist." He lets out a guttural cry.

Unable to hold it in any longer, my sobs join his. I think of two brothers. Twins. Best friends. Up on that mountain, each trying to save the other.

Chapter Twenty-five

Cooper

She pushes off the couch and comes to me. "It's not your fault."

"The hell it's not. I could have done it. I should have. We'd both be here if I wasn't such a coward."

"That's not true. You were trapped. There was no way both of you were getting out of there."

"I could have made it to the road if I'd just—"

"Stop it, Cooper. You wouldn't have. You'd have died from blood loss. There was no way to cauterize it, even if you'd been able to do it without passing out. Don't you see? You would have died, too."

"Maybe I should have."

She pulls me into her arms. "No, you shouldn't have. And even if you'd made it to the road, if by some miracle you'd survived the amputation and hiked down the mountain on one leg, you said yourself the boulder was holding him together. It was essentially keeping him alive. As soon as rescuers moved it, he'd have died anyway. He knew it and it's why he slit his wrist. He knew you'd do anything to save him. But he also knew he was beyond the point of saving. He did what he had to do. He knew it was the only way one of you would live. It's not your fault. God, Cooper, have you been thinking it was for the last four years?"

I fall to my knees. She falls with me. Her arms hold me tightly. Her words soothe me. Her body presses against me. Then her lips are on mine. And my god, I need them. I need her lips. I need her body. I need *her*. I'm removing her clothes before my fuzzy brain catches up to my actions. I strip her naked. I strip me naked. Without a thought, I press her to the floor and push myself inside her like a caveman taking what he claims as his. My thrusts are demanding, brutal even, as I fuck the images of my bloody twin out of my head. I grunt as I come hard, then I collapse and pass out.

~ ~ ~

Dawn wakes me. My pounding head reminds me of how much I drank last night. It hurts as I turn over. Then all thoughts cease as I see Serenity staring at me. I gaze into her dark eyes, wanting to cradle her and tell her everything will be alright. But I can't. I don't know that. And I certainly shouldn't be promising it.

"Are you okay?" she asks.

She's naked, covered to her chest by a sheet. *I'm* naked. The events of last night come rushing back.

I lie back on the pillow. "Fuck, I'm sorry."

"I'm not."

She scoots over and lays her head on my chest. Good sense tells me to move it. But I can't. I can't because I want it there. "Don't you hate me?"

"I told you last night, there's nothing you could have done."

I close my eyes, knowing there was. "Even so, when I promised to take care of you, I'm fairly sure this isn't what he meant."

She lifts herself on an elbow. "You promised to take care of me?"

I laugh sadly. "Just another way I failed him. The night before he died, he made me promise to take care of you. I also promised him we'd get out of there. So you see, I'm shit at keeping my word. You should run away now."

She snuggles into me. "I'm not going anywhere. I'm right where I want to be."

"People won't understand. They'll say we shouldn't be together."

"Who cares what they say?"

"It won't bother you if they assume you're with me because I look like him? Or if they think I'm only with you because I feel sorry for you?"

"Are you?"

"Damn it, Ren. No, of course not."

"Well, me neither. I told you last night, you're different than he is. It's you I want, Cooper." In her hand, she holds the ring on the end of her necklace. "This is only a reminder of him, just like my mom's photo on my dresser. If it bothers you, I won't wear it."

"It's not on your finger anymore. That's all that matters."

She lifts her head, the edges of her sexy mouth turning up into a seductive grin. "Did we just turn a corner here?"

My dick stirs. "Are you sure this is what you want?" I nod to the boxes in the corner. "I come with a bit of baggage now."

"I happen to be quite enamored with your baggage. He's a wonderful boy."

"He is kind of amazing."

"Like his dad."

"I still can't believe it whenever someone calls me that."

She runs a finger down my chest, teasing one of my nipples. "While I really dig your kid, I'm wondering if you want to lie here and talk about him, or maybe do something else."

Fully stiff now, I pull her to me. "Serenity, I'm going to do things to you I've been wanting to do for a long time."

She giggles. "Thank God."

I unwrap her from the sheet, gaze at her naked body, and push away the guilt I feel over her being the only woman I've ever truly wanted. The air around us electrifies. Desire warms her delicate features. Her breasts rise and fall with shuddering, uneven breaths as sexual vibes pour off her in waves.

"You're so damn beautiful."

She pulls the sheet off me and stares at my cock. "So are you."

Amused, I say, "Nobody has ever called the general beautiful before."

She laughs. "The general?"

"He does like to stand at attention."

When she puts her hand on me, I groan. It's better than I remember. It's everything I've dreamed of.

I cup one of her breasts, silently cursing the cast that prevents me from palming them both. I dip my head and run my tongue across the sensuous path between them. I pull a nipple into my mouth. A mewl escapes her.

Say my name.

My fingers glide along her wet folds. My god, she feels exquisite. She's like a fine wine; I want to drink her yet savor her at the same time. I slip a finger inside her, then pull it out and circle her clit. Her back arches and a breathy "yes" dusts across my hair.

Say my name.

Her hand works me harder, and I struggle not to come. I want to be inside her when I do. I want to be inside her when it's *me* there, not the memory of someone else, not the pain we were both feeling, not the comfort we were both seeking. *Me.*

I lift my head. "I probably should have asked you before, because the last thing we need right now is another surprise, but are you on the pill?"

She raises her arm. "Implant. I'm not even sure why I got a new one when they took out the old one. It wasn't like I was, well… active."

My fingers still. "You haven't been?"

She shakes her head.

"Since…?"

"No."

I swallow with the knowledge that I'm one of only two men who have been with her, the other being my twin.

"It's okay," she says, sensing my hesitation. "I want this. I want this like you wouldn't believe."

The sinfully erotic movement of her fingers dancing across my cock has me drowning in her. Her taste. Her scent. Her beauty. I pause to tame my rapid breathing and pounding heart. To take stock in what I've done. What we're about to do. I push away the guilt, hoping it's me she wants and not a reminder of her past.

"It's okay," she repeats, her breathy whisper stroking me with the same fiery effect as her hand.

"I want it too," I murmur against her silky hair.

Her hand falls away from my cock when I work my mouth down her abs, across her stomach, and right to her stiff little nub.

I circle her clit with my tongue. I suck on it. She moans loudly when I graze it with my teeth. I stick my tongue inside her, fucking her with it, tasting her, worshiping her. My tongue goes back to her clit while my fingers search for the holy grail. I crook them against each fold inside her, needing to find the spot that will drive her wild.

Moans coming from deep within her let me know I've found it. Her muscles tense. I can practically count down in my head to her detonation. *Three, two, one…*

"Oh God," she shouts, her voice strained and taut with need as she clamps down on my fingers.

Say my name.

I let her ride out her climax on my mouth, but before she can recover, I climb up her body and sink myself into her. Her hands clamp my rear. She pulls me close, bucking her hips into me as she searches for another.

I've been with my share of women, but the sensations building inside me are like nothing I've felt before. It's always been the same, like I'm on a roller coaster, heading to the top and about to rocket down a huge hill. But it's different with Ren. Just when I think I'm at the top, I go higher. Just when I think I'm about to go over the edge, there's more. A voracious, mind-shattering thirst I've never experienced.

Then, as she falls apart beneath me, shouting *my* name, I see a life in front of me that I've never imagined. And I come, the sensation transcending a pure physical feeling, it's a whole body and mind numbness that for a few seconds has me feeling helpless, yet in complete control all at once.

I lie next to her, both of us breathing hard. Both of us staring. Both of us laughing.

"Oh. My. God," she says.

And I smile. Because I'm the king of the fucking world.

Chapter Twenty-six

Serenity

Standing in the shower, the ball in the box hits the pain button head-on. I sink to the floor, my tears washing down the drain along with the water. Chaz slit his wrist to save his brother. Four years ago, I was told the boulder had killed him. I knew Cooper had been trapped, but I had no idea he had to endure days of watching Chaz slowly waste away. And Chaz—he knew he was dying. He made the ultimate sacrifice so Cooper wouldn't die or maim himself. I cry for Chaz and the life he gave. I cry for Cooper and the horror he had to live through on that mountain. But most of all, in this moment, I cry because I'm so relieved Cooper wasn't taken too.

When I come out of the bathroom, Cody is standing with Tag and Cooper.

"I, uh… we just got done hiking." I can feel heat cross my face as Tag smiles knowingly.

"Ren!" Cody says. "Are you going to the house too?"

"House?"

"Cody and I are going to look at a house this morning," Cooper says. "You're welcome to come if you want."

"Please, please?" Cody begs.

I check the time. "I guess I could, as long as I'm at work by ten."

"It shouldn't take long," Cooper says.

Tag drops Cody's backpack on the floor as I hastily make the bed, hoping Cooper has the good sense to wash the sheets later.

Cooper walks Tag out. Cody picks up his bear off the floor.

"Oh, I'm sorry," I say. "I didn't mean for him to fall. Does he have a name?"

"Ozzy."

I fluff the bear's head. "Hello, Ozzy. You know, Cody must be a pretty big boy if he didn't need you to go on his sleepover."

Cody giggles. He looks at my damp hair. "Do you know how to do hair?"

"You mean, like cut it?"

He shakes his head. "Mommy would do my hair."

I remember the pictures of him and realize what he's talking about. "You want me to spike it up for you?"

"Dad tried, but it didn't work."

"I can give it a go if you want."

He pulls me into the bathroom and holds up a bottle of hair product. I squirt gel onto my hand, rub it into the top of his hair, and then try to bring it to a point in the middle. "Like this?"

He stands on his toes and looks in the mirror, smiling. "Are you a mom?" he asks.

"No."

"But you do mom things. Like hair and books and muffins and stuff."

"I guess I do. Speaking of muffins, did you have breakfast yet?"

"Uncle Tag made pancakes. He has a dog. Her name is Sissy. He said Uncle Jaxon has a dog too, but I didn't meet him yet and I forget his name."

"Heisman."

"That's a weird name."

I laugh. "It is."

"Do you have a dog?"

"No."

"Do you think Dad would let me get a dog? Mommy said it was too hard to have a dog in our 'partment."

Cooper appears in the doorway. "Why don't we concentrate on finding a house first, eh, sport?"

Cody looks excited. "Is there a backyard? I always wanted a backyard."

"There is. And a swing set. But don't get too excited. I'm not sure we're going to buy this one or another one."

"What house is it?" I ask.

"Did you know Roger Dellsbury?"

"Sure, he was the owner of the auto parts store over on Eighth Avenue. My dad went to his funeral." Suddenly, I'm the excited one. "His house isn't too far from mine."

Cooper's roguish grin makes an appearance. "It's not. But there's another one across town I was going to look at on Monday."

"The market is hot these days. If you like Roger's house, you might want to jump on it."

He chuckles. "Is that so?"

I shrug. "Just saying."

Cooper takes a quick shower, grabs his keys, and the three of us exit the cabin. He stops on the front porch. "Um, the van only seats two."

I look at the Mustang. When I gave it to him, I never thought about the possibility that we'd be in it together. I wonder how weird it would be—for both of us.

"Maybe we should walk," he says.

"It's fine," I say. "Unless you plan to get rid of the car, we'll have to do this eventually. Might as well be now."

"You don't like the car?" Cody asks. "I think it's cool."

"No, I do. It just holds some sad memories for me. You know, like your book *Are You My Mother?* This car used to belong to your dad's brother, the one who died."

"And that makes you sad?"

"It does. Chaz and I were very close. Just like you and your mom were."

Cody puts his hand in mine. "It's okay, Ren. I can help you."

I gaze down at him. "Thank you, Cody. You're a sweet boy."

The drive to the house isn't as hard as I thought it would be, especially after last night, learning what I did, and this morning, when it hit me again. And even though I'm in the passenger seat— a place I've sat in a thousand times before—it's not Chaz I see driving. It's Cooper.

He glances over at me. I grin and nod. He looks back at the road with a satisfied smile.

"It's blue!" Cody says as we pull up.

"Yeah, I'd probably paint it," Cooper says.

"Aw," Cody pouts. "I love blue."

Cooper stares at the house. It's really blue. Like, overkill blue. The siding is dark, like the deeper parts of the ocean. The door and shutters are light, like Cody's and Cooper's eyes.

We get out of the car, and a woman approaches. "Mr. Calloway, I presume? I'm Kendra Wilkins."

Introductions are made and she leads us into the house. Cody races through the rooms. "It's like a castle," he says, rejoining us in the living room.

It's not, of course. According to the stats, it's just under two thousand square feet with three bedrooms, three bathrooms, and an office. But for Cody, even with his mom's business doing well, living in the city was expensive, and their nice apartment was less than half this size.

Cody looks out the back sliding doors. "There it is! And there's a slide. And a trapeze bar." He turns. "I want this house, Dad. Can we get it?"

"Hold on there, sport. I'd like to see it for myself."

Cody trots over and pulls Cooper by his arm. "Come on, I want to show you what room I want."

He drags Cooper down the hallway and stops at a bedroom. The walls are painted blue in various shades of horizontal stripes.

Cooper laughs. "That old man really did like blue, didn't he?"

"Look," Cody says. "There is a bathroom here, and it's really neat because if you walk through it, you go to another room. But that one is pink. Yuck."

We follow Cody through. Cooper cringes at the walls. "Why would an old widower have pink walls?"

"He had a lot of grandkids," I say. "Let's go see the master."

The largest bedroom is a neutral beige. The bathroom is nice, much nicer than the master bathroom at Dad's house. There is a raised vanity with double sinks, a separate toilet room, and both a tub and a shower—both big enough for two.

Cooper comes up next to me, his shoulder rubbing against mine. "Like what you see?" he asks with a dirty smirk.

Yeah, we're both thinking the same thing.

The realtor comes up behind us, ruining the moment. "The kitchen appliances are all new. Did you see the double oven? And the roof is only two years old. You'll want to see the garage. While it's only a two-car garage, it has an extended work area off to one side.

Still looking at me, Cooper asks, "Do you like it?"

"I think it's... kind of perfect."

I don't tell him it's a place I could see myself living one day. With him. With *them*. I don't tell him, but somehow, I think he knows anyway.

"When can we write up an offer?" Cooper asks, eyes still on me, his grin both boyish and roguish.

"You, uh, don't want to see the rest of it?" Kendra asks.

"Don't need to. The lady says it's perfect." Cooper's lips twitch in amusement. "I just realized this is the second house I've bought from a dead old geezer."

"We can get this one?" Cody asks. "And we can keep the swing set? And the blue?"

Cooper finally breaks our stare. "Yes, little man, we can keep all of it. Well, not the pink. What do you say we paint that room and make it into a playroom for you?"

His face lights up. "I get *two* rooms?"

"Sure. Why not?"

Cody catapults himself at Cooper, hugging his lower half tightly. "I love you, Dad."

Cooper's breath hitches. His eyes glisten. He looks down at Cody as if his whole world just changed. I'm certain this is the first time Cody has said the words. Cooper drops to Cody's level and puts a hand on his shoulder. "I love you too, son."

My heart lurches as I watch father and son bond in a way they never have, grateful I'm here to witness it. Cooper looks up at me a different man. A changed man from the one I knew. The past twelve hours have been cathartic for him. Maybe even healing.

He holds a hand out to me. "Get in here."

I fall to my knees and wrap my arms around them. My guys. My future. And in many ways, my salvation.

Chapter Twenty-seven

Cooper

In the restaurant office on Sunday morning, Cody is playing with the Game Boy, and I'm reading up on CoGS. I'm not exactly sure why. Donny will be coming back full time in four or five weeks. I'll no longer be needed. A week ago, I was looking forward to that. My cast would be history, and I'd pack up the van and be on my way.

Thompson Wagner, one of my major sponsors, had me slated to do an adventure in Vietnam. I was going to hike into Hang Son Doong, the largest cave in the world, and do a live broadcast. The cave is so dangerous that more people have climbed Mount Everest than have hiked into it. And it's so large that an entire New York City block could fit inside, including skyscrapers.

But now, after putting a deposit on the house and giving Wagner back the money he'd fronted me for the excursion, my bank account is getting thin. I watch Cody play and realize I'm going to have to figure something out. I have no intention of being a leech on his trust fund.

Leaving Calloway Creek isn't an option. Cody needs to grow up around family. I could learn a trade; become a plumber and work for my dad. Maybe even take over his business one day. But the thought is unappealing. *Every* thought is unappealing. While I've no desire to go risking my life and leave Cody an orphan, I still love the outdoors. But I realize what I love even more is being here at the pub with Serenity.

Ren enters the office. My brows go up. "You're here early. Couldn't stay away?"

She greets Cody and smiles. "Well, when you figure out what you want in life, you kind of want that life to start right away."

I stand and trap her to the wall behind Cody's back. "What you want out of life, eh?"

She bites her lower lip and slowly nods, looking at me through long, thick lashes darker than her hair. And damn if her sexy, wicked smile isn't as much a challenge as it is an invitation.

Jesus, I'm standing two feet from my kid, and my cock is dancing in my pants. All I could do last night was think about her. Her in my bed. Her in my shower. Her… everywhere.

Addy comes around the corner. "Hey, Cody." She spies me leaning into Ren. "You two, really?" she says, her eyes darting between us and Cody.

I go back behind the desk lest my little sister see the tent in my pants.

"You're acting strange," she says. "Did something happen yesterday?"

"Something did happen," I say. "I bought a house."

Her eyes go wide. "Are you going to live together?"

"What? No. I mean, not now. Or maybe ever. But, I don't know, maybe sometime. But, just, no."

Addy chuckles at my rambling. I give her the stink eye. She always says exactly what's on her mind, even if it's inappropriate. Ren and I have been together for, what, thirty-six hours? And technically, are we even together? Am I supposed to ask her to be my girlfriend or something? She seems like she is. We're both acting like she is. But, damn, making her my girlfriend—isn't that the ultimate betrayal? No matter how much I want it? Maybe we can just keep doing what we're doing without having to put a label on it.

Addy motions for Ren and me to step out of the office. "Seriously, guys. It's clear something is going on between you two. But that kid in there just lost his mother. If all you're doing is messing around, maybe you shouldn't make it so obvious."

"Obvious?" I ask.

"Oh, come on. You guys were all over each other yesterday. Sneaking back to the storage room when you thought nobody would notice. Believe me, people noticed. I'm sure Cody noticed. And the last thing you want to do is give him something else to be upset over if this doesn't work out."

I lean against the wall. "Shit. Did anyone say anything?"

"This is Calloway Creek, of course people said stuff. Just not to your face."

"What did they say?" Ren asks.

Addy shrugs. "Mixed reactions. Some people seemed genuinely happy for you. A few thought it wasn't right. Someone even might have used the word taboo."

"That's ridiculous," Ren says. "It's not like we're related."

"What do *you* think?" I ask Addy.

"I think it's great. The two of you have moped around long enough. And it makes sense. Not only do you have a shared tragedy, but it's apparently ingrained in your DNA or something that you be attracted to each other. Anyway, all I'm saying is you shouldn't give a shit about what anyone thinks except that little boy in there."

With that, she walks back out front.

Ren looks at me like she's been given a dose of bitter medicine. "Maybe she's right. We shouldn't give Cody the wrong idea."

"Five minutes ago, you said something about figuring out what you wanted in life."

"But if we're not on the same page…"

"We are. I just need time to get my head around some shit."

Shit like I'm fucking my brother's girl. Shit like I want her in my life—permanently. Shit like I think I'm falling in love with her.

"Well, while you do"—she glances around to make sure nobody is watching—"keep this in mind." She fists my shirt, pulling me to her exactly like the day I gave the speech for Chaz. Our lips collide. I do nothing to stop it. The heated intensity of our kiss brings back the feeling from yesterday—the roller coaster. The *more*. And I know that although my head keeps telling me it's wrong, my heart is the one winning this battle.

A giggle comes from the doorway. Cody is watching us. "Do you like my dad?" he asks Ren.

"Yes," she says, locking eyes with me. "I really, really do."

Cody smiles. And I can't help it—I do too. And I realize I don't care that he saw us. Hell, I don't care if anyone sees us.

Cody hands her a drawing.

"Is this me?" she asks, pointing to a stick figure with brown hair and pink lips.

"Uh-huh, and this is me. And that's Dad. And this is Donovan's."

"I love it. I know exactly where I'll put it."

"Where?"

"It just so happens there's a lot of blank space on my bedroom walls. Maybe you could help me fill them up."

Cody looks pleased.

I tug on his sleeve. "Come on, sport, you can help me turn on the OPEN sign."

Waiting outside, our first customers enter. It's Maddie's grandmother, Rose Gianogi, and her uber-rich boyfriend, Tucker McQuaid. They've been the talk of the town since last fall, when they got together. They'd been living in the same retirement community, him in the castle-like VIP home he expanded to suit him, and her in a small apartment. Word is, she's no longer living in the apartment. The man must be eighty-five years old. I've got to hand it to him, the sly devil.

"I had to come by and see for myself," Rose says, looking at Cody. "Oh, you're as delicious as a ripe apple." She leans down as far as her aging body allows. "Cody, dear, I'm your Uncle Tag's grandmother-in-law. I suppose that doesn't make us technically related, but who cares about technicalities. I think you should call me Granny Rose. What do you say?"

Cody looks to me.

"Up to you, sport."

"Granny Rose," he repeats.

"He's a strapping little boy," Tucker says. "Good of you to do right by him."

"Thank you. Sit anywhere you'd like."

Even though Tucker McQuaid is the grandfather of my archenemies, my beef isn't with him. As far as I know, he's never said a single bad word about my family.

"Will the two of you join us?" Tucker asks.

Cody tugs on my shirt. "Can we, Dad? I'm hungry."

"I'll sit for a minute and order you some food, but then I have work to do."

Addy comes over and takes orders for the three of them.

Tucker seems quite interested in Cody and me. "The two of you appear to be settling in well. I heard you're going to be living in Roger Dellsbury's house."

"Word travels fast."

He eyes me sternly. "Does this mean you're giving up the reckless behavior?"

"I suppose it does."

He nods. "As you should. You have a boy to think about. I wish my grandsons would take note at what you and your brothers have accomplished this past year. With all you've done, I believe there's hope for them yet."

I laugh. "Your grandsons couldn't care less what Tag, Jaxon, and I do, sir."

"Yeah, well that's a cryin' shame. They'd all do well to quit their philandering and settle down."

I try to keep a straight face. "With all due respect, weren't you a philanderer yourself?"

He takes Rose's hand and holds it on the tabletop. "It's amazing what the love of a good woman can do."

I peek over at Ren, who's getting the bar ready.

"Then again, seems you already know that," Tucker says.

"Why don't you hate me like all the other McQuaids?" I ask.

"My mama was a Calloway. My brother married one, too. Hell, all of us McQuaids and Calloways seem to be related in one way or another. Besides, life is too short to hold grudges. I wish I could get that through to my grandsons."

Rose catches my eye. "His grandsons aren't the only ones who need to let it go."

Food arrives and I stand. "Cody, I'll be over by the bar or in the office, okay?"

"Granny Rose will keep a good eye on him," Rose says.

"Granny Rose, are you going to make me eat *all* the green beans?"

"Of course not, cutie pie. That's your father's job," she says with a wink before I walk away.

I join Ren behind the bar and line up clean glasses.

"He sure does have a lot of people who love him," she says. "He's a lucky boy."

"I guess he is."

"And especially because you're his dad."

I shake my head. "I still have no clue what I'm doing. I'm just winging it."

"You're exactly what he needs, Cooper."

"Maybe you are too." I drink in her smile. "You're so goddamn beautiful. Do you know how hard it is to get any work done with you being so close to me?"

My phone vibrates with a text. I pull it out and read it. "It's from the realtor," I say. "They've tentatively set the closing date for July 15th." I lean against the bar and close my eyes. "I'll make her change it."

"Maybe you shouldn't," Ren says.

"You think I should close on my new house on the anniversary of his death?"

"I think maybe you need to not sit around and think about it. Maybe moving into a new home and starting a new life with Cody is the perfect thing to do that day."

Memories of the past three anniversaries of Chaz's death flash through my mind. The first year, I hiked the peaks of Mount Huashan in China, with its network of steep trails and rickety planks bolted onto the mountainside at 5,000 feet. The second year, I hiked the treacherous Skellig Michael in Ireland, where no handrails, sheer drops, and rockfalls have led to more than a few fatalities. Last year it was Villarrica, Chile, where the volatile volcano's snow-clad slopes are popular with daredevil skiers. Three years. Three mountains. I knew what I was doing. But none of the mountains agreed to take me like they had my twin. I left all of them virtually unscathed, and with fat bank accounts, which left me feeling even more guilty.

"Cooper?"

I look up to see her waiting on an answer.

I nod. "Maybe you're right. Will you help me move? I get the feeling we might both need a distraction that day."

She smiles. "I'll bring the paint."

Chapter Twenty-eight

Serenity

Dad comes into the office, thanking Kelly for another great lunch on the way. "Hey, pumpkin."

"Hi. How's Patricia?"

"She's fantastic. Had to go back to work. Thought I'd take a look at the books."

"You don't think I've been doing them the right way?"

"Guess I'm about to find out." He nods to Cody's play table in the corner. "How does the boy like it here?"

"He wants to help out like I did. I was thinking of giving him a small job to do."

"You used to love rolling up crayons inside kids' menus."

"Good idea. I'm sure he'd love that."

"And you and Cooper? How's that going?"

"Fine, I guess. It's still new."

"Don't you let anyone give you any flak. If he's the one who makes you happy, then he's the one you should be with."

"They both make me happy."

"The boy is growing on you, is he?"

"He's amazing. You should see them together. Watching them bond has been incredible. Cody is still coping with the loss of his mom, and I'm sure he will be for a long time, but somehow, Cooper is the best person for him, having lost someone so close."

"Cooper isn't the only one who's good for him in that respect."

"Yeah, but he's his dad. And every day, I see more similarities in them. The way Cody cocks his head to the right when he watches TV, just like Cooper does. The identical dimples in their left cheek when they smile really big. The goofy grin they both share. They are more than father and son, they're friends. And in a way, they are growing up together."

"And in order to recognize all those things, you've had to spend a lot of time with them."

"I have been. In some crazy, unexpected way, this past week has been one of the best I can remember."

He smiles proudly. All he ever wanted was for me to be happy. Well, I'm happy. I just hope Cooper feels the same way.

Dad stares at the computer screen, moving the mouse around, squinting at the numbers. I bite my nails. I'm pretty sure I've been doing an okay job of things, but it's been years since I've done this. After a while, he looks up. "Seems like I left the place in good hands."

"Cooper is great at managing front of house, giving me a lot of time to take care of all this."

"So I was right, you make a good team."

I give him an eye roll. "Yes, Dad, you were right."

"You might even say I'm responsible for you kids getting together."

"I suppose you could."

"Is it safe to say you're home for good, then?"

"I believe it is. I'll have to go back to Sitka and get my things out of the duplex so Hilda can find another renter. I'll wait until you're working full time to do that."

"What if I don't come back full time?"

"What do you mean? You love this place."

"Patricia and I were thinking maybe we'd do some traveling. Weekend trips down the coast. Maybe even hop over to London. I've always wanted to go overseas."

"Wow. The two of you are getting serious, then."

"There's something else I wanted to talk to you about. I know this seems sudden, but the past six weeks with her have been the best I've had in a good, long while. She says it's been the same for her."

My mouth hangs open. "Dad, are you in love?"

"I think that's safe to say."

I run around the desk and hug him from behind. "I'm so happy for you."

"No happier than I am for you," he says. "Falling in love is a powerful thing, isn't it, pumpkin?" He gives me an all-knowing stare.

"You think I'm in *love* with him?"

Oh, my god. Am I?

"Uh… hey," Cooper says from the doorway.

I feel the color drain from my face. *How long has he been standing there?* I try to play it off. "Hi, um, we were just talking about Cody. Where is he?" I crane my neck to see behind him.

Cooper studies me as if he knows I'm full of shit. "My mom took him for the afternoon."

"I'm glad you're here, Cooper," Dad says. "I wanted to talk to the both of you."

Cooper comes through the doorway and puts his hand on the knob. "Is this a closed-door conversation? One where you're going to thank me for helping you out in a jam, but then lead into telling me you're coming back to work and with the two of you running the place, I'm no longer needed?"

Dad laughs. "Leave it open, son."

Son?

"Sit." Dad motions to the couch and turns his chair to face us. "I wanted to let both of you know how much I've appreciated you taking things over. I'm not sure what would have happened to this place if you hadn't. It's a lot of work. I should know. I've been doing it for almost thirty years. And the past six weeks have shown me it's really too much work for any one person to take on. I've put my life on hold for far too long. And not being tied to this place twenty-four seven has been quite freeing. So while I still plan to be a presence here, I'd like you both to stay on. But I'm not the only one who needs a life here. You two—you're young. And with the whole Cody situation, you can't be working every night. And I don't want to either. I guess what I'm proposing is that the three of us manage this place together. We'll be able to take days off when needed. Go on vacations. Attend parent-teacher meetings." He looks at Cooper. "I realize it's not nearly the money you were getting with your YouTube adventures, but I've overheard you talking with friends and family the past few days, and if my hearing hasn't deceived me, it sounds like you're getting out of that business. So while you know working here isn't the most glamorous job in the—"

"Yes," Cooper says. "My answer is yes. Yes for now anyway. I can't say it'll be forever, but while Cody is young, it seems like the perfect opportunity. He likes it here. It's close to my new house. And like you said, with the three of us sharing duties, it'll be flexible for everyone." He turns to me. "That is, if this is what *you* want."

I can't help my face-splitting smile. "It's exactly what I want."

"Then it's settled," Dad says. "You can work me back into the schedule a few hours a day over the next couple of weeks, and then up from there as my hip can handle it." He stands. "For now, it looks like you have everything under control. So I'm going to have Kelly cook me up a steak to go so I can have it for dinner later."

"You really should start cooking at home, Dad."

"Don't need to. Besides, Patricia is a great cook, and you never know, maybe she'll be the one cooking my meals after not so long."

"It's been six weeks. Do you mean to tell me you're actually thinking about living together?"

"Just might be," he says, walking through to the kitchen. He looks back. "And if I were a betting man, I'd say we're not the only ones."

"Dad!" I give him a death stare. "Don't mind him," I say to Cooper. "He's old and obviously off his rocker."

"You really want to do this?" he asks.

For a minute, my brain goes in the other direction, right to the blue house with the blue shutters. "I, uh—"

"Run Donovan's together," he says with a smirk.

"Right. Yeah, I knew that's what you were talking about. Yes, of course I want to."

He steps close, leaning in so his hot breath flows over my ear. "Fuck, you're beautiful when you blush."

My knees get unsteady. I try to ignore the heat between us. It's completely inappropriate having this moment here. Inappropriate but utterly amazing. I look into his inviting icy-blue eyes. "We're going to have some nights off. *Together.*"

The dimple appears. "So I can take you on a proper date."

He walks out, leaving one word echoing in my head. *Date.*

My heart pumps fast knowing that maybe he wants this as much as I do. It's hard to know for sure when he's the king of sending mixed signals. But he wants to take me on a date. This *is* happening. And suddenly, I know what I have to do. I remove my necklace and put it into my pocket. And when I get home, I'll put it in the keepsake box with all of my other stuff from Chaz. The box that symbolizes the past. Because while Chaz will always be the boy who was my first love, I hope Cooper is the man who will be my last.

Chapter Twenty-nine

Cooper

I'm up early, sipping coffee on the front porch so I won't wake Cody. In a few more weeks, I won't have to worry about it. He'll be in his own bed in his own room. And the best part—Ren will be able to sleep over. We won't have to sneak kisses and gropes in the restaurant storage room. Or send Cody on a sleepover so we can have a night together.

It's hard to even count how many times one of us has brought up how she'll be able to stay late, sleep in my bed, and leave the house before Cody is any the wiser. Or—and this was my idea—bring hiking clothes with her and pretend she just showed up in the morning. That way she'd never have to leave.

In the past few weeks, the overwhelming guilt over who I'm sleeping with has given way to my constant need to have to be with her. It's like the ball in the box. Only instead of a pain button inside the box, it's a guilt button. And although the ball is getting smaller and not hitting the button constantly anymore, it still stings like a bitch when it happens.

Like the other day when that dickwad Hudson McQuaid saw Ren and me together and called me Chaz. Or when I took the

Mustang in for service, and all the old records had his name on them. Or when I saw Serenity's bare neck the day after she removed the necklace with the ring. I thought I'd be happy to see it gone. Instead, I felt guilty knowing she was letting go of him because of *me*. Or when I look at Cody and think how he'll never get to meet his uncle—the most important person in my life. Until now, that is. Somehow over these past weeks, a five-year-old kid with spiky hair has taken over that distinction. Followed a close second by someone slightly taller and curvier.

The cabin door opens, and Cody sits next to me, still in his SpongeBob pajamas, holding his bear.

I ruffle his messy hair. "Morning, sport."

He yawns. "Morning."

"You know what we have to do soon? Sign you up for school."

"Gigi's school?"

"That's the one. Only, you won't be in her class. She'll be in first grade. But maybe you'll see her at lunch."

"I get lunch at school?"

"Sure. You'll be there all day, from eight thirty until three, I think."

"Can I have grilled cheese?"

"Probably not. It would be soggy by then. But maybe peanut butter and jelly."

"Will you make them like Aunt Maddie? She does dinosaur shapes."

I chuckle. "Dinosaur shapes it is." I stare into my coffee cup, unsure how to broach the subject that's been bouncing around in my head for a few days. "So, Cody, I want to ask you about something. I know you're only five years old, but this is kind of a big decision, so I want us to make it together."

"What's a big decision?"

"Let's see. A big decision is kind of like buying a house or moving to a new city. Not like small decisions such as picking out clothes to wear or choosing a place to eat. Big decisions are something that can last a long time, and maybe you can't even take them back once you've made them."

"Like Uncle Jaxon having babies?"

"Yes, exactly like that."

"Are you and Ren having a baby?"

I cough. "No, we're not. This isn't that kind of big decision. This has to do with your name."

"My name?"

"When I started filling out the papers to enroll you in school, there was a place to write in your first name, and a place to write in your last name. And that's when I realized I wanted to write Calloway instead of Putnam. But like I said, it's up to you. And if we do change your name, that doesn't mean we're taking anything away from your mom. A lot of kids have their dad's name, even if their parents weren't married. And I understand if you don't want to be a Calloway right now. But I just wanted to put it out there. So, what do you think?"

"They let you change your name?"

I nod. "They do."

"To anything?"

"Yes."

"Would they let me change it to Thor?"

I laugh. "I suppose, but I'd strongly advise against it. I was thinking we'd just go with Cody Calloway for now."

"Cody Calloway." He says it two more times as if testing the name. While I'm sure it's crossed everyone else's mind, he had no idea it was a possibility. "Do you think Mommy would be mad?"

"No, little man, I don't. Your mom wanted us to be together. She thought that's what would make you happy."

His lips morph into a grin. "I want to be Cody Calloway." He squeezes his bear. "But Ozzy still wants to be Ozzy Putnam."

"As is his right," I say.

Inside, I'm bursting. "I'll get started on the paperwork so by the time you go to school next month, you'll officially be a Calloway."

"Can I have breakfast now?"

"Sure thing, Mr. Calloway."

He giggles and we go inside.

~ ~ ~

"Grandma," Cody says excitedly when she picks him up for an afternoon of school clothes shopping followed by a sleepover. "I'm going to be Cody Calloway!"

"Is that so?" She looks more than a little pleased.

In the past year, my mother has gone from having no grandchildren to having four. And she couldn't be happier about it.

She hands me a stack of mail. I still use their address since the cabin doesn't get mail delivery, and I never bothered to set up a post office box. No need to now, with my pending home purchase.

"I'll drop him at Donovan's tomorrow around lunchtime."

I try not to seem too excited about tonight being my first official date with Ren. We're going to take the train into the city, have dinner, and stay overnight at a hotel along the Hudson River.

The ball gets dangerously close to hitting the guilt button. I don't let it. I busy myself filling Cody's backpack. "Have a good time with Grandma." I hold up my phone. "Call me if you need me, okay?"

"Grandma makes smiley-face pancakes," he says.

"I know. I had them all the time when I was your age."

He regards his bear, contemplating whether or not to take it. He scoops Ozzy into one arm and then hugs me with his other on the way out. "Bye, Dad."

It's been weeks now, and still, every time he calls me Dad, he wedges himself deeper into my heart. I had no idea I could ever feel this way about a child, let alone one I haven't even known for an entire month.

"Bye, little man."

After a run, a shower, and a grilled cheese sandwich (because like Cody, they've grown on me), I sit with a cup of coffee and go through my mail. It's mostly the usual junk, until I come across a large envelope. The return address is that of Tilly Putnam in New York City. Maybe some more of Cody's records. I open it. There is another, smaller envelope inside with a sticky note attached.

> Found this when I got back from my cruise. I'd forgotten that I told Jennifer I'd give it to you. I hope you and the boy are getting on fine. Best, Tilly

It's been weeks. *Weeks*. And the woman hasn't called. She hasn't asked to see Cody. Nobody seems to give a shit about what happens to him with the exception of Shawn Waylen, who checks up on him quite frequently.

I open the letter. A picture falls out. It's a selfie of Jennifer and me. I set it aside and unfold the letter, eager to find answers to the many questions I've had since the day I found out about Cody.

Cooper,

I can't imagine what you must be feeling right now, finding out you have a child you didn't know about. I'm not going to say I'm sorry. I'm not. The only thing I'm sorry about is not being there to see Cody grow up.

I was always going to tell him about you. I'll admit, however, if I hadn't gotten sick, it may have been when he was eighteen. Call me selfish, but I didn't want anyone else raising him. And quite frankly, based on our one night together, I was sure you'd want nothing to do with him. In fact, I was pretty certain you were either married or in a serious relationship based on your behavior. But I didn't care. The truth was, you were exactly what I was looking for at the time. A younger man. Strong. Handsome. Someone who didn't want a girlfriend but who might, albeit unknowingly, be able to give me the child I'd always wanted. You see, we didn't say a lot to each other about our private lives that night. You didn't tell me why you wanted to be with me, and I didn't say why I needed you. I didn't tell you that I'd suffered a miscarriage two months before, and I was devastated and desperate to have a child. I didn't tell you that at thirty-three years old, I felt the clock was ticking. I didn't tell you there was a void in my life that I knew could only be filled by a child.

And it was. Cody is the best thing that ever happened to me. And for that, I thank you.

But life had other plans for me. For us. From the minute I found out I was sick, I introduced him to you via your videos. Cody now thinks the world of you and is excited to meet you. Selfishly, I wanted to live my last days and weeks with him without complication. Shawn and Tilly will help with the transition. But honestly, other than missing me, I believe Cody will be happy with you.

And here's where I beg. Please take Cody and be a father to him. He truly has no one else. I know you have a choice. I know that by doing what I did, I was taking a risk that you might not want him. But I know my son. He's wonderful. He's smart and funny and polite. And he comes with a trust fund, but I'm hoping that's not what draws you to him. I'm hoping it's his goofy grin. His captivating eyes. His zest for life.

Teach him not to fear anything—including death. But maybe hold off until he's older to strap him into a hang glider or a bungee jumper. Teach him to live and love fiercely. Teach him to seize the day, because trust me, you never know what tomorrow holds.

I hope you are a good man, Cooper. Or at least I hope you can be one for him. He deserves one.

One final request. Even if you hate me for what I've done, please remind him how much I loved him.

Thank you for giving me the most amazing five years of my life. And thank you (I pray) for giving Cody the next best years of his.

Jennifer Putnam

P.S. One day, when you tell Cody how we met, maybe leave out the part where he was conceived in the dugout of a baseball field in Central Park.

I reread the last line three times. I've never been to a baseball field in Central Park. Hell, I've never been to Central Park. *What the hell?* Blood pounds in my temples, and my stomach tightens with an intuition that never precedes anything good.

The photo of us lies on the counter. I pick it up and study her, trying my best to remember her face. For the life of me, I can't. Then I look at myself in the picture, and the air rushes out of my lungs. My jaw clenches. My broken fucking heart falls into the pit of my heaving gut. Because the man in the picture isn't me at all. The man in the picture has a small scar over his right eye. The man in the picture is Chaz.

That motherfucker. He must have told her he was me.

He's the one who went to Central Park.

He's the one who slept with her.

Holy mother of God… he's the one who's Cody's father. Not me.

I glance out the window, at the Mustang parked beside the van, and the guilt hits me with the force of a tsunami. I'm driving his car. Fucking his girl. Raising his child.

I'm living his goddamn life.

I drop the photo and run to the bathroom, vomiting grilled cheese and coffee into the toilet.

~ ~ ~

"Let me get this straight." Tag pushes another shot of whiskey across his kitchen table. "Chaz is Cody's father, but the paternity test you took says *you* are?"

"I looked it up," I say after downing the shot. "A standard paternity test won't be able to tell which identical twin is the father."

Jaxon shakes his head. "And I thought *my* situation was screwed up."

"What are you going to do?" Tag asks.

"What the hell can I do? There's a genome test that might be able to prove it, but it costs tens of thousands of dollars and would require DNA from Cody, me, and two dead people. Even then, there's a chance it might not be conclusive."

"And you're sure it's not you?" Tag asks. "You're absolutely sure you weren't with her? I mean, this is Chaz we're talking about. If he did this…"

"It means he cheated on Serenity." I point to the picture of them. "Yeah, I'm sure." I gaze into the brown liquid in my shot glass. "I can't tell her. It would kill her." I close my eyes. "I can't tell Cody. We're just starting to connect."

"You can't keep this a secret," Jaxon says. "Believe me, secrets always come back to bite you."

Tag looks displeased. "Hold on now, in this case, maybe not telling the truth is better for everyone. Chaz is gone. He can't be a father to Cody. And what would be the point in telling Serenity? Like Cooper says, they share so much of the same DNA, he might as well *be* Cody's father. Nothing has changed here. You still have custody. No matter what any genome test would say, you have guardianship papers."

"Guardianship papers that would have named Chaz had he not lied about who he was."

"Yeah, but don't you get it?" Tag says. "If he had told the truth and Jennifer had named *him*, that lawyer guy would have found out he was dead, and then what would have happened to Cody? So if you think about it, him lying is the best thing that could have happened."

"Or maybe him *not* fucking around on his fiancée would have been the best thing," Jaxon says angrily.

"While I agree," Tag says. "I'll also point out the obvious fact that Cooper wouldn't have Cody had he *not*." He turns to me. "You love that kid, right? Even after knowing this?"

"Of course I do."

The three of us look at one another, all probably thinking the same thing—that the universe is a perverted, fucked-up place.

"So where the hell does this leave me? Serenity must know something's up. We were supposed to go to the city tonight. Then I got the letter and canceled. Told her I was sick."

"Then I'd suggest you figure out how to barf up a lung, brother." Tag refills our drinks.

Jaxon scoffs. "You really don't think he should tell her?"

"It won't change anything, so no, I don't think he should. At least not now. The kid just lost his mom. He's finally bonding with Cooper. The last thing he needs is another devastating blow."

"That's true," Jaxon says. "But say you wait. When is the right time to tell him you're his uncle and not his dad? When he's eight? Thirteen? An adult? There's no way to tell if he'll be mad or not."

I run an agitated hand through my hair. "Shit."

"All I'm saying is you don't have to do this *right now*," Tag says. "Telling him in a few weeks or a few months won't make any difference."

"And Ren?"

"Serenity thought she and Chaz were the ideal couple. Everyone did. And I'm not too keen on her hating our deceased brother for being a stupid twatbag. Especially when none of us will ever know what drove him to do it."

It's something I've asked myself a dozen times since I read the letter. We were twenty. Life was good. He and Ren were happy. We were planning our business. *Why the hell did he do it?*

"You think this Jennifer woman was the only one?" Jaxon asks.

The three of us seem deflated by his question. Was he messing around on Ren the entire time? If so, he's not the brother I thought he was. And damn… I thought we knew everything there was to know about each other. Suddenly, I think of something.

"What is it?" Jaxon asks, seeing my demeanor change.

"Something Chaz said on the mountain. The night before he died when he asked me to take care of Ren, he said she deserved so much better. I thought he meant better than him dying and leaving her alone." I stand and pace Tag's kitchen. "Fuck, he meant she deserved better than the cheating, lying bastard he was." I look at them. "That's what he meant, didn't he?"

"I don't know, brother," Tag says, shaking his head sadly.

"So we're in agreement?" I ask. "Nobody says anything until I figure out how and when I'm going to tell Cody."

"Fine," Jaxon says.

Tag holds out a shot. "Just remember, Coop, it's not blood that makes someone a father. You've taken him in. You've loved him. You've sacrificed your career for him. He's going to have one hell of a future because of you. That's what makes you a father. Not some genome test."

I hear what he's saying, and I know he's right. But… *fuck*, I really did want to be his dad.

Chapter Thirty

Serenity

I fidget with a pencil, attempting to get work done, but not doing a good job of it. Cooper pops in to check on Cody, who's happily tracing letters on his notepad. Cooper seems fine today, despite having to cancel our date last night. Our *first* date. Because of a migraine, he said. But I'm not so sure. He's different today. Off. Except with Cody, who he's giving even more attention to than usual.

Cooper lifts his chin and salutes me on his way out.

See—odd.

I give up at trying to run any semblance of numbers. On my way out of the office, I glance at Cody's pad. He's practicing writing his name. Cody Calloway is written several times. It reminds me of the days when I used to doodle my name all over my notebooks in high school.

Serenity Calloway

Ren Calloway

Serenity Donovan Calloway

Serenity Grace Donovan Calloway

My heartbeat quickens as I realize I *still* want to doodle those names.

Cody looks up. "Dad says I can be Cody Calloway."

"That's fantastic. And very phonetic."

"What's phonetic?"

"It's when two words sound good together."

"You should be a teacher," he says. "You know a lot."

I laugh. "I'm glad you think so, but I think I'll stick to working here if that's okay."

"That's okay. Besides, you get hamburgers and French fries any time you want."

"It does come with perks." I belatedly notice the spike in his hair. "Hey, look at that. Your dad finally figured out how to do your hair."

"He said I can play baseball. Will you come watch me?"

"I'd be happy to. I'm going to go help with the lunch crowd now. Need anything?"

He shakes his head and goes back to writing letters.

I almost run into Addy, who's carrying a huge tray of food. I follow her out to a table of teachers, who are enjoying their last few weeks of summer, and help distribute the plates.

Calista Hilson is among them, with her adorable baby girl, Ashley, on her lap.

"Hey, Calista," I say. "You change your mind about going back to teaching?"

"And leave this gorgeous creature? Not on your life. I just like to hang out with everyone."

Cooper's brothers walk in. Jaxon comes over and picks up Ashley, fawns over her, then sets her back on Calista. He and Tag take a seat on some barstools. Nobody's behind the bar right now, so I go over. "Here for lunch?" I hand them some menus. They both look at me strangely. Almost like Cooper did earlier.

I fill some water glasses for them and take their orders. When I return from the kitchen, Cooper is talking with them. I stand back and watch, busying myself rolling utensils inside napkins. Every once in a while, one of them will look over. *Are they talking about me?*

Cooper hasn't touched me all day. Hasn't snuck into the back and kissed me. Is he going to break up with me? Not that we're officially together or anything. Except that we are. *I think.*

He glances over and smiles, but awkwardly. He wouldn't be smiling if he's about to dump me.

The chime over the door jingles, and Hunter and Hawk McQuaid stroll up to the other end of the bar. I hurry over because Cooper is the last person who will want to serve them. "Lunch?" I ask, handing them menus.

Hawk's eyes pinball between Cooper and me. "Is it true?"

"That we sell the best Philly cheesesteak in town? Yes. Yes, it is."

"You don't think it's a little bit creepy boning your dead fiancé's twin brother?"

I glance over my shoulder, hoping Cooper and his brothers didn't hear. "The grilled cheese is also very good. Can I put you down for two?"

"Seriously," Hunter says. "You and Cooper? That's some fucked-up shit."

"Is there a problem here?" Cooper says, coming up behind me.

"No problem," I say. "Hawk and Hunter were just ordering lunch."

"Didn't sound like it to me." Cooper's arm comes around my shoulder, and he pulls me against him. Like he's claiming me. I want to shrug him off yet bask in him at the same time.

Hawk taunts him with a nasty laugh. "Wow. Out of the hundreds of available twenty-somethings in this town, you choose Chaz's widow."

"They weren't married," Cooper hisses between clenched teeth. "Now if you aren't ordering, you're welcome to get the hell out."

Tag and Jaxon both sit tall on their stools, ready to help their younger brother if needed.

Kelly comes out of the back with Cody and three plates of food. Cody climbs up onto a barstool next to Jaxon and stuffs a fry into his mouth.

"Oh, look." Hawk stares at Cody, his eyes dripping with spite. "Another illegitimate Calloway."

Cooper leans close to them. "Leave my kid out of this, you fuckwad. And you're hardly one to talk. At least I stepped up."

"Greer's derelict fetus isn't mine," he says. "She's a gold-digging tramp."

"How about we keep the trash talk down," I say, nodding to Cody. "And a nice booth just opened up in the corner." I stare down the two McQuaid brothers. "I think you'll be more comfortable eating there."

Addy strolls by and gives them a warning. "Watch your mouths around my nephew, or you're getting sneezers for sure."

"Addy!"

"I'm kidding," she says, then turns to them and waits for them to get up. "Maybe."

Hawk's eyes travel down to Addy's prosthesis. He stares at it pensively before dragging his eyes away.

Tag gets up and strides over. "You look at my sister like that again, and you'll be eating my goddamn fist for lunch."

Addy pushes Tag away. "Sit down. All of you need to bottle up the testosterone and get along already." She turns back to Hawk and Hunter, then points at the booth. "You two, go." She takes their menus. "One burger medium rare, hold the pickles, and one French dip without cheese coming up."

Everyone stares at Addy.

"What? You think because I'm new that I don't know what every customer likes to order?"

A guy at a nearby table asks, "What happened to your leg?"

She rolls her eyes at me and turns. "Got run over by a jilted lover on a lawnmower. Then I picked up my severed leg and beat him to death with it. So, do you want to ask me out for a date?"

Laughter comes not only from her brothers but Hunter McQuaid. I swear, if anyone could end the Calloway-McQuaid feud, it would be Addy. That girl may have lost her leg, but she seems to have magical powers. Everyone loves her.

Addy gets them seated in the booth and walks back by the bar. "Hey, Cody *Calloway*."

Cody smiles. "Hi, Aunt Addy."

Cooper catches my eye and thumbs to the back. I follow him to the office. He shuts the door. "You okay?"

"I'm fine. I don't let them get to me like *some* people do."

"Do you... feel like a widow?"

"No. Are you... having second thoughts?"

"About Cody?"

"About *us*."

"You think because I canceled on you last night that I don't want this anymore?"

I shrug. "I don't know. Sometimes you send mixed signals."

He studies me. There's a war going on in his head. I can only pray the right side wins. He crosses the room, pushes me against the wall, lifts my chin, and kisses me. When his tongue enters my mouth, I melt into him. His casted arm pulls me against him, allowing me to feel his growing erection. His hand travels from my face, across my shoulder, down my arm, then up my ribs to cup my breast. It's only been days since he's touched me, but it feels like years. It's become an obsession, having his hands on me. A drug I'm addicted to. A feeling I never want to go without.

He pulls his lips from mine, shimmying his hips into me as a tantalizing smile creeps up his face. "Does it feel like I don't want this?" he asks, his voice deep and sinfully rich, like aged whiskey. The work schedule is taped to the wall on his right. "Donny's closing Friday. We're going on that date. Now if you'll excuse me, I'm going to splash cold water on my face."

He leaves. I sink down to the couch, relieved beyond belief. Because, no, I don't feel like a widow. More like a love-sick schoolgirl.

Chapter Thirty-one

Cooper

I twist my arm around. After six weeks in a cast, it feels weird without it. It looks strange, too. My skin is pale and flaky. And rank smelling.

"You can wash it in the sink over there," the doctor says. "Take it easy for a few more weeks. Best to ease back into any sports or heavy lifting."

A month ago, I'd have taken issue with that. I'd probably have gone straight to the airport, ignoring doctor's orders, ready to do something that could have me ending up with bigger problems than a broken arm. But that was before.

Before Cody.

Before Ren.

Before my life did a complete one-eighty.

"Your arm looks funny," Cody says on the way back to the car.

"Not as funny as your goofy grin."

"Grandma says we have the same goofy grin."

"I guess we do."

Then it stabs me right in the heart. Sometimes, for a few minutes or a few hours, I'll forget that he's not really my son. And that one day, I'll have to tell him.

I talked to the counselor Shawn recommended. He suggested telling Cody sooner rather than later. I know I have to do it. But I also know it could very well affect my relationship with Ren. I think that's the main reason I'm waiting. She'd be pissed at Chaz for sure, but the real question is, would she see Cody in a different light? The product of an affair. A constant reminder that her first love cheated on her. Could she be around him? Around me?

I'm being selfish and I know it. But damn, I *just* got her. I can't lose her.

"I'm going to pick up Ren and then drop you off at Uncle Tag's house for your sleepover."

"So you can go on a date with her?"

"That's right."

"Can *I* go on a date with Ren?"

I laugh. "No, sport, you can't."

"Why not?"

"Because dating is for two people who really like each other."

"I like Ren."

"It's a different kind of like. The kind that makes your heart flutter and butterflies dance in your stomach."

"Because you think she's pretty?"

"Because I think she's gorgeous."

"What's gorgeous?"

"It's more than pretty."

"Will you marry her?"

"I think it's too soon to talk about that."

"Gage's dad got married, and he got a new mommy. I already have a mom, even though she's gone to heaven."

"Yes, buddy, you already have a mom. No one will ever take her place. If I ever get married, and that's a big *if*, the woman I marry would be your stepmom."

Except that she wouldn't, my brain reminds me. *She'd be your aunt.*

"What's a stepmom?"

"It's someone who marries your dad and does mom things like help get you to school and fix your dinner."

"Would I have to call her Mom?"

"You'd get to call her whatever you want. Listen, we're almost to Ren's house, so let's talk about something else."

"When do I get to play baseball?"

"Soon. I signed you up yesterday. And guess what? The back of your jersey will say Calloway."

I see him smile in the rearview mirror.

Ren is standing outside her house, overnight bag in hand, when we pull up. I get out and load her bag into the trunk, trying not to think about how fucked up it is driving her to the city in Chaz's car so we can have a romantic night at a hotel.

"Hey there, Cody," she says after getting in.

"Dad says if you get married and are my stepmom that I can call you whatever I want."

I guffaw, certain I'm three shades of red when I've never blushed in my whole goddamn life. "Uh, no. Jesus, Cody. I swear, he was just asking questions. He's five. You know how inquisitive he is. I never said anything about—"

She puts her hand on my arm. "Cooper, it's fine. I know how he is." She turns to look in the back. "Your dad is right, though. When he gets married and you get a stepmom, you can call her lots of things. One of my friends calls her stepmother 'Mama.' Another one calls her 'my other mother.' And a lot of people simply call their stepparents by their first names."

Samantha Christy

"Gage calls his new mommy *Mom*."

"Well, yes, there is that option. It's really up to you, Cody." She glances at me. "But I think you have plenty of time before you have to make that decision."

"Do you think my mommy in heaven would get mad if I called someone else Mom or Mama?"

"No, I don't think she would. In fact, I think she'd be happy if you loved someone else enough to honor her with that name."

Cody looks out the window, silent for the rest of the drive to Tag's.

Back in the car after I drop him off, I apologize to Ren. "I didn't mean for that to get uncomfortable. He was asking about our date, and it kind of blew up from there."

"It's not a big deal, Cooper. He's curious. Curiosity is a sign of intelligence. You should be proud of him. Your son is one smart kid."

Bam. There it is again. The stake through my heart.

Tell her.

No, don't.

Shit.

"What is it?" she asks.

I shake my head. "Nothing. You ready for a great night? I called ahead. The hotel will have a bottle of champagne chilling in our room."

"Can I let you in on a secret?" she says with a wry grin. "I'm kind of a sure thing. You don't have to wine and dine me."

I chuckle. "Can I let *you* in on a secret?" I blow out a breath. "I'm fucking nervous."

She scrunches her brows. "You are?"

"I've never really done this before."

"You've gone on plenty of dates, Cooper."

"Yeah, but not like this one. This one is different."

"Different how?"

"It… *means* more than all the others."

"Wow." She bites her lower lip. "I think I just got butterflies in my stomach."

I lean over and pull her to me. "Just wait. I promise you that with what I plan on doing to you, by the end of the night those butterflies will be fire-breathing dragons."

"Cooper?"

"Yeah."

"Thank you."

"For what?"

"For doing this. For taking a chance on us. For… everything."

Chapter Thirty-two

Serenity

I pull up to Cooper's cabin in Dad's SUV. Today is moving day. But it's so much more than that. It's the fourth anniversary of Chaz's death. How will he handle it? How will I?

He's sitting on the porch drinking his usual morning cup of coffee. I get out of the car, walk over, and sit next to him. He drapes an arm over my shoulder, his finger casually caressing my neck. "You okay?"

"Mm-hmm. You?"

"I'm trying to think of good things. Like how you'll be able to sleep over."

I give his leg a squeeze. "Like how nice it will be waking up in your arms."

"Like how I can take showers with you," he whispers. Then he looks pensively into the woods. "Shit, Ren, is it wrong of us to be talking like that on today of all days?"

"Stop it," I say. "Let's not go there."

"What were you doing on this day last year?"

"Way to not go there."

"It's not like I can go all day without thinking about it, Ren." His voice is torn, rough, and thick. He picks up his phone and glances at the time. "I mean, shit, it was right about now that I woke up and saw him."

I scoot closer. I knew there would be memories today. And now that I know what really happened up on that mountain, it makes it even harder to stomach.

"Do you know how hard it was to leave him there? He was gone, but I still sat with him for hours. I knew that if I left, I would never see him again. Never talk to him. Never, anything."

His words become soft and stuck in his throat. He pulls me closer instead of pushing me away, for which I'm grateful. Today, we share our tragedy together instead of suffering apart.

"I should have sent someone looking for you," I say, quiet desperation coating my words. "You'd been out of touch for days. It wasn't unusual for that to happen when you went off together, but if I'd had the sense to sound an alarm…"

"This isn't on you, Ren. Not in the least."

"What did you do? How did you finally get him down?"

He swallows. The memory is painful. But I get the idea he needs to tell me. "I covered him with my jacket and a few branches. I didn't want any animals—" He curses and scrubs a hand down his face.

"And then?"

"I hiked down to the road. It took over an hour even though it couldn't have been more than a mile. I was hungry and dehydrated, and it was painful walking on my ankle. When I got there, no cars came. I couldn't go any further. If I was going to die there, so be it. In fact, part of me hoped it would happen. So I sat down in the middle of the pavement, right after a bend in the road."

A hand muffles my cry. "Oh, Cooper."

"Sometime later, I heard it. The noise of an engine. A truck probably. I'd been sitting there for God knows how long, thinking of everything that happened over the past three days. What I should have done differently. How I could have saved him. As the noise became louder, I didn't bother moving. How was I going to tell my family? How was I going to tell you? It would just be easier that way."

Ugly tears stream down my face. I came so close to losing both of them. I *did* lose both of them for almost four years.

"But you moved."

"I didn't. The truck came barreling around the corner, right toward me. I didn't move a single goddamn muscle. I watched it come closer, adrenaline building inside me. An excitement almost. The high of knowing it would happen quickly. And it wouldn't be any worse than the suffering I'd already been through. But at the last second, it turned and missed me. Hell, he was lucky he didn't go over the side. Gave me an earful before I could tell him what happened."

"That's why you do what you do, isn't it?"

He turns, questions looming in his bloodshot eyes.

"All your adventures. The risks you take. That day on the mountain when the truck was coming toward you, even after what happened to Chaz, you felt an exhilaration. And that feeling gave you something you needed, something to strive for as you missed him, even if it meant you were trying to join him."

"Are you psychoanalyzing me, Ms. Donovan?"

"It just makes more sense now is all." I take his hand and rub his left arm where his cast used to be. "Do you still have the urge to do it? *Will* you do it?"

"I bought a house, Ren. I have a"—he hesitates and draws in a shaky breath—"kid. And now, a permanent job. Those things don't exactly lend themselves to my former life."

"You forgot one more thing, Cooper. You have *me*. That is, if you want me."

He pulls a strand of hair off my wet cheek. "I do. I really, really do. Even if that makes me a horrible excuse for a brother."

"You're not a bad brother. You're an honorable man. Look at how you've stepped up to raise your son."

He pinches the bridge of his nose. "Ren, I need to—"

The door opens behind us. "Moving Day!" Cody sings. Then he sits next to Cooper and sees how devastated we both are. "Dad, are you okay? Are we still moving to the blue house?"

"We're moving, sport."

"How come you and Ren are sad?"

"Remember how I said my brother died? Today is the day he died four years ago."

"Will I still be sad on the day Mommy died in four years?"

"I think you will, little man. It never quite goes away. Someday, Ren will tell you about the ball in the box." He looks over and gives me a sad smile.

I hand a bakery bag over to Cody. "I brought extra muffins today. We'll need a lot of energy to move all your stuff to the new house."

"I can't wait to have my own room again. Dad snores."

Cooper chuckles and ruffles Cody's messy morning hair. "I do not."

I lean close and whisper, "Yes, you do."

His eyebrows go up. "I hope that won't keep you from—"

"Wild horses couldn't keep me away."

He smiles, but it's still sad. Then he hops off the porch steps. "Cody, go eat breakfast. We have lots to do today."

"You okay?" I ask after Cody goes inside. I nod to the woods. "Do you want to go to the clearing?"

"Maybe later. I think I just needed to get it all out there. Thanks for listening."

"That's what girlfriends are for."

His lip twitches. "Girlfriend, huh?"

"Yeah, girlfriend. Get used to it, Calloway."

He wraps an arm around my waist and tugs. "I think I just might have to do that."

~ ~ ~

"That's the last of it," Cooper says, dropping a box in the dining room.

"I can unpack the kitchen stuff if you want to get started on Cody's playroom. I know he's eager to get rid of the pink."

"You're not going to work?" he asks.

"My dad is almost back to one hundred percent. And it's Wednesday—slow day. He promised to take lots of breaks."

He looks around to make sure Cody isn't watching and pulls me into his arms. "Maybe I should have my mom pick up the kid so we can christen every room."

"It's not my house," I say with a laugh. "I'm not sure that applies."

"It could be." His heated stare slays me. "Someday."

My insides get all warm and tingly at the thought of sharing a house with him. Then again, it was only three hours ago that he finally admitted I'm his girlfriend.

"Dad!" Cody calls, ending the conversation that never started. "There's a spider in my room."

Cooper chuckles. "Duty calls."

I take the opportunity to run out to the car and bring in a few boxes of my own. After Cody is saved from the spider, I hold out a box for him. "This is for you."

"You got me a present? It's not my birthday."

"It's a housewarming gift. That's something you give to someone when they move into a new home."

He plops down on the floor and tears into it. It's the photo album I promised him. In the slot on the front is a picture of Cody's mom back before she got sick. She looks beautiful and full of life. He opens it to a picture of her, heavily pregnant and cradling her belly. Then one of her holding him in the hospital. The other pages have photos of vacations, birthdays, and random selfies. His eyes glisten as he turns every page. Finally, he looks up. "Can we make another one with pictures of me and Dad?"

"I think that's a fine idea." I pull out my phone. "In fact, let's take one right now. How about outside in front of your new house?"

Cody hugs the album, puts it on the counter, and runs outside.

I nod to the other box I brought in. "That one is for you," I tell Cooper. "It's the photos from Jennifer's bedroom. I thought you'd want them since you missed all his birthdays. Every parent should have pictures of their kids' birthdays. I switched out the frames to ones not so girly."

"Thanks."

For a moment, he looks sad. I get it. He loves Cody. And he's missed so much of his life already.

"Come on," he says. "Let's go take that picture."

While Cooper spends the next hour taping baseboards and windows, I sift through boxes. It's like he just threw stuff into them regardless of where they belong. Some of Cody's clothes are in with the housewares. Cleaning supplies have been packed alongside shoes. Toys and games are packed with bottles of body wash and shampoo.

Cody walks into the room. "How about you tackle that box there," I say. "It looks like it contains mostly your stuff."

He pulls out some books. Then he sits down and pages through them. I laugh because he's easily distracted and not the best at unpacking. When I finish putting away some dishes, Cody is on the floor staring at a photo. He looks up. "Which photo book should we put this one in?" he asks. "It's got both my mom and dad."

"Really? Let's see."

He holds it out to me. I look at it, appreciating the fact that he has at least one photo of the two of them together. Then my heart completely stops beating when I see the small scar over his right eye. "Cody, where did you get this picture?"

"It fell out of this." He holds up an envelope.

My mind has lost all grasp on reality. I swallow hard. "Cody, why don't you take the rest of this box into your bedroom?"

"Okay."

I stare at the envelope, my butt blindly finding the kitchen chair behind me. Hands shaking, I pull out the letter and unfold it. It's addressed to Cooper. I glance back at the picture, confused beyond belief.

I read the letter three times, looking for clues. There are none, other than the scar.

Cooper walks into the room and sees me with the letter. I show him the picture. "What the hell is going on here? This is Chaz, but the letter is made out to you."

Hands rake through his hair. "Oh, Jesus."

"Cooper?"

"He lied, Ren. He told her his name was *Cooper* Calloway. She had no reason to believe otherwise. So when she got sick, it was me she went looking for."

I glance back toward Cody's room—the gravity of the situation slapping me square in the face. Bile rises, burning my throat. "He's... *Chaz's?*"

He approaches me. "I was going to tell—"

I stand, toppling the chair to get away from him. "Stay away from me. He... oh, God." I can almost hear the hysteria in my voice. "He cheated on me. And you knew and lied about it."

"It's not what you—"

"Stop." I hold out my hand. My stomach is churning. My head is spinning. "I can't be here." I grab my purse and head for the door. "Don't come after me. I can't look at you."

"Dad!" Cody calls. "Another spider!"

"Serenity!" Cooper shouts from the front door.

I reach the car and turn. "Go. Your *nephew* needs you."

Driving away from his house, I get to the end of the block and have to pull over, unable to see through my tears. Chaz cheated on me. I do the math in my head. We were twenty. We were happy—or so I thought. I pound on the steering wheel. "Damn you!"

My phone rings. Cooper's face appears on the screen. I don't answer. It rings again, and I turn it off. I can't look at him. His face. Scar or no scar, I'm not sure I'll ever be able to look at him again and not think of the man who cheated on me.

Choking down my feelings, I drive the few blocks to my house. Sadness turns to fury by the time I reach my bedroom. I rip open the closet door, pull out the keepsake box, remove the lid, and sift through it until I find the binder with all of Chaz's letters.

"Liar," I say, opening the binder and ripping the pages from the rings. "Cheater." Page after page, I tear them in half and let them float to the floor.

My engagement ring sits in a corner of the box. I pick it up and twist it around on the tip of my index finger, sick to my stomach that for all those years, I actually thought it meant something. I lob it across the room and into the wastebasket by the door.

Leaning against the bed, I look up, my walls lined with drawings from Cody instead of pictures of Chaz. But even without him on my walls, I can't get away from him. I stand, retrieve my backpack, pack it with the essentials, and head out. At the bedroom door, I glance into the trash can, the ring reflecting light from the lamp. I don't know why, but I pick it up and shove it into my pocket. There's only one thing I can do. It's the same thing I did three years and fifty-one weeks ago—the night of Chaz's funeral.

I get back into the car and turn on my phone just long enough to text my father.

Me: Your car's at the train station. I'm going back to Sitka. I love you Dad.

Chapter Thirty-three

Cooper

"We have to leave, Cody."

"But we just moved in."

"We'll come back. Right now, Serenity needs us."

He looks around, confused. After all, she was just here a minute ago.

"I'll explain on the way. Let's get in the car."

When he sees where we're going, he asks, "Did you forget something at the cabin?"

I park. "Come on." I lead him past the cabin, down the trail a ways and under the tree tunnel. But she's not here. I sit on the rock.

Cody has questions I don't know how to answer. "What's wrong, Dad?"

"Ren is upset. I have to find her."

"Maybe she's in her bedroom. When I got mad or sad in the 'partment, that's where I would go."

"Right. Let's go by her house."

Five minutes later, we're pulling up. I jump out of the car and knock on the door. No answer. "Ren!" I shout. *Nothing.* I go over to the garage and peek through the small square windows. No car.

"She's not here. Let's stop by Donovan's."

"Can we eat lunch? I'm hungry."

"Yeah, sure, we can eat."

The lot isn't full yet. It's not quite noon. Cody shouts as I pull him along to the back door. "Why are we running?"

"Sorry, buddy. I guess I just really want to find her." I swing open the back door and race to the office.

Donny looks up, sees my face, and shakes his head. "She's not here."

"Do you know where she is?"

"What happened?"

I lean against the doorjamb, not wanting to divulge too much with Cody by my side.

He gives me a pointed look. "Did you hurt her?"

"Not in the way you might think. It was unintentional. But it was only because I was trying to protect her, Donny. I swear it. I…" I close my eyes and finally say the words out loud. "I'm in love with her."

"I believe you. But, son, you've got a situation on your hands. My daughter is on her way to Alaska."

I slump into the wall. "Alaska? Oh, fuck."

"*Daaaaad,*" Cody scolds.

"Sorry. I have to go after her. Donny—"

"Don't worry about me. I've got things under control here."

"Maybe I can catch up with her at the airport before she even leaves. Cody, just in case I can't, let's call Grandma and see if you can stay with her for a day or two."

He frowns. "But I want to go to Alaska."

"This probably isn't the time for a family trip."

"But you said we were a team. If Ren is sad, I want to go. She helps me when I get sad."

"The boy may have a point. Two of you going may be better than one."

"Okay, fine. I don't have time to argue. Donny, can you feed him? I'll run back to the house and pack a few things."

"Go."

"Yay!" Cody squeals behind me. "I love airplanes."

At the house, Tag's SUV is in the driveway. I forgot he still had some of my things in his garage. Hell, in the past thirty minutes, I forgot this is moving day.

"Where's the fire?" he asks as I race past him.

He follows me inside, and I toss him the house keys. "I'm going after Ren. She found the letter from Jennifer. She knows everything."

"Oh, shit."

He stands in the hall, watching me go from my room to Cody's, filling a backpack. "Donny said she took off to Alaska." I get a bad feeling in my gut and park myself on a kitchen chair. "Maybe it serves me right. She was never mine." I rake my hands through my hair, refusing to look up at Tag. "What if… What if in some way I wanted him to die?"

He steps back. "Jesus, Cooper. You're a fucking idiot if you believe that. You two were as close as any brothers could be."

"But I wanted his girl. I wanted his life. And now I have it." Finally, I make eye contact. "Am I being punished?"

"We've all been to hell and back. You and Serenity especially. You deserve happiness, Coop. If that's with each other, so be it."

I gaze out the window. "I'm beginning to think happiness is an illusion. It's like the horizon—you can chase it, but you can never quite get there."

"You can. Look at Maddie and me. Jaxon and Nicky. Believe me, brother, you'll get there. Sometimes, however, you have to sail right through the storm to find clear skies."

"Since when did you become a goddamn philosopher?"

He laughs. "Don't you have a plane to catch?"

~ ~ ~

Ninety minutes later, as I'm at JFK trying to get the quickest flight out, I keep looking around the airport hoping to see her. I figured there would only be one or two flights to Sitka, and surely I'd catch her before she was even able to board the plane. I was wrong. There are a dozen flights going out from here, LaGuardia, and Newark that fly into either Seattle, Juneau, or Ketchikan, and then on to Sitka.

She could be at any airport, in any terminal, on any flight.

Still, as we wait for Delta's 3:55 p.m. flight to Seattle, I look at all the faces in the terminal. Then, as our flight gets called, I hang back and watch as others board, hoping she'll be one of them. After we get on the plane, I put away my backpack, which holds a change of clothes for each of us, a few toiletries, and Ozzy Putnam. Then I check my phone one last time. She hasn't answered any of my texts, emails, or phone messages.

"Cool," Cody says, looking out the window as luggage gets loaded into the belly of the plane.

"You're going to want to sleep," I tell him. "We won't get into Seattle until after your bedtime, and it'll be the middle of the night our time when we get to Alaska."

"Our time?"

"The sun goes down later on that side of the country, so they change the time. It's four hours earlier there. So when we finally get to Sitka, it will feel like one thirty in the morning."

"Neat. I've never stayed up late before. Except at Uncle Tag's. He let me and Gigi stay up in the dining room fort until the stars were out." He looks back out the window as we take off, practically bouncing in his seat. "Look how fast we're going! Dad! Dad, can you see?"

Dad. Every time he says it is another reminder that I'm not. He's going with me to find her. He's bound to hear us talking. Maybe even fighting. I have to tell him before he hears it from anyone else. Besides, my main reason for not saying anything was to protect Ren. That no longer applies.

When the flight attendant comes by, I order an apple juice for Cody and a stiff drink for me. Liquid courage for what I'm about to do.

When we're far above the clouds and there's nothing else for him to look at, I pat his hand. "Cody? There's something I need to talk to you about."

"My name again?"

"No. Not your name. This is more about my name. You know how Gigi calls Uncle Tag Daddy? Well, he's not really her dad. Her dad died when she was a baby. But she loves Uncle Tag a lot and he loves her, so she wanted to call him by that name. I guess what I'm trying to say is that just because someone isn't a real dad doesn't mean they can't love you as much as a real dad would."

He stares at me. I'm not sure he's understanding anything.

"Sport, I love you lots. And I'm so happy we bought our house. I want you to live there with me until you go off to college or do whatever you want to do. But there's something I found out recently. Something nobody knew, not even your mom. So the thing is… Well, the thing is, I found out I'm not really your dad. My brother Chaz is."

"Chaz? Your brother in heaven?"

I nod.

"But the test said we matched."

"That's the funny thing about identical twins." I pull out my wallet and show him an old picture of Chaz and me. "This is us when we were about fifteen. You couldn't tell us apart. And twins like us even share the same blood. That's why the test said I was your dad even though, technically, I'm not."

I don't go into details about Chaz lying. Cody probably isn't even old enough to understand sex and the fact that it leads to babies. That's a conversation for way in the future.

"If you're 'dentical, and you have the same blood, and the test said we match, then it's *kind* of like you're my dad."

I chuckle. "I suppose you could look at it like that. Kind of, but not really."

"If you're kind of but not really my dad, do I have to stop calling you Dad?"

"That's up to you, little man. You could always call me Uncle Cooper." I try not to let on how upsetting that is for me. That a mere two months ago, I didn't want to be anyone's father, and now, I'm cursing the universe because I'm not his.

"I can still live with you even though they are both in heaven?"

"You bet you can. For as long as you like. We're family. And we're still a team, you and me."

He plays with the extra length of his seat belt. "I don't want to call you Uncle Cooper."

"Okay, sport. Then you don't have to."

"Dad?"

My heart fucking soars. "Yeah?"

"I love you lots too."

I swallow my emotions, put an arm around his shoulders, and pull him close. "Try to sleep now, son. We have a long flight."

Chapter Thirty-four

Serenity

Chaz cheated on me. And Cooper lied about it. How long had he known? We were friends back then, good friends. But in no world does being friends trump being twins. He would protect his brother at all costs.

How could he have cheated? We were in love. He always told me I was his forever.

I do the math in my head. Then I get out my phone and scroll back through pictures of our summer six years ago. He was twenty. I was nineteen. We were engaged. Happy. Deliriously so—or so I was led to believe. There are all kinds of pictures around their birthday. We took a trip to Moab, Utah, that year. Most of the pictures are either of Chaz and me or Cooper and Chaz. But a few times, we'd asked a fellow hiker to take one of the three of us.

I stare at one such photo. We'd arrived at the Delicate Arch before dawn. We were the first ones there and had to wait half an hour for someone else to arrive to snap a picture of the three of us under the iconic rock formation. We were so young. So carefree.

My heart hurts knowing that not so long after that, Chaz impregnated Jennifer Putnam.

Did he know? Then I remember what Jennifer wrote in the letter. *No, he didn't.*

Chaz was a risk-taker, a thrill seeker, but he was a decent man—he'd have stepped up if he'd have known, even if it had meant losing me.

I look out of the small airplane window. Oh god, he was a risk-taker and a thrill seeker. Is that why he did it? Was he doing it all along?

Looking at the photos, it dawns on me the shift that has occurred. It used to be I couldn't look at Cooper without seeing Chaz. Now I can't look at Chaz without seeing Cooper. And as I sit here, staring at the pictures, I'm not sure which is worse—loving a man who looks like my dead fiancé, or loving a man who looks like the man who betrayed me.

I turn off my phone and try to sleep.

I can't.

Every time I close my eyes, I see him.

I'm just not sure which *him* I'm seeing.

~ ~ ~

My layover in Seattle isn't long. Still, I sit here and think.

Am I doing the right thing, going back to Sitka? Life was easier there, when all I had to think about was going to work. Wasn't it? Hilda will give me my job back. I still have my place there. Most of my things. Maybe it was meant to be this way.

I finally turn on my phone and take it off airplane mode. Twelve unopened texts from Cooper. Three voice messages. One email. I turn it off again. There's nothing he could say to make this any better. To assuage his guilt over keeping his brother's infidelity a secret. To change the fact that my past was a lie of epic proportions. To excuse the harsh truth that my dead fiancé had a child with another woman.

I try to decide if I hate Chaz. Can you hate a person who isn't even around to be hated?

I hated Cooper. For years, I hated him merely for looking like his twin. And then I loved him despite it. And as much as I want to hate him for keeping Chaz's secrets, I can't help but miss him. It hasn't even been twelve hours, and I miss him so much.

I miss the way he looks at me like he can't get enough of me. The way he sneaks back to the office just to tell me I'm beautiful. I miss the way he whispers my name when we make love. And how he looks right into my eyes after he comes, as if thanking me for the experience. I miss all the ways he's uniquely Cooper.

I miss the way he loves Cody.

Cody.

Chaz's son.

Tears clog my throat at what this means. Then it occurs to me that Cody was still calling Cooper his dad. Did Cooper have any intention of ever telling him?

Lies. So many lies.

I think about what Cooper told me this morning, how he didn't want to leave Chaz up on that mountain. I close my eyes. Four years ago today, I lost him. Four years of thinking I'd lost my soul mate. The man I was going to spend my life with. The person who would have never ever lied to me.

I pull the ring out of my pocket. I'm not sure why I brought it with me. It symbolizes something that no longer exists. A past that was an illusion. A future that had no foundation.

A woman's voice comes over the loudspeaker. "Now boarding flight 1365 to Knoxville, Tennessee, at gate thirty-two."

Suddenly, I know why I brought the ring. I know what I have to do. I approach the man behind the desk at gate thirty-two. "I'd like to buy a ticket for this flight."

He taps on the keyboard. "You're in luck. There's one seat left."

I pay for the ticket, put in my earbuds, and board the plane.

Chapter Thirty-five

Cooper

It's 10:00 p.m. New York time when we land. And we have a ninety-minute layover. Cody napped a bit on the flight, and right after I get him a snack and drink in the terminal, he's asleep in the chair next to me, his head in my lap.

I stare at my phone, noting none of my texts to Ren have been read. I glance at a sleeping Cody, wondering if it was a mistake to bring him. Is it me she's running from, or him? I try to put myself in her place. She feels betrayed by a man who can no longer defend himself. And by me, a man she thinks lied to her. I suppose I did, if only by omission. Maybe in some strange way she even feels betrayed by Cody, who she must realize can't help who his father is.

I think my eyes deceive me as I gaze at the gate across the terminal. Is it? Can it be Ren?

I stiffen. Of course it can. We're going to the same place, and this is a major hub to get there. I go to stand, but it's difficult with Cody's head on me. "Wake up, sport."

He mumbles, eyes closed. I try to juggle him into my arms, wrestle the backpack onto my shoulder, and keep my eyes on her all at the same time. She's in line to board a plane. She must have gotten an earlier connecting flight than we did. I race over. "Ren!"

She doesn't answer.

"Serenity!" I shout louder.

Not even a flinch.

When she turns the corner into the jet bridge, I catch a glimpse of an earbud. I sit back down, Cody becoming heavy in my arms, and surmise I'll catch up with her soon enough. Our flight leaves in forty-five minutes.

"Last call for flight 1365 to Knoxville, Tennessee," the woman at the gate announces over the loudspeaker.

What the hell? I look at the illuminated sign at the gate. This flight—the one Ren just boarded—is going to Knoxville. Not Sitka. Did she board the wrong flight? I know with today's policies that could never happen. But why is she going to Tennessee?

My stomach flips with the realization of what today is. And the fact that there's only one reason she would go there. I pick up Cody and go to the gate. "I need two tickets for this flight."

"I'm sorry, sir, the flight is full."

Fuck.

"Can I get a message to a passenger?"

"Sure you can. There's this new-fangled contraption called a cell phone. You can text them. Or call them even. Easy peasy."

"She's not answering my calls."

He eyes me suspiciously. "Maybe there's a good reason for that."

"There's not. A misunderstanding. Listen, I really need to talk to her. Can you please go on the plane and get her a message?"

"Despite what you may have seen in movies, sir, that's not the way it works."

I turn around and see the last few people boarding the plane. I approach them. "I'll pay you for your tickets," I say. "Five hundred each? I can Venmo you right now."

"Sir," the guy from the counter says. "Do I have to call security?"

"Dad." Cody stirs. "You're squeezing too hard."

"Sorry." I loosen my grip and walk back to the counter. "I have to get on the next flight to Knoxville."

He taps on his keyboard. "That was our last one out today. You can check with other airlines—"

I'm walking away before he can finish. I put Cody down and pull up my flight app, finding one that leaves in an hour from another airline in another terminal. I hike Cody up on my shoulder again and start the trek.

Before we board, I call my sister. "What's going on?" she asks. "Donny said you and Ren are both out of town. I thought you were moving today."

"It's a long story, and one I can't get into right now. Listen, I need you to meet me in Knoxville. I'll pay for everything. There's a flight from LaGuardia that leaves in two and a half hours. If you leave now, you'll just make it. You'll land right before we do. I'll text you my flight info."

"Where are you?"

"In Seattle."

"How come you're in Seattle if you're going to Knoxville?"

"Like I said, long story. I promise to tell you as soon as I get there. But I'm going to need someone to watch Cody tomorrow."

"Because?"

"Because I know where she's going, and it's not someplace I want to take Cody."

A long sigh comes through the phone. "I'll go pack a bag."

~ ~ ~

It's the middle of the night in Knoxville. Cody is sleeping in one bed, and Addy and I lie on the other after talking for hours.

She cranes her head and stares at Cody in disbelief. "I can't believe he's Chaz's," she whispers. Then she swats me. "And you—you should have told her when you found out. You might have avoided all this."

"When I found out, things were still new between us. I didn't want to lose her."

"Seems you still may have."

I eye the clock. It's almost four in the morning. I grab a bottle of water and the keys to my rental. "Get some sleep," I say. "I'm not sure how long I'll be gone."

"You're leaving *now?* It's not even light out."

"It's an hour's drive to Gatlinburg. I plan to be on that mountain before she gets there."

"Why the rush?" Her expression flattens. "Cooper, you don't think she'd do anything stupid, do you?"

"Let's see, I recently told her that her fiancé killed himself. And now, on the anniversary of his death, she finds out he was a douchebag cheater whose affair produced a kid. I don't pretend to know what she's thinking. All I know is halfway to Alaska, she changed her mind and decided to come here."

"Go," she says. "Just find some caffeine. I don't want you falling asleep on the road."

"I got a few hours of shut-eye on the second flight. I'll be fine."

"But you're going back to—"

"Addy, I'll be alright. I'm done doing stupid shit. I have Cody to think about."

She hops off the bed and hugs me. "I don't think I've ever been as proud of you as I am right now. I don't care what any stupid test says, you're that boy's father." She turns me toward the door. "Now go get your girl."

The entire way to Gatlinburg, I try to put it out of my mind that I'm going back to where he died. I've traveled all over the world since then, but the one place I swore I'd never set foot in again was Tennessee.

After my third cup of drive-thru coffee, I'm weaving through hairpin turns at dawn, climbing the mountain road that leads to the trail. The last time I was here, Chaz and I started at the foot of the trail, hiking eight miles to the summit. This time, I'm driving most of the way. I make it to the place where the trail splits off from the road, the very same place I hiked down to and sat on the pavement, hoping maybe death would take me as it took him.

I pull over onto the first shoulder area I find, get out, and race the mile to the top, hiking so fast I don't have time to think about where I'm going or what I'll find when I get there. Out of breath, I stop dead when I reach the top. I'm inundated with memories. The area looks untouched since I was last here. The boulder that trapped us still sits where it fell. The sign warning not to climb on the rocks still stands twenty feet uphill.

The sun rises over the adjacent hill, shining upon me as I fall to the ground in the spot where he died. There's no more blood on the ground or on the rock. Time has washed it away. There's no indication we were here. No remnants. No name etched in stone. No cross erected showing someone died here.

And no Ren.

Maybe I was wrong, and she wasn't coming here. Perhaps she was going back home, and Knoxville was her connecting city.

Tears fall. Emotions I haven't felt in years flow through me like hot lava. I sit and lean against the rock, cursing it for falling. Cursing us for being so stupid.

Trees rustle somewhere down the trail. I sit up and look in the direction. A family comes into view. A mom, a dad, and two boys older than Cody. The man approaches. "Are you okay?"

I nod and try to find my voice. "Fine."

He surveys the area. "Are you sure? Do you need water or food?"

"No. Thank you."

"Dad, look at me!"

Oh, Jesus. A kid climbed up on the rocks. I scramble to my feet and yell, "Get off the rocks! Get down! Get down now!"

"Easy, buddy," the man says like I'm some psycho.

"You don't understand." I point to the sign. "This is here for a reason. Please, get your son down."

"Christopher," the woman says to the child. "Come on down."

"Take a picture, Mom!"

"Christopher, now." The woman looks at me the same way her husband did. "Bruce, maybe we should go."

"Yeah," he says, keeping a close eye on me. "Let's go find that other trail Michael saw a little way back."

I sit back down by the boulder and watch them disappear into the trees. Then I shake my head. If only a family had come up here four years ago. If someone had found us right away, things might have turned out differently. Chaz could still be here.

I study the boulder. It's bigger than I remember. Somehow over the years, my mind made it smaller. I truly believed I would have been able to save him. Looking at it now, I know it's not true. I'd have died right here with him.

He fucking saved me.

There's more rustling by the trees. I wonder if the man has come back to give me a piece of his mind. But it's not him. It's Ren. And she stares at me like I'm a ghost. Her face goes completely ashen, and her legs threaten to come out from under her. I run over and steady her. "Ren."

Her eyes focus on the area above my right brow. She's looking for a scar that's not there. "Cooper... What... How?"

"I saw you at the Seattle airport. You were getting on a plane to Knoxville."

"You followed me?"

"I guess Donny thought you might need someone. And I needed to explain. Serenity, if you won't open my texts or take my calls, you'll never know what I need you to know."

"Did you know he was cheating on me?"

"No. I swear to God, I didn't. I was as surprised as you were. Cody being his never crossed my mind. I slept with a lot of women back then. And the paternity test..."

"Identical twins will both test as a child's father."

I scrunch my brow. "You know that?"

"Mia told me once. She's a twin, though not identical, but she's obsessed with all things twin. She once told me that if Chaz and I had a kid, genetically you could be the kid's father too. But I have to know, when did you find out?"

"Jennifer's stepmother sent me the letter a few weeks ago. The picture was included. I knew the second I saw it. Not to mention, I've never been to Central Park. I'm so sorry, Ren. I had no idea he posed as me. I can't imagine how you must be feeling."

Her eyes close briefly. "The day you canceled our date."

I nod.

"So why didn't you tell me?"

"There are so many reasons. I don't even know where to start."

"Try."

"You have this ideal version of him in your head. I know, because I had it myself. It's like after someone dies, you remember only the best things about them. Not the things like the times he'd gotten me into trouble with our parents. Or the time he swiped twenty bucks from me to buy you flowers. He was this perfect person who was supposed to give you a perfect life. I didn't want to be the one to ruin that when there was no point."

"Except there was a point," she says sadly. "Cody."

"That's the second reason I didn't want to tell you. God, Ren, this past month or so with you has been something I never dreamed of. Even as guilty as I was feeling about it, it was still the best thing that's happened to me. And Cody, he's a big part of why it's been so incredible. And I thought if I told you, you'd…"

I swallow, unable to even say the words.

"You thought I'd what?"

"I thought you wouldn't want to be around him. That maybe you'd even hate him."

"Cooper, I—"

"Let me finish. Please. I get that you hate Chaz now. And you hate what he put you through these past four years. You have every right. Believe me, I hate a lot of things about him too." I point behind me. "I hate that he went up on those rocks. I hate that he took away my choice by killing himself. I hate that he left me to go it alone. But, damn it, for the life of me, I can't hate what he did to make Cody. Because even though he's not mine, that kid is a part of me and I love him. And I couldn't stand it if you didn't want to be around him. Because, fuck, as much as I tried to fight it, I love you too."

She steps back as swiftly as if I'd pushed her. "You *love* me?"

My empty stomach churns as much as if I'd eaten an entire pan pizza and dove off a ten-meter platform into a swimming pool. "I know this isn't the ideal place to say it, but yeah, I love you. I've loved you since the day I kissed you in high school. I loved you that day on the beach when Chaz put a ring on your finger. And I loved you the first time we made love in the clearing. As wrong as it's been, Serenity, it's always been you."

"Cooper." The tears welling in her eyes finally give way and fall. "I love you too."

It takes a moment for her words to sink in. I want to reach out and pull her into my arms. I want to kiss her and hold her and never let her go. But I can't. Because it's not just me anymore. "And Cody? What about him?"

"Unlike you, I hate what Chaz did to make Cody. It's something I'll never forgive him for. He ruined everything we had. Every perfect picture I had of our past. But I could never hate Cody. It's not his fault. And you're right, he's still a part of you. And I love every part of you, including him. And I need you to hear this and understand it. It's *you* I love, Cooper. Not your face. Not a memory of someone else. You—the man who's never met a challenge he couldn't overcome. The man who is fiercely loyal to his family. The man who wants everyone to think he's this big tough guy but who's really an old softy. And the man who loves that little boy as if he were truly his own."

Relief floods through me. "Say it again."

"I love him." She steps forward and threads her arms around me. "I love *you*."

I kiss her. I hold her. I wrap her in my arms. I breathe her in, sighing in pure delight as I rock us back and forth. I stand with her in my arms until something finally occurs to me. "Ren, why did you come here?"

She sticks a hand into her pocket and comes out with her engagement ring. "For this. I was on the way to Alaska. I'm not sure why. It was a place I felt safe after he died. I suppose I was looking for a safe place again."

"Me," I tell her. "I'm your safe place."

"Thank you." She regards the ring. "But somewhere on the way to Alaska, I knew I finally had to let him go once and for all. Even if you and I weren't going to be together, I still had to let him go. And I thought coming here to where he died would be the best place."

I keep an arm around her and turn. I stare at the boulder. "It was over there."

Her hand covers her mouth. "*That's* the boulder? It's still here?"

"Yeah. It's a big motherfucker."

She approaches it. "And it was *on* you?" She runs a hand down my chest. "You're lucky to have gotten out."

"Only because of what he did."

"So this is where it happened?"

I nod and she sits. She takes a handful of dirt and sifts it through her fingers. "I could never entirely hate him. You're alive today because of him." She shows me the ring. "Over the past few weeks, I've wondered what I should do with this." She grabs a thin, flat rock and uses it to hollow out a hole in the ground. "Now I know." She drops the ring into the hole and covers it with dirt. She stands, wipes off her hands, and smiles. "Now let's go back to Calloway Creek and spoil the hell out of your nephew."

"Just so you know, I told him. And he decided he still wants to call me Dad. So I guess to simplify things, legally and otherwise, we're just going to roll with that. Oh, and he's in Knoxville with Addy."

"He came with you?"

"He insisted on it. He wanted to come so he could make you feel better like how you've made *him* feel better when he's sad."

I can tell she's biting back tears. This time, however, they're happy ones. "You have one hell of a kid... *Dad.*"

I take her hand in mine and lead her back down the trail. "I sure as hell do."

Chapter Thirty-six

Serenity

"I wonder if there's ever been a kid who has traveled on an airplane as much as you have in the past twenty-four hours," Cooper says to Cody.

Cody turns away from the large window he's been staring out of in the Knoxville airport. "Dad, could I be a pilot?"

I try not to laugh. Seems Cody has already caught the Calloway adventure bug.

"You can be anything you want to be, sport."

"Is it hard?"

"I don't know," Cooper says. "I was going to learn myself, put it on my YouTube channel. Then I broke my arm."

"Maybe we could learn together."

Cooper puts a hand on his shoulder. "Maybe we could."

Cody goes back to watching planes come and go.

A group of teenage girls carrying backpacks walks by, approaching a departure gate. One stops and stares at Addy's leg, looking repulsed by the prosthetic exposed by her wearing shorts.

"Oh. My. God," she says. "What happened to your leg?"

Addy looks up from her magazine. "Plane crash. Senior class trip. I was the sole survivor." She pops her gum and goes back to flipping pages.

The girls go ashen, whispering to one another as they shuffle away. One even says she's not going to get on the plane.

"You're terrible," Cooper says and laughs.

"Serves them right," I say. I move over and sit next to Addy. "I owe you an apology."

"For what?"

"We were like sisters, Addison. I should have been there for you after the accident. I was so caught up in my own grief that I didn't stop and take time to think about how awful it was for you. I ran. It was selfish. I hope you can forgive me."

She closes her magazine. "We all lost someone close to us that day. And we all grieved in different ways. Cooper went rogue. You disappeared. I got drunk and stupid. There's nothing to apologize for, Serenity."

"Still, I'd like to get back what we had. Can the two of us go out sometime? Share a bottle of wine maybe?"

"I'd love that." She rolls up the magazine and hits it against her titanium calf. "We'll Uber, because, well, I'd like to keep my only remaining meat leg."

I love the way she can laugh at herself. "It's a date."

Cooper leans across me. "Addy, I've wanted to ask you something for a while."

She rolls her eyes. "If one more person in this family asks about grad school again, I'm going to beat them over the head with my prosthetic."

"I couldn't give a shit if you go to grad school, Addy. You of all people should know that."

"Spit it out, then. What is it?"

"What did you do with his ashes?"

"I scattered them under the overpass where I had my accident."

He regards her inquisitively. "You did?"

"It was about six months after. That's how long it took me to come to terms with losing my leg, and in some way, losing him. I guess it was my way of letting them both go."

Our flight gets called. Our tickets have Addy and me sitting a few rows away from Cooper and Cody. But when boarding, Addy holds a hand out to Cody. "If you sit with me, I'll give you the window seat."

Cooper nods his thanks as Cody scoots in next to her.

Once everyone has boarded, Cooper summons a flight attendant.

"Something wrong?" I ask.

"I have an idea."

"Sir?" a flight attendant asks.

Cooper gestures to Cody a few rows back. "I was wondering if it's possible to give my boy a tour of the cockpit."

My face breaks out in a smile hearing him call Cody *his boy*.

The woman looks over at Cody. "We have a few minutes. I'm sure the pilots would be delighted."

I turn around and watch Cody's face light up when the flight attendant tells him what's in store. They pass our row and he says, "Dad! I'm going to meet the pilots!"

"That's amazing, Cody." He unlocks his phone and holds it out to the flight attendant. "Miss? Would you mind taking his picture?"

"Come with us and you can take it yourself."

Cooper scoots out of his seat and escorts an excited Cody to the front.

Five minutes later, Cody is trotting back down the aisle, smiling from ear to ear. "Ren! I was a pilot. I got to put on the white hat and push a button that made the whole room light up like a Christmas tree." He points to his shirt. "Look! Wings. They said only real pilots get to wear them."

"Okay, Pilot Calloway," Cooper says. "Let's go get you to your seat."

Cody turns and hugs Cooper, the boy's eyes squeezed so tightly shut you know he's having one of the best experiences of his new life.

Cooper gets Cody situated next to Addy and slides back in next to me before showing me the pictures he took.

I page through the photos then stare up at Cooper.

"What?" he asks.

"You thought you couldn't do it. Be the person he needed. Someone he could look up to. A mentor. But you're all those things and so much more. He doesn't even know how lucky he is to have you."

He looks beyond me, out the window, seeming sad by my declaration.

I put a finger under his chin and force him to look at me. "Cooper, that boy loves you as much as any child loves a father. For all intents and purposes, that's what you are to him. You're always going to be the man who raised him. And years from now, he's going to remember this day, when his dad took him into the cockpit of an airplane. He's going to remember how you held him when he cried. How you celebrated every milestone. How you took him in when he had no one. And how fiercely you loved him."

He tucks a piece of loose hair behind my ear. "There's one more thing I'd like him to remember."

"What's that?"

"The day we became a family. Move in with me, Ren. With us. Do it today. I don't want to spend another night without you. I know it's too soon. I know it's crazy. But you and I know more than anyone how fragile life is and how easily it can be taken away. I don't care what anyone else thinks. We need to live our lives for today, right now, this moment. And someday, not too long from now, I'm going to get down on a knee and ask you to be my—"

"Yes," I say, tears streaming down my face.

His Adam's apple bobs as he swallows, staring at me as if he's not sure he heard me correctly. "Yes?"

"To all of it. The moving in. The living in the moment. The… someday."

As the plane accelerates down the runway, he cups my face in his hands, and I look into the eyes of the man I once feared. The man I couldn't look at because he reminded me of a future I'd never have. The last man on earth I ever dreamed would be my saving grace. My kindred spirit. My one true soul mate.

Breathe.

Chapter Thirty-seven

Cooper

We drop Addy at Mom and Dad's and head back to the new house. Although Ren agreed to move in with me, she said she wouldn't do it unless Cody was on board.

"I'll make lemonade," she says, giving us a moment alone.

I follow Cody to his room. I know he's eager to finish unpacking. "Hey, little man, can we talk about something?"

"Again?"

"I guess we have been having a lot of deep conversations lately, haven't we?"

Worry creases his brow line as he looks up at me. "You still want to be my dad, don't you?"

I sit and pull him onto my lap. "More than anything. Being your dad is one of the best parts of my life. But I wanted to ask you about the other best part. I was wondering if you'd like to have Serenity come and live here too."

He looks through his bathroom into the other bedroom. "Would she sleep in there?"

I chuckle. "No, sport. She'd sleep in my room, with me. You can still have your playroom."

"With you? Like how moms and dads sleep in the same room?"

"Yes, exactly like that."

"But she's not my mom."

"No, she's not. Your mom in heaven will always be your mom, no matter what happens."

"Will she make me grilled cheese dinosaur sandwiches?"

"I think she would love that."

He picks up his bear, holding the stuffed animal's mouth to his ear. "Ozzy says yes, Ren can live here."

When I look up, Serenity is standing in the doorway, tears in her eyes. "Did someone say something about grilled cheese?"

"Our first meal together in our new house," I say. "Grilled cheese sandwiches and"—I wink at Ren—"champagne?"

She laughs. "Sounds perfect."

"Dad?"

"Yeah, sport?"

"Ozzy said he wants a dog."

"Does he now?"

"He said that Uncle Tag and Uncle Jaxon have one, so it's only fair that we have one too."

Ren fluffs Ozzy's scruff. "It's kind of hard to argue with that logic."

I raise a brow. "Teaming up on me, are you?"

"I'll walk him and feed him like Gigi does," Cody says. "And we have a fence so he can't get out. And we can play in the backyard. Heisman likes tennis balls. We could get tennis balls. And Sissy likes chewy sticks. We could get those too. I promise I'll take care of him. And he can sleep with me and Ozzy. And maybe we could call him Ozzy. They'd have different names because Ozzy the bear is a Putnam and Ozzy the dog would be a Calloway. Like us."

"Maybe you should join the debate team and become a lawyer," I say. "You make one heck of an argument."

"I don't want to be a lawyer," he says. "I want to be a pilot."

"Oh, right. Well, one thing at a time. Dog first, pilot school later."

"Did you hear that, Ozzy? We're getting a dog!"

~ ~ ~

After dinner, Ren walks back to her house to pack some clothes. She doesn't have much to move. We don't need her bedroom furniture, and the rest of her belongings are still in Sitka.

She comes through the front door pulling a suitcase. I hand her a key. "Welcome home."

Cody eyes her sole bag. "You don't have a lot of stuff."

"You're right. I don't. I have a few more things at my dad's house, but most of my things are in Alaska. I guess I'll have to go back and get them."

"Can I come?" he begs. "I want to go to Alaska, and we didn't get to go."

She looks at me and I shrug.

"You know what?" she says. "Maybe we'll all go. But I think we should wait a few months."

"How come?" he asks.

"There's a very cool thing that happens at night in Alaska, but not until September, when it stays darker at night. It's called the Aurora Borealis, or Northern Lights. It's when electrons in the earth's atmosphere collide with nitrogen and oxygen molecules."

Cody's head tilts. "Huh?"

Serenity pulls out her phone, googles it, and shows him a picture. "These amazing lights can only be seen in the far north, and I was lucky enough to be able to see them often. To me, it looks like heaven, and I liked to pretend the people I'd lost, like my mom and"—she glances at me—"others, were somehow connected to me through the lights."

"Do you think my mom is there, too? And Uncle Chaz? And my grandpa?"

"I think they just might be."

"Then we should go, right, Dad?"

"Yeah, sport, I think we should."

"It's settled then," she says. "In September, we'll go collect my things and then visit old friends."

I kiss the side of her head. "I hope you know that you're amazing."

Cody gives her the drawing he'd been working on. It's of three stick figures in front of a blue house. I think he also drew a dog. But he's five and can barely draw a circle, so it's hard to say. She fawns over it like it's the Mona Lisa. "The very first artwork to go up on the refrigerator."

He watches proudly as she uses a magnet to display it. Then he yawns.

"Come on," I say. "It's been a long couple of days. Let's get you in the tub, and then it's off to bed."

Serenity nods to the bedroom. "I'll go unpack. Is there a certain side of the closet or dresser or whatever that you want?"

I kiss her on the way by. "Whichever side you don't."

Later, when I join her in the bedroom and see how she's perfectly organized the closet, having unpacked some of my things as well, something occurs to me. Neither of us has lived with anyone else before. The thought makes me smile. Because although she had a lot of firsts with Chaz, this one belongs to me. And I damn well will be having *all* the lasts with her.

I look at the dresser. There's only one photo on it. It's an old picture of the three of us—Ren, Chaz, and me. Ren is standing between us, all of us in our caps and gowns looking like we were ready to tackle the world.

She comes up behind me and threads her arms around me. "I hope this is okay."

"Of course. I wasn't sure you'd want any pictures of him."

"He's still your family. And a big part of our past. And in a way, he's the reason we're together." She stares at the picture. "This photo reminds me of a happy time. Before he was with, well… you know."

I turn and hold her tightly. "He was a fool, Serenity."

"Please tell me you won't ever—"

"I'm done doing idiotic things. And believe me, after what we've been through, I'm not about to fuck this up. Ever."

"And the other stuff? The jumping out of planes and off bridges? Will you miss it? The excitement. The adrenaline."

I pull her shirt over her head, remove her bra, and cup her breasts. Her nipples quickly pebble under my touch. Then I take her hand and put it over my pounding heart. "Feel this? This is all the adrenaline I need. You're the only mountain I want to climb. The only slope I want to ski. I'm afraid you're stuck with me, like it or not."

She untucks my shirt and runs her hands underneath it. "Like it," she says. "Definitely like it."

I walk her backward until her calves hit the edge of the bed, and she sinks back onto it. I stare at her, half-naked, my cock straining the fly of my jeans. "Time to christen our house."

"Our house." She smiles. "I like the sound of that." She nods to the door. "But you'd better get used to locking that when we, uh, *christen*."

I snicker as I swiftly lock it. Then I join her on the bed, climbing over her, happy to be rid of the cast so I can have both my hands to do everything I want to do to her amazing body. Straddling her, I tease her nipples, working them between my fingers as she moans helplessly beneath my weight. Her arching back tells me she wants more.

Lifting myself off her and bracing one foot on the bed, I remove the rest of her clothes. I push her legs apart and find her wet and glistening. *Fuuuuck me.* I have to taste her. I slide off the end of the mattress and pull her by the legs until her pussy meets my lips. She whimpers as I dart my tongue inside her. I know she loves the sensation of my beard against her delicate skin. She practically howls when my mouth circles her clit. She's completely under my spell and my control, and it feels better than any high from any drug or any adventure.

She's close. I've come to know her body and how it works. I know that when she's on the verge of coming, she relaxes her hips. I think she does it to try and hold off, build up even higher, make her come harder. Then, when she's past the point of no return, her stomach muscles clench, her head falls back, her eyes close, and she lets herself go completely, unabashedly, and fantastically. It's like watching the last lap of the Indianapolis 500, when the lead car rounds the fourth turn and is on the way to the checkered flag.

I'm the driver. She's the car. Together, we get her to the finish line.

The shudders subside. Her body goes languid, sagging into the mattress. She exhales a gust of air, and I can almost see years of frustration and pain leave her body with that one giant breath.

Then, with a sudden, fierce awakening, I know for certain that *I'm* the one she wants. And I damn well plan on being the only man she'll ever need.

Her eyes open and a throaty, seductive laugh escapes her. "Just… Wow."

I want to stand and take a bow, but my throbbing dick begs to be inside her. I quickly get naked then move up her body and sink myself inside, her pussy wet, warm, and welcoming. Heat envelops me, warming my skin like I've been dipped in lava. It's a cocoon I never want to leave. A feeling I never want to forget. I stop moving, brace myself above her, and gaze into her chocolate eyes. "I fucking love you, Serenity."

She brushes a clump of hair off my brow. "Promise me you'll say it every day."

"I promise."

"Promise me you'll keep your promise."

My throat burns as I remember another promise I once made. I lean down and whisper, "I promise to love and take care of you every day for the rest of my life."

She holds my face close to hers. "And I promise to love and take care of you for the rest of mine."

"Are you sure? I'm talking forever here. You. Me. Cody."

She glances at the picture on the dresser. "I'm lucky in so many ways because I get to have the best parts of both of you."

Her words resonate with me. And in this moment I realize that while I'll miss Chaz every day of my life, having Cody means we'll always have a piece of what we both lost when he died.

My hips start to move as I make love to the only woman I've ever dreamed of, knowing she's the only woman I'll ever make love to again.

I swallow back tears as I quietly thank my brother, my other half, my twin. I finally understand why he did what he did back on that mountain. He still loved her. Even after everything he did, he loved her, and he gave his life for that love. And I vow right here and now that I'll love her for the both of us. That I'll live a life full enough for two men. That I'll raise Cody in a way that would make him proud.

That I will never again take for granted the gift he gave me by leaving me the untaken twin.

Epilogue

Cody Calloway – age 16

"Easy there," Dad says as I expertly lift us off the runway in the Cirrus SR22 G6 single engine aircraft.

"Dad, relax. I know what I'm doing. I've logged all the hours. Passed all the tests. I've been cleared to fly solo. And someday, I'm going to be the youngest commercial airline captain."

"I don't doubt it for a second. You're a good pilot."

I spare a glance in his direction. "Yeah, well it takes one to know one."

"I'm really proud of you, Cody."

"Don't forget to take a picture. I promised Mama."

"You know she'd be here if she could."

"I know. There will be plenty of other times I can bring her up."

He takes at least a dozen pictures, scolding me when I turn, smile, and give him the peace sign.

I laugh. "It's not like driving a car, Dad. You *can* take your eyes off the sky, you know." I look off at the horizon, certain I was born to do this. And I know one day, I'll pilot an airplane in Canadian airspace and fly at night until I find the northern lights we've gone to see from the ground every year since I was five. My mother is in those lights. My father, too. Well, my biological father; the man sitting next to me is my dad.

I grew up watching Dad's old YouTube adventures and wanting to follow in his footsteps. But he raised me to be a rule follower. Adventurous, yes, but careful. Not reckless like he used to be. That's not to say we haven't gone on our share of excursions. He's taken me to the tops of mountains and to the deepest canyons. We've been whitewater rafting, rock climbing, and spelunking. But my first love has always been flying. To be up in the sky, defying the laws of physics. Ignoring mathematical equations that fail to explain why aerodynamic lift occurs.

This is where I belong. And learning to fly together over the past few years has been one of the highlights of my life. And I'm fairly sure it's also been one of his.

The satellite phone rings. The one Dad takes everywhere. He's long since told me the story of how his twin died. And now he refuses to go anywhere without it.

But it only gets used for emergencies. It's never rung. Not one time. Until now.

Dad and I look at each other. We both know this can only mean one thing.

I turn the plane around as he answers. Because I know what he's going to say. He's going to tell me I'm finally getting what I've been wishing for over the past eleven years. I'm going to be a big brother.

Dad smiles as he talks, confirming my suspicions. Mama's water has broken.

My twin sisters are coming.

Acknowledgements

Untaken Twin is my twenty-fourth book. Although it was heartbreaking to write at times, I'm so proud of Cooper and Ren's path to finding peace, love, and happiness after their shared tragedy.

Without my steadfast team of supporters, experts, editors, and beta readers, I wouldn't be able to live this fulfilling life and do what I do.

My amazing list of beta readers is long: Michelle Fewer, Joelle Yates, Shauna Salley, Laura Conley, Heather Carver, Ann Peters, and Tammy Dixon. The honest critiques I get from you only make my books better, and for that I'm eternally grateful.

Thank you to my copy editor, Amanda Cuff, and my promo peeps at Greys Promotions.

Last, but certainly not least, thank you to my wonderful assistant, Julie Collier, who makes me feel like I'm her one and only client.

If you loved these trash-talking Calloway Brothers, I can't wait for you to dive into the McQuaid brothers' books. Hawk, Hunter, and Hudson have a rich, meddling grandfather who will stop at nothing to make sure his grandsons find love.

About the author

    Samantha Christy's passion for writing started long before her first novel was published. Graduating from the University of Nebraska with a degree in Criminal Justice, she held the title of Computer Systems Analyst for The Supreme Court of Wisconsin and several major universities around the United States. Raised mainly in Indianapolis, she holds the Midwest and its homegrown values dear to her heart and upon the birth of her third child devoted herself to raising her family full time. While it took time to get from there to here, writing has remained her utmost passion and being a stay-at-home mom facilitated her ability to follow that dream. When she is not writing, she keeps busy cruising to every Caribbean island where ships sail. Samantha Christy currently resides in St. Augustine, Florida with her husband and four children.

You can reach Samantha Christy at any of these wonderful places:

Website: www.samanthachristy.com

Facebook: https://www.facebook.com/SamanthaChristyAuthor

Instagram: @authorsamanthachristy

E-mail: samanthachristy@comcast.net